Death in a Perfect Town

A Cramer Creek Mystery

Sharon King

To Judy,
God bless and Good reading!
and
Sharon King
3/15/03

PUBLISH AMERICA

PublishAmerica
Baltimore

First printing

ISBN: 1-59129-464-9
PUBLISHED BY PUBLISHAMERICA BOOK PUBLISHERS
www.publishamerica.com
Baltimore

Printed in the United States of America

This book is dedicated to Mary Kaplan, 9th grade English teacher, who inspired me to reach higher, and to Alan Klaus who helped remove many stones and boulders from rocky soil.

ACKNOWLEDGMENTS

Thanks to Jennifer Adkison, Sally A. Wilson, and Rebecca Graff, for their insightful reading of the manuscript and their constructive suggestions; Rev. Darryl Ridgely, for checking the Biblical accuracy of Pastor Sharpe's sermon and counseling sessions; Jeff Wilson, for his time and technological expertise; and to my "Experiencing God" group, who loveth at all times, for their encouragement.

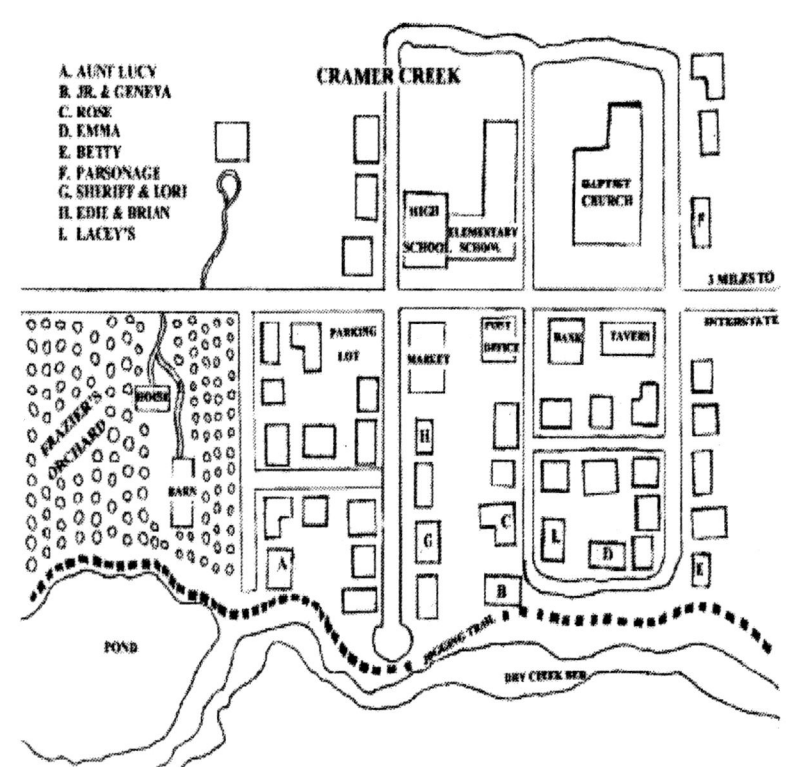

CHAPTER 1

The older woman sat at the old Formica kitchen table, with its legs of tubular steel, husking two ears of corn. She was built like a scarecrow with bones. Wisps of gray flyaway hair over a wrinkled forehead, large nose, and round, slightly bulging, cat yellowish-green eyes topped her syncopated frame. She rarely scrutinized her face in a mirror, but constantly monitored those of others. She didn't own a full-length mirror, but pictured herself as young and desirable, the epitome of a 1942 pin-up girl with Betty Grable legs.

This morning there were too many things for her muddled head to think about. For starters, there was Junior's lunch to prepare. You couldn't just put a tuna sandwich in front of him, she thought, even if you grilled it in butter with a bowl of soup on the side. "He's a 'meat and potato' man," she said aloud. Food had to be bulky going down, stick to his ribs a couple of hours, give gas, heartburn, indigestion, or constipation before her baby would admit to having eaten. But, for all her son's intemperate gluttony, she considered his resultant bulk as solid as a steel locomotive. She sighed, and began whipping milk and butter into the potatoes. He really was a strapping young man (a saying her father had used) and handsome too. From the moment he was born she had known the kind of adult male he was going to be, and she had watched and molded his precious little body and soul, using a unique neurotic and smothering process of her own, from that moment to the present. After her husband, Ram, had left them, Junior was all she wanted and she had nurtured and protected him always, except for his "ridiculous marriage to that slut, Betty Abbott."

Geneva Bryson, Junior's slightly built, hawk-nosed, sixty-eight-year-old mother had been heard on numerous occasions to refer to Betty Abbott, now Bryson, in those terms. The wrathful comment never failed to raise eyebrows and raise hands to mouths, mostly to conceal and fight back chuckles, as her listeners tried to picture the friendly, somewhat matronly school teacher as "that slut, Betty Abbott." This particular slur, as well as gross others, caused many of her sisters and brothers at the church to find creative ways to avoid her company. The young, and usually friendly, pastor, when trapped by Geneva, listened to her caustic diatribes with a knot in his stomach.

"Yes," she spoke with satisfaction, "my boy finally seed the folly of that marriage!"

It was true. Junior had run back home to her after the tragedy. Being her only child, and raised tied to her apron strings, he had regressed to a child once again after the murder, and sought her familiar kind of neurotic care and comfort. The day he and Betty had found their child, Karen, stabbed numerous times in the back and left wedged between a forked limb in an apple tree in Frazier's orchard, he had left his wife, run through his mother's kitchen door, sobbing, and he had stayed.

"The child weren't his anyways," Geneva spoke aloud with venom, "and I din't mind tellin' him so! Karen was too pale and weak, and downright pitiful lookin' to have been sired by my boy."

"What's that, Mrs. Bryson?" a pert blond head spoke through the kitchen screen door. "You know what they say when you talk to yourself?"

Geneva flapped her right hand to her heart. "My stars, Edie, you jest took ten years off'n my life." Then suspiciously she asked, "How come you din't ring the front bell?"

"I did," Edie giggled, "I guess you were too busy talking to yourself and didn't hear me."

Edie, trim in a close fitting lime green chemise with two side slits, and pretty with a peachy cream complexion, was ready to do business. In cosmetic sales she had found the better she looked the more she sold. However, with some of her older ladies, especially Geneva, she found good looks and a charming personality were wasted, even a detriment.

The older woman stared at the visitor for a minute and wiped her hands on her gunny-sack apron, but made no move toward the screen door (kept locked, she had asserted to Junior, "in case some pervert might wander into town and do no telling what, like what happened to little Mary Jane Oglesby last year").

"Well, at least I weren't talking back to myself," Geneva finally countered. "Anyways, Edie, I don't have time for you now. Junior will be home any minute and his steak ain't ready." Determined to rid herself of the young Vision Cosmetic representative, she abruptly changed her strategy, and pointed to the small clapboard house next door. "Say, why don't you go next door and meet up with our new neighbor. I ain't seen hide or hair of her since she moved in a couple of days ago. Old Aunt Lucy rented to her and she ain't seen her neither, done it all through the mail. Guess the only ones to actually talk to her's Willow, down to the post office. Willow says she got off the bus with her suitcase, walked into the post office to register her name and address, and it weren't nobody Willow'd ever heard of, then walked straight to the house, din't even stop at the market. I reckon she ain't even et since she moved in. I'm aimin' to take a little stew over later." As an afterthought, Geneva added encouragingly, "You know, Edie, I bet you'd make a sale over there. Willow says she's got nasty scars all over one side of her. She's bound to need a lot of makeup to cover all that up."

Geneva was red-faced and out of breathe from her long speech, and decided to unlock the screen door, not to let Edie in, but to step out onto the small landing for a minute of fresh air. No way in the world would she let Edie in the house just before Junior was due home. No one had to tell her what little Miss Priss, Edie, was up to. Geneva snorted to herself, Why, the girl was hot for anything in pants, and Junior, she reckoned, being the most eligible bachelor in town, had to be her target. "So you jest come back in an hour or so, and I'll look at your book. I might try that new perfume you're peddlin'. What's it called?"

Edie frowned at her customer, and shrugged her slim, angular shoulders as she turned toward the side of the new neighbor's house. Then, remembering to be polite, further augmenting Geneva's theory, said, "Well, I'll just leave my book with you, and if Junior needs any soap or aftershave, let me know."

Geneva smiled to herself as she hooked the screen door. "I will, dear." Then turning back to the stove, dropped two fresh ears of corn into boiling water. Both ears were for Junior. Perhaps she would eat some stew later before taking it to the new neighbor.

Geneva didn't analyze why she never shared the noon meal with Junior, she only knew she preferred to sit and perhaps talk to him while he ate, and then, later, eat by herself. In a somewhat similar vein, she used to wait up for him on the occasional evenings he frequented the Drinking Trough Tavern, or at least would lie awake in her bed listening until she heard him come in, but had finally stopped that activity from sheer exhaustion. At her age, she decided, she could no longer stay up until the early hours of the morning, and then force herself to "get up with the chickens" a few hours later. She felt, with remorse, that she was letting him down in this small way, but for the most part, considered herself a worthy woman and mother, and she was happily content with her life. After all, she had neighbors who liked to gossip, fair to middlin' health, a small, but nice house, a big healthy garden, and of course, the pride of her life, Junior.

"I'm home," he yelled through the door.

Geneva hurried to unlock it. "Just in time, honey, everything's hot off the stove and biscuits are just about ready. Hurry up now, worsh up while I git it on the table."

Junior, with his 260-pound girth, lumbered through the door and tried to sidle past his mother. As his large belly touched her, his face knotted with rage, "Woman, get out of my way!"

Geneva closed her eyes, shivered, and stepped back to let him pass, then turned toward the stove and filled his plate.

* * *

Edie was a liar. Most everyone in Cramer Creek knew it. Whether Edie, herself, knew it was debatable. Some people argued the pretty girl had to know she was telling a pack of lies. She had to know her house didn't burn down ten years ago, that she didn't brave the fumes and flames and death itself to rescue her little brother, Brian, then give him artificial respiration until his limp little blue body turned pink again. Some people insisted she had to know she wasn't raped by a large man in a ski mask with a knife at her throat while her parents slept peacefully in the next room. "The police never caught the man," her critics would announce with a wink. And Edie had lots of stories.

Cramer Creek's current favorite, much to her pastor's chagrin, was the story in which Edie's heart stopped beating after a nasty fall down a flight of stairs. As desperate paramedics tried to resuscitate her, her spirit was irresistibly drawn into the bright light of Heaven. Her description of the streets of Gold, the Crystal River, the Emerald rainbow about the throne of God, the blissful atmosphere of Eternity, and then the agonizingly reluctant trip back to soiled Earth was nothing short of art.

Whether Edie did or did not know she was a liar was a question no one could resolve for certain, and whatever the true answer, or her detractors might argue, she was an artist. She painted unforgettable scenes in the mind's eye, and Meryl Streep could not have played the many diverse roles in which Edie starred, again and again, and not on any stage, but in the small town of Cramer Creek.

Being a door-to-door Vision Cosmetic representative was a perfect job for her. She could tell her stories over and over, not only matching her customers' tales of woe, but always topping them and lessening their real-life anxieties and troubles with dramatizations of fires, deaths, stabbings, and rapes. Edie's best days were those few when she could welcome a newcomer to town with cosmetic samples and the story of her life. Like an ornate embroidered sampler, her life's story held many colored threads, intricate designs, and a variety of subject matter. And as she wove her tales, needless to say, the listener would be overwhelmed and devastated by the young girl's history, but would simultaneously admire her courageous spirit "in spite of it all." Her new customer would invariably offer to help in any way they could and would begin with a large cosmetic order. After Edie had gone, the new residents would wonder if they had inadvertently moved into a particularly dangerous and lawless community.

Some townsfolk say the real catastrophe was inevitable, that she had tempted providence for it to happen, even though they felt sorry for her. When it struck, most expected her to crumble; a real-life tragedy they thought would destroy her. But Edie surprised everyone after she and Brian buried their father and mother; and Edie, with exquisite decorum, a few discreet tears, appropriately thanked the funeral director, staff, and the mourners who had brought food and flowers, and then went on with her stories as before. The exception being the added tale of how her parents had been "murdered" in a hotel fire by a careless woman who fell asleep while smoking in bed.

Edie took the short cut between the Bryson's side door off the kitchen and the new neighbor's front porch, passing through an old knotted grape arbor, two ancient apple trees, which, miraculously, in spite of their age, still bore pale red apples, and under the large Poplar tree. Fall was definitely in the air she thought, noticing the grapes had begun to turn from the green to purple stage. School had already resumed, which kept her pesky, but sweet, teenage brother out of her hair, and kept her customers' children out of theirs, allowing more interesting gossip and larger orders. With Christmas only a few months away the orders would triple. These thoughts in mind, she climbed her prospective customer's porch steps.

Edie opened the storm door of the house and knocked loudly on the leaded glass pane of the old carved weather-beaten door. Looking through the glass, she could see a small female figure rise slowly from a reclining position on a flowery overstuffed couch. As the woman approached, Edie's eyes were drawn to the right side of the woman's face and neck where hideous pink and white flesh was pinched and pleated together in chaotic and grotesque patterns. The flesh surrounding the right eye was particularly unnerving to the observer for the skin here was permanently stretched and plastered to the cheekbone, while the eye seemed to be in a state of floating and searching on a sea of vitreous fluid. Edie wondered if the eye could "see." The woman's face on the left side, however, was scarless and attractive and it was this side she turned toward Edie as she opened the door.

"Yes?" she asked.

Edie focused her eyes just beyond the woman's left ear and speedily sang out her memorized new customer banter. "Hello, my name is Edie Bentley. Welcome to Cramer Creek. I am your sales rep for Vision Cosmetic, and because you are new in town and have been referred to me by one of my regular customers, I have a free sample product for you." She held up a small bottle of Vision Cosmetic's newest perfume. "For just a few minutes of your time. May I come in Mrs...?" Edie's arched eyebrows rose to a question mark.

"Findley, Rose Findley. But...I'm sorry...I would like to invite you in...uh, Miss...uh...I didn't catch your name."

"Just call me Edie."

"Uh...but...I have an awful cold and I wouldn't want to give it to you." Rose retreated a step and began to close the door.

"Oh, I never get colds, Mrs. Finley, may I call you Rose? This will only take a minute or two." Edie stepped forward.

"Well," Rose acquiesced grudgingly, "come on in then."

Edie smiled and chirped brightly, "You know, Mrs. Findley, I mean Rose, you should call Aunt Lucy about that cold. Folks around here go to her when they're under the weather. It saves a lot of doctor bills. She just prescribes, and prays for you, doesn't charge anything. Aunt Lucy knows everything about vitamins and herbs. People call her a witch doctor, behind her back, of course, but she generally cures them of whatever they got. Last winter, I was at death's door with double pneumonia and Aunt Lucy brought over a tea made of rose hips, chamomile, honey, slippery elm and a bunch of other things, I forget them all. Well, anyway, I sipped it day and night, and before you knew it, I was as good as new." To crown her testimonial, Edie gave Rose her brightest smile.

"That sounds very nice," said Mrs. Findley cautiously, "but, who is Aunt Lucy?"

"Why, she's the old lady you rent this house from," answered Edie, "don't you know her?"

"No, well, I've never actually met her," admitted Rose. "The transaction with Miss Kirby was done by correspondence. I read the advertisement for the house in the *Democrat Advertiser* and answered the ad by mail. After I mailed the deposit, she sent me the key and said she would drop by and meet me after I was settled."

"Yes, she'll probably drop by after school to welcome you. She's the school principal, you know."

"Oh, really?" Rose yawned.

Edie answered, using her wizened Yoda face, "Oh yes, old as the hills, but still won't retire. Everyone in town, including me, has had her for a teacher or a principal. And lots of us have felt her paddle on our bottoms. She's all strict and no nonsense, but everybody likes her anyway. Most folks say they wouldn't have grown up as well if it hadn't been for her. I tell you what, Rose, if I see Aunt Lucy today, I'll ask her to bring you something for your cold."

"Thank you, Edie, but I'm sure I'll feel better in a day or two."

Then struck by an idea, Edie blurted, "I bet she'll have something to heal those scars on your face too!"

Rose's face turned pale as Edie spoke, and her trembling right hand absently touched and caressed her wounded cheek. She stared out a lace-covered window at the large Poplar and wished her visitor would go away.

"Forgive me, Mrs. Findley, I didn't mean to..."

"That's all right, it would be difficult not to notice," Rose murmured, with a voice that alternately sighed and faltered. "I...suppose you must be wondering what caused these horrible scars."

"Well," granted Edie cautiously, "I am curious, but I assume you must have been badly burned, perhaps in a fire."

Rose nodded assent, but said nothing.

"I can certainly sympathize with you," she said with compassion, "because I was in a horrendous fire, myself." Edie paused, centered and focused on the familiar script, then began. "Ten years ago when I was just a child living with my parents, God rest their souls, they're both gone now," she whispered, bowed her head, then continued. "I had awakened in the early hours of one of the most terrible mornings of my life and heard strange hissing-type sounds in the house. It sounded like steam escaping from a tea kettle before it starts to whistle." She made a hissing sound through her teeth. "Then, I was horrified to hear the unmistakable sound of crackling flames and I smelled the stench of smoke coming into my bedroom from under the door. The night before, I had shut the door to my bedroom, because, well, I guess a premonition had come over me before I went to bed. For one thing, the sky had been a funny color that evening, you know that yellow-gray color the sky gets before a bad storm or a tornado hits? And another thing, the house had been making more creaky noises than usual. Anyway, when I finally registered that the house was on fire, I tried to get out my bedroom door, but it was too hot to touch, and thick, black smoke had begun to roll into my bedroom from the small crack beneath it." Pausing to glance at her audience, Edie was rewarded by the look of abject terror on Rose's face. "Believe me, I wasted no time getting out my window, and then I ran to my parent's window screaming at the top of my lungs and banging frantically on the glass with my fists. After what seemed like forever, my parents woke up. They couldn't get into the hall either but were able to escape through their bedroom window. The first thing my mom asked me was where was Brian. He's my brother. When I told her he must still be asleep, she started screaming for my dad to save the baby. He really wasn't a baby, he was six years old. Anyway, Mom got more and more hysterical and kept screaming for Brian, and Dad and I began pounding on his window, but he didn't answer. So, my dad threw a drain-tile through Brian's window. We called frantically to Brian, but no sound came from his bedroom. Black smoke began pouring through his broken window though. My dad tried to climb in but the window was too far off the ground, so I begged him to boost me through the window and let me get Brian. He didn't want to let me go back into the house, but he finally had to agree. Inside his room, the smoke was so thick and black; I was blinded and lost my sense of direction. Trying not to breathe, I felt myself around the room. But in a matter of seconds, I was crying and coughing uncontrollably and decided to get back to the window to save myself. Struggling back to the window, I actually tripped over Brian's unconscious body. Quickly, I gathered him in my arms and stumbled toward the hysterical voice of my mom and dad at the broken window. Through his tears, Dad lifted Brian and then me to the ground. Brian was lifeless and we all thought he must be dead. Without hope, I lifted his small blackened head, pinched his nose shut and began to blow breath into his mouth."

Edie, caught up the emotions of her own drama, with wide stricken eyes, spoke in a well-rehearsed mesmerizing desperation, while Rose, suffering her own remembered nightmare, could only nod her head, tears dripping on one smooth cheek and one miniature, scarred wasteland.

With the final curtain and happy ending in sight, Edie paused for effect, and then passionately soliloquized, "After what seemed an eternity, Brian choked. His small, hot desert breaths smelled of ashes, but he began to breathe. His chest raised and lowered. He coughed some more and started crying. We all cried. I felt as though I had died and been resurrected with him."

Her monologue screeched to a halt, and she looked tragically into Rose's eyes and saw her stark immutable face mirroring her own. Then, with a heavy sigh, Edie backed onto the old couch and sat. Her eyes caught the vacillating light and shadow of the early afternoon sun shining through the leaves of the tall Poplar tree outside the south window. She listened, as its crisp, paper-like leaves seemed to be shattering in the wind.

Rose catatonically stared through the leaded glass of the front door. She hadn't told her story to anyone before; would she dare open her soul now? It seemed she and the girl shared a special kinship, as if an invisible thread connected them. She didn't analyze the attachment, but felt an overpowering need to release the hated memory that filled her with self-loathing and recurring nightmares, poisoning her life. She thought perhaps Edie would understand her guilt and need for absolution. If the girl could understand and forgive, would this be the beginning of forgiving herself? She slowly lowered herself to the other end of the couch and faced Edie. Then, fighting for control of her emotions, she began forcing the words.

"Yes, a fire did this to me," she whispered. "It was my fault. I...I...caused the fire. A huge hotel fire. You must have read about it in the newspapers...about two years ago. I...fell asleep...was smoking in bed, I...guess."

While Edie's story had been told with the same ease as driving a heavy car with an automatic transmission, Rose's simple straightforward truth came in spurts, jerks, and pauses, like one's first experience with a stick shift. She continued, "I awoke to find the mattress under me and...and the right sleeve of my gown...on fire. I didn't...know what to do...couldn't think. I panicked and ran. My hair caught on fire. It must have been instinct brought me into the bathroom...turned the shower on. By the time the flames were extinguished on me, the entire bedroom was on fire. I was rescued through the bathroom window." Rose paused, hardened her jaw, and determinedly continued, "It was too late to stop the fire. Several...people...were...killed. I don't know how I could be so careless. I hate...you see, I can't seem to live with myself...I've even left my husband."

Rose sat, as in prayer, with bowed head and clasped hands, hopefully raising her eyes to Edie for the forgiveness and understanding she craved. However, the look she received from the young girl was unfathomable. Rose couldn't remember seeing such a look before and was afraid to read it. But Edie recovered quickly, and without speaking, slid to Rose's side, opened her arms, and held the older woman silently for some minutes.

CHAPTER 2

The pleasant town of Cramer Creek is situated as an oblong rectangle on a 100-acre tract of land in central Missouri. It consists of one wide main street stretching east and west, which was only named recently because of the 911 system, and seven lesser streets, some crossing it, which end after a block or two, or circle back to the main street. Thus, it is a town determined by its innate structure to witness any travel, however seldom, in or out of its boundaries. The post office, bank, grocery store, and combination pool hall/tavern line the middle two blocks on the south side of the main street, while the Baptist Church and public school occupy a larger area on the north (the latter three establishments supply the majority of Cramer Creek social life). Closed years ago, the only gas station in town was rebuilt near the interstate three miles away. To the chagrin of realtors and investment-prone individuals, future housing developments or proposed industry is categorically refused by the multi-termed elected city council.

Surrounding the downtown area are small, mostly white, well-kept houses on grassy lawns splattered with ancient hardwood trees, many with white picket fences, rose bushes and other perennial plantings such as Irises, Daylilies, Poppies, Hollyhocks, Phlox and Peonies. Most homes boast a large garden plot with the usual fare of green beans, tomatoes, onions, radishes, peas, spinach, summer squash, cucumbers, a couple of hills of watermelon and cantaloupe, and two to four rows of sweet corn. Occasionally, in order to upstage neighbors, or satisfy a creative urge, an avid gardener will grow a small crop of ornamental gourds, spaghetti squash, burpless cucumbers or Indian corn. This renegade action causes a fair amount of jealousy in the neighborhood and a call to arms by the old guard to better the upstart gardener the following year with purple chard, Kohlrabi, popcorn, or snow peas.

Residents enjoy the wide range of all four seasons: hot, dry and dusty in summer; falling musty colored leaves and crisp fresh air in autumn; snow-cover and brittle cold temperatures in winter; and chilly, damp, and prone to flood waterways in spring. Understandably, therefore, conversations involving weather forecasting and the subsequent effect on crops are paramount and unceasing. However, the change of seasons, the mimic of all life from birth to death to new life, does not bring with it a natural shift in point of view for residents of Cramer Creek. For, ignoring their own mortality, testified by the forces surrounding them, most folks live day-to-day, unconcerned by wars and rumors of war in the outside world, and concern themselves mostly with professional sports, soap operas, who did what to whom, dirty dishes and children's runny noses.

The ladies, mostly housewives, middle-aged and older, can be seen daily, from spring to fall, hoeing stubborn weeds or gossiping over back fences in their colorful cotton housedresses and occasional shorts and halter-tops, while their sons' and husbands' overalls flap in the breeze on the clothesline. In colder weather, sewing, baking and television become the major pastimes. Several women work in Cramer Creek: one in the post office, four in the bank, one in the market, nineteen in the school system, three as secretaries and one as a Vision Cosmetic representative.

Only a few young people remain in town after high school, preferring the larger towns nearby, or better yet, distant cities, to the culturally confining atmosphere of Cramer Creek.

Most of the men work on farms, or in the apple and pecan orchards skirting town. Some rent nearby pastures to graze what cattle they can afford to buy. A mere handful own and operate, or are employed in the town's businesses. An even dozen commute to work in another community.

To sum it up, Cramer Creek is an isolated town, exuding a pastoral atmosphere like a picture postcard from the past. A nostalgic and friendly town presents itself to the uninitiated visitor with sunny smiles, promises to visit, and pleasant conversations. Seemingly, no constant state of flux is exhibited here as in most of the civilized world. That natural law of change is non-evident to the naked eye and most residents prefer it that way. The social upheaval caused by rampant drugs and gun-carrying children as witnessed in other communities on the nightly news seems far removed. It is a source of pride that once, a few years back, a famous Missouri artist captured the town on canvas and labeled the painting, "A Town Caught in Time." A print of the painting currently hangs inside the school, in the hall just inside the front entrance, on a wall across from the elementary school office, and serves to remind the young students of their heritage. Only an occasional confession by one of the 250 residents admits to a vague uneasiness, an undefined fear, or an inability to sleep well. Otherwise, the little town seems to remain the same, its surface calm and elasticity closely resembling the small, secluded pond, separated from living water with barely a ripple to mar its serenity. Of course, there was a murder about eight years ago.

* * *

Aunt Lucy, with a crackled parchment face like ancient paint on a Renaissance masterpiece, was dressed in a magenta double-knit pantsuit. Her transparent pink-rimmed glasses were pulled to the end of her nose, as she sat hunched over the desk in her second-story office observing the tranquil scene below her window. Her office was in the nearly one-hundred-year-old, two-story brick structure that housed the high school classes, and was attached to the thirty-year-old "new" wing addition housing the air-conditioned classrooms of the elementary school. Suddenly, she opened her eyes a bit wider as an incongruent element appeared below her window. Marjorie Jacob and Ivan Phillips, previously engaged in a lively conversation outside the market, had turned to stare at Edie, running full speed past the market with her cosmetic case held tightly to her chest. She quickly turned left at the corner near her home and disappeared from sight.

"What is the matter with that girl today? Well, no doubt we'll hear the whole story, sooner or later." The warning bell commanding all high school students to their fifth hour classes, and the second through fourth grades in from recess interrupted Aunt Lucy's thoughts concerning Edie. She turned from the window, returned her glasses to the bridge of her nose, and reentered her workday with vigor.

Behind the school, on the playground, elementary students continued their joyful mayhem even after Ms. James blew her warning whistle. While most of the young students obediently formed two lines at the rear door, waiting for the signal to return to their classes, a few rebellious others pretended deafness. Shrieks of outrage from second grader Mary Thomas echoed over the playground as Tommy Samp strutted to the end of the line with her shiny blue hair ribbon dangling from his upraised fist. Fourth grade students, observing their younger schoolmates, rolled their eyes with haughty disgust and natural superiority.

"It's begun already," Aunt Lucy said aloud, "another year of unbridled chaos to channel into constructive chaos." She pushed each jacket sleeve up past her bony elbows with determination, and busied herself with first quarter objectives.

Abruptly and simultaneously with the first knock, the principal's door opened, and Ms. James, a petite, African-American second grade teacher entered. Out of breath and shaking her head, she pushed Tommy Samp through the door ahead of her, her fist wrapped tightly around the back of his collar. "He's up to his old tricks," she snapped. "Tommy grabbed Mary's hair ribbon and flushed it down the toilet, and Mary's making a big fuss claiming her mother will spank her for losing it."

Squinting at Tommy through one eye, Aunt Lucy reached for a tissue to clean her glasses. Tommy, on the other hand, looked at various objects in the room: the old picture of President Kennedy, the tall black file cabinet, and the round frayed rug at his feet. He didn't look at Aunt Lucy. After facing her desk in many somewhat similar circumstances the past two years, he knew not to look at the "old sourpuss, with her wrinkled face, frizzy white hair and one eye that nailed you in your tracks."

Ms. James continued, "I've had about all I can take from him today." She released his shirt and turned toward the door. "Well, send him down when you're through with him." She sighed, then turned on her heel and clicked back to her classroom.

Continuing to fix her eye on the young rebel in overalls, the imposing matron slowly rose to her feet. "Can't leave the girls alone, Tommy? We'll see about that. Young man, look at me when I speak to you!"

Tommy, seemingly engrossed in his new cowboy boots, locked eyes with the one opened steel-blue eye of Aunt Lucy and began to chew on his lower lip. He wondered how old she was, and when she might be expected to die a natural death. "She'll probably live to be a zillion," he surmised.

"Mr. Samp," she commanded, "I don't need to tell you teasing girls will get you into trouble. Later on, they get around to enjoying it, but, then, it's not as much fun for you. My advice is to keep your hands to yourself, and horse around with the boys. If, however, you continue your current behavior," she threatened, "I'm afraid we will have many long, illuminating discussions like this one throughout the year. For now, drag yourself to the floor outside my office and write a note of apology to Mary. If you don't know how to spell 'I'm sorry,' I will help you. After I approve your effort, we will take the note to her, together."

Tommy again studied his new boots. He couldn't figure out why everybody was making such a fuss about Mary's stupid ol' ribbon. Girls were so stupid.

"Well," queried the old woman, "what do you have to say?"

Shrugging his shoulders, he wondered what he was supposed to say.

Usually, when his mother asked him that question, she wanted him to say "Thank you," but that didn't seem to fit this situation. He hazarded a glance upward.

"Alright, get started on that note." She sighed, and handed him a pencil and piece of paper.

As Tommy worked on his apology, Aunt Lucy reseated herself and began revising schedules and reviewing the IEPs of the six handicapped students. She liked Public Law 94-142, providing a free public education for all disabled children, but she despised the paperwork that accompanied it, and all government programs. An hour later, after she, and an embarrassed Tommy, had delivered the apology to the gloating Mary Thomas, she again tackled the government forms. When she closed the last file with satisfaction, she turned again to the window and surveyed Cramer Creek, and the nearby pond. A cool breeze swept off the dirt-packed cobblestone street, and whipped the dusty curtain toward her face as she considered that body of water.

The pond had been rejected with great alacrity and threat of litigation against the Corps of Engineers, but the townspeople had eventually been forced to accept the exchange of their wild flowing creek for the small pond. Now, the picturesque, rocky, sand-bottomed, rippling creek was gone, replaced by the pond and a dry creek bed that meandered on the south side of town. To further placate the town, in addition to the pond, a jogging track had been constructed on the bank of the old creek bed.

Soon after completion of the government's hateful project, there had been a movement to change the town's name of Cramer Creek to something more apropos, but a suitable name was never found. The populace had considered the name, "Cramer Pond," a poor substitute, and "Cramer Lake" was vetoed as a euphemism and giving too much prominence to the outrage enacted upon them by the "powers that be." So, the town's name remained Cramer Creek, and continued to be the impetus of a wound rubbed raw.

Before he died, Aunt Lucy's father had grieved and waxed eloquent about the lost creek, and had despised the investors, with their inside information buying the soon-to-become-prime real estate before the ancient creek was diverted into the new 6500-acre recreational lake and playground twenty miles to the north. He had been alternately angered, then intrigued and fascinated by the small, isolated body of water left for the town by the engineers. The old Cramer Creek, with its freely flowing water, and prolific life, that sang and sparkled as it raced or meandered through the town's boundaries was forever lost, and her father had felt the loss deeply. The ignoble pond was unacceptable to him as a substitute, but, still, he had sat beside it, fishing pole in hand, through the final season of his life. In the nearly dead body of water he caught few fish, but became fascinated by the pond's mysterious and unpredictable capacity to turn itself over and periodically expose the hidden, dormant slime and teeming life beneath the surface. The "awful" would simply and stealthily appear, becoming an eyesore to passersby, obliterating the previous placidity and reflective beauty of the water. The following stagnation and resultant stench would endure for an indeterminate season until clump by clump the insidious mass would again sink to the pond's depths, leaving the surface undisturbed, calm and beautiful as before. He had kept vigil over the pond before his death.

"Lucinda," he had told her, "it's all down there, no inlets or outlets, nothing can escape."

CHAPTER 3

Edie, out of breath, her heart beating rapidly, flung open her front door and raced through the living room into the kitchen at the rear of the house. Throwing her cosmetic case on the kitchen counter, she began to pace with nervous energy on the old linoleum floor. Blinded to her surroundings, the only colors in her consciousness, other than a misty whiteness, were blurry swatches of red and black linoleum squares passing rapidly beneath her feet.

She felt nauseous and thought she would vomit soon. Confused and numb, her mind couldn't concentrate. It seemed only the oldest, most primitive brain was functioning, for she was conscious only of hatred, anger, revenge, the desire to cause physical pain, even to kill. Her mother's face hung for a moment before her eyes, but then blurred into hideous pink and white scarred flesh. "Mama!" she screamed at the top of her voice, then, her energy depleted, she leaned against the old refrigerator and slowly slid to the red and black floor.

Drifting smoke and high dancing flames entered and consumed her thoughts, still fragmented and obscure, and bore large black holes in the red swatches of her memory. She felt his hand again, beneath the blanket pushing her cotton gown aside, and his alcoholic breath whispering ugly words in her ear. Crushing her face into the kitchen floor, she screamed again, "Daddy, help me! Mama, I need you!" Then the smoke and flame became a raging fire in her head causing the blurry red swatches to shrivel into nothingness and the black to seep into every corner of her consciousness.

* * *

The teacher's lounge was exceptionally smoky. Emma and Betty stood outside the doorway, waiting for the meeting to begin. They rarely visited the teacher's basement enclave, preferring the sanctity of their classrooms, or the cafeteria, to the gossip and smoke-filled room. Today, however, their presence was mandatory as all teachers were expected to participate in the after-school discussion and planning of the annual chili supper. The money raised by the event would be used to purchase much-needed software for the high school library's reference section. Emma Cleates, the young, black, London-bred English teacher, was excited about the project for she expected quality research papers with many footnotes and lengthy bibliographies as a result of the purchase. On the other hand, her middle-aged friend, Betty Abbot Bryson, was less enthusiastic because of the unmet needs existing in her own Home Living classroom. She sighed in defeat, knowing her classroom's needs were a low priority in a technological age.

The meeting began promptly at 3:30, as Sarah Frazier, the arthritic, gray-haired Social Studies teacher brought the meeting to order, and immediately asked the second grade teacher, short, dark-skinned Opal James, to record the minutes. Emma and Betty entered quietly and sat near the open door. All issues were voted on quickly following last year's format. The chili supper was soon scheduled the second Saturday of October, leaving them a month before the event. The elementary teachers would serve the meal, buy supplies, create games and carnival booths, and decorate the gymnasium/cafeteria, while the high school teachers would procure donations of pies, cakes and homemade ice cream, as well as cook the chili and vegetable soup.

As the final order of business, Sarah appointed the high school teachers to various areas in the community to solicit dessert donations. "Miss Cleates, your assignment will be the homes behind the tavern to those behind the bank. Ms. Bryson: the homes behind the bank to the post office. Mr…"

"Uh…excuse me, Sarah," Betty objected, "but I would like to switch my area with someone else."

Sarah was quick to understand. "Oh, how remiss of me," she acceded, "of course you do. I'll take that neighborhood myself, Betty. You may canvass the homes behind the market." After Betty nodded assent, Sarah continued. "Mr. Warmbrough, and Miss Jones, you two will please split up the area from the west side of the market to the western city limits. Ms. Gilmore and Ms. Patton, please take the area east of the tavern to the eastern city limit sign. Mr. Lacey, I have a list of twenty past contributors living outside the city proper for you to contact. Now," she queried, "do these assignments suit everyone?" No one voiced disagreement, so Sarah concluded, "Each of you try to get a variety of desserts so we have a balanced selection." Then, a last minute reminder to Opal, "Ms. James, you are constructing a similar schedule as last year, noting the duties and serving times for each teacher, are you not?" Opal indicated with a curt nod she was doing just that. "Well, then it seems everything is taken care of," Sarah pronounced, and declared the meeting adjourned.

As the teachers filed out, Sarah congratulated herself the meeting had gone so well and was over so quickly, but chided herself for her unthinking assignation of Betty to Geneva Bryson's neighborhood. She was not particularly anxious to visit her either, since Geneva's granddaughter had been murdered on Frazier property, but she admitted it would be worse for Betty. Asking her to go to Geneva's was like inviting Daniel into the lion's den without the subsequent miracle. Except for those chance encounters on the street and at church, Sarah had been more or less successful in avoiding Geneva for almost twenty years. On the street, Sarah feigned hurriedness and was generally allowed to rush past with a perfunctory nod, or "How are you?" At church, she attended a different Sunday school class and usually managed to sit on the opposite side of the sanctuary during services.

"Well, I might as well get it over with," she thought, and started walking the two and one half blocks to Geneva's house.

By the time Sarah reached the Brysons', it was after four and Geneva was already cooking what she called supper, and Sarah called dinner. This suited her admirably, for Geneva would have little time to gossip, and be frantic to serve Junior the minute he got home from working at the orchard, usually between five and five-thirty.

The visit, therefore, was necessarily brief, with only a smattering of local gossip, mainly about the mysterious new neighbor, Rose Findley, and concluded with Geneva's promised donation of peanut butter pie for the chili supper, Junior's favorite dessert.

* * *

Emma and Betty were first out of the building after the meeting. As was their custom, they walked slowly together across the street, two blocks east past the Tavern, two blocks South to Betty's house, then Emma walked alone one half block west to her home.

Emma glanced curiously at her friend. She had met Betty only a month ago, when Emma, a new teacher at Cramer Creek High School, introduced herself to the middle-aged tenured teacher as they prepared their classrooms for the coming school year. The two had hit it off from their first meeting and grown closer through their daily walks to and from school. Lately, they had spent a few evenings together as well, grading papers, baking cookies, and having quiet talks. Still, Emma didn't want to delve into Betty's personal life without invitation. A glance at Betty's face assured her Betty was her normal, pleasant self, so Emma attempted to appease her curiosity.

"Betty," she asked tentatively, "would it be too personal to ask why you didn't want to canvass the area behind the post office?" Emma winced, "that was blunt," she thought, "Just call me Miss Tactful."

But Betty tossed her medium length hair, the color of dark maple syrup, and seemed amused by her friend's question. "Oh, you know," she chuckled, "I told you about my ex-husband and mother-in-law."

Emma remembered, "Yes," and smiled conspiratorially.

"Well, they live a street over behind the post office. I would be wasting my breath to ask Geneva for a glass of water if I was dying of thirst! The names she still calls me after all these years you would not believe! To put it delicately, according to her I'm a scarlet woman; the Jezebel that seduced her innocent son, and worse, bore him an illegitimate child. Where she got that idea I don't have a clue. After eight years you would think she'd cool down. Anyway," Betty shook her dark head and giggled, "I am a jaded woman to anyone who will listen to her."

"That's terrible, Betty!" Emma wrinkled her wide nose and cocked her head toward her friend. "It's really weird, too. She must be bloody crazy."

"She is. You'll have to meet her sometime." Then as an afterthought, Betty quipped, "And if you do, act as though you are interested in Junior, then you'll get the full effect."

"She'll be like a tigress protecting her young, huh?"

"Exactly. The entire time Junior and I were married, Geneva and I were in constant competition. There wasn't enough room in Junior's life for both of us. I don't take it personally, because she would have reacted the same way to anyone Junior had married. She was jealous, always picking at me, waiting to point out and exaggerate any mistake, no matter how trivial, and of course, I made plenty." Betty's speech lost its lightheartedness and became more stressful. "She constantly criticized my cooking, said I didn't feed him properly. When he stopped by her house, she always sent food home: leftovers, cake, cookies, pumpkin bread, baked ham, you name it. And when we visited her together, she would manage to make a comment about my size, while she, believe it or not, would hike her dress up, exposing her bony legs and thighs. Looking back, it seems hilarious, but back then I took it very seriously." Betty sighed. "I guess the worse part was Junior usually took her part and blamed me for not getting along with his mother. It's so funny," Betty said, "and tell me if you can figure this out. One afternoon, before Ram left Geneva, I dropped by their house, and found them in bed together. When I casually mentioned it to Junior, he refused to believe it; he couldn't believe they still had sexual relations. He called me a liar!"

"Blimey, that's too deep for me," Emma said quietly. "Betty, you sound as though it still bothers you."

"I hate to admit it, but I guess it does. I worked so hard at our marriage, and I loved Junior in spite of his faults. There was something very sad and vulnerable about him." Betty smiled. "He used to thank me for loving him. Emma, it's simply this, I was committed for a lifetime. I wanted to raise kids and grow old together. And then," her voice rose and hardened, "and then, after our little girl, Karen, died, he left and refused to come back home, except to get his stuff. Overnight, we became adversaries. He suddenly believed his mother's lies about me. The truth became so twisted, and what truth I thought he knew, he denied. There is so much pain that will never go away. I lost my little girl and my husband at the same time." Tears began filling her eyes, threatening to fall, but Betty appeared to be angry with herself and swiped at her eyes with both fists. "It is so stupid, but I still believe someday he'll see through all the lies."

Incredulously Emma demanded, "You don't mean you would actually take the bugger back?"

Betty replied simply, "Yes."

Leaving Betty at her door and walking toward her home, Emma realized with surprise that her friend's answer had shocked her, not because she doubted it, but because it seemed so outdated, a fully antiquated response, Evangeline stuff. In Emma's young world, words like love, marriage, commitment, and "till death do us part," was an if, but, and, or, and a however situation. Those words were relative, like everything else in the world. When spouses, children and other alliances were disposed, there were counselors, self-help groups, doctors, and other caretakers whose sole occupations were to make pain and separation relative. In addition to emotional Band-Aids were money, toys, pets, addictions, and other available substitutions to make separation even more relative. "Me First" was the religion of today: selfishness without guilt, sex without love, love without commitment, everything with relativity and no regrets. The world, as she saw it, was mostly material after all. Martyrs were definitely out of vogue, and her friend didn't seem to recognize it.

"Betty apparently doesn't know how to shed a few tears and go onward and upward," she mused, "and that makes her totally vulnerable."

Emma had no experience with love or marriage, only the usual boyfriends in secondary school and a few fleeting affairs during college. However, she knew instinctively she would not have Betty's strength and loyalty in a serious relationship. On the other hand, if she ever needed a friend, she knew she could trust Betty to be there for her.

Betty was different. The physical attribute most noticeable about her was not her large solid frame, but her intense gray eyes that appeared to hold simple purpose and resolve. Similarly, her face, while not beautiful, had a certain courageous intensity, which might be called beauty. To Emma, Betty reminded her of an unflinching and determined Jeanne de Arc, or some other martyr, but decided that was too fanciful an idea, even for an English teacher.

CHAPTER 4

Sarah Frazier stepped rigidly off Geneva's front porch, holding her straight, iron-gray hair away from her face, as a cool stiff breeze blew out of the north. Walking down the sidewalk she felt her arthritic joints protesting the changing weather, and debated whether to continue. The worse visit over, however, she felt a sigh of relief, and decided to at least visit Geneva's new neighbor, Rose Findley, and ask her for a dessert donation for the chili supper. "It would be good," she surmised, "to get her involved in community affairs."

* * *

"Are you going to church tonight, Brian?" asked sixteen-year-old Elizabeth Lacey. "Remember, that guy from Calvary College is coming to talk to our youth group." Elizabeth smiled demurely up at six feet, three inch Brian Bentley's face. She knew his answer of course because he was wrapped tightly around her little finger and she had only to wiggle it to get the response she wanted! Her extensive power over the opposite sex began two years ago when she was a freshman, and she was enjoying it immensely. Her father, a widower, and the high school math teacher, was greatly alarmed by her sudden blossoming, but was relieved when she began dating Brian Bentley, a serious-minded student and dedicated Christian.

"Sure, I'll be there, but I have to work on my chemistry tonight too." Brian squeezed her hand, and then headed toward the home he shared with his older sister, Edie. "See you later." Waving to her, he crossed the street, turned left past the market and walked the short distance home. Elizabeth had to wait at school until her father was ready to leave.

Brian yelled to Edie as he banged the screen door, "Hey, I'm home." Receiving no answer, he flung his backpack down on the couch and headed for the kitchen. "Hello-o." He spied her legs first, stretched out on the floor and protruding into the center of the kitchen. Running to her, he worriedly entreated, "Sis, what's wrong?" Edie didn't look up at him, but he could see her face was pale and she had been crying. "Edie, what's wrong?" he repeated.

She slowly struggled to her feet and moaned as Brian put his arm around her. "I'm sick, I'm going to bed, I'll be all right in the morning." As he walked her slowly to her bedroom he told her, "I'll stay home from church tonight and take care of you; should I call Aunt Lucy?"

"No, Brian, go to church without me, I need to rest. I'll be fine in the morning." She braved a short-lived smile for his benefit, then settled into bed with her face toward the wall.

"Okay, if you're sure." Brian returned to the kitchen, microwaved two large pieces of leftover pizza, then settled down with his chemistry textbook.

Edie, herself, continued to be lost in an inner world of self-pity, hatred and confusion. "Oh, God, why did you take my mother and daddy away?" she cried, heartbroken. "Why didn't you protect me? Why did you deliver Rose Findley…this…murderer into my hands?"

* * *

Sarah's husband, James, was ready to call it a day. He, and his field supervisor, Junior Bryson, had worked solidly since lunchtime, and they were both tired. Although James was ten years older than Junior, he was in excellent health, slim and muscular, and more energetic than the younger man. "Junior, why don't you and your crew take off now, it's past five, and we can finish this row first thing tomorrow," James Frazier shouted above the clicking roar of the fruit picker motor. His sorters and packers had already left for the day.

"Sure thing, Jim," Junior shouted, then motioned with a wide arc of his arm to the pickers to go home, and then disengaged the machine's gear and guided the arm to the ground. Although there was a cold wind out of the north, there was no rain in the forecast, so he left the machine uncovered, and waved to James. "See ya in the morning."

"Yeah." James stepped up into his high pick-up truck and headed for the house, a quarter mile away on well-worn tracks through the orchard, two fenced and gated pastures, and past the large red barn. As he rounded the barn, he was relieved to see his wife's classic '51 yellow Plymouth not parked in its usual spot in the driveway, even though this meant dinner would be late. Usually, she beat him home, and was preparing their evening meal when he walked through the kitchen door. Tonight, he would take a shower and have time to think before having to talk to Sarah. The call he received this morning from Rose had shaken him to the core. Thank God Sarah was just leaving for school when the phone rang and he had answered. Rose had whined into the phone that she just needed to talk. But thoughts of why she needed to talk after two years and the bigger question of why she was now living in his small town of Cramer Creek had debilitated and angered him the entire day. Promising to stop by her house soon, he had alternately begged and adamantly commanded her not to call him at home again. As far as he knew, Sarah had never discovered his clandestine affair with Rose, or any of his other secret practices, and he wanted to keep it that way. He was not in love with Sarah and never had been, but their marriage worked. Sarah kept the household in order, was faithful to him and tolerated his late nights out. As a base of operation, he couldn't ask for better.

James grabbed a large thirsty blue towel and stepped out of the steamy ceramic shower stall. Usually the ultra hot water he preferred relaxed and invigorated him, but tonight his muscles remained tight, and his brow, furrowed. "Damn, damn, damn," he ranted.

* * *

Instead of turning right at the bank, Junior drove one block further east and parked in front of the tavern. Often, he stopped in for a quick beer before heading home for supper, even though this practice irritated his mother. The thing that really bothered her was when he missed the evening meal entirely. Not that she complained aloud, but her feelings were made manifest by the banging of cabinet drawers and doors, and the heavy stomping of shoes across the floor throughout the evenings in question.

A hand waved to him from the darkened bar. "Come ova here, Junior, and shettle thish argument." Junior sidled up to the bar, ordered a beer, and lit a cigarette, keeping a fixed eye on his buddy, Doug Patton. He and Doug had been friends since before they went to school. Later, in high school, they shared the similar interests of girls, cars, fishing, the Kansas City Chiefs and beer, but as Junior went on to other pursuits, Doug became enmeshed more deeply into alcohol. He owned and operated his own over the road rig, and had just finished a long trip through Detroit, Minneapolis, and Omaha. When he wasn't on the road, he was on call as a volunteer 911 First Responder for the county, and could usually be found at the tavern, much to his wife, Cheryl's, displeasure. Currently, he was in the middle of a heated argument with another regular.

"Red, I know you or nobody elsh pulled a catfish outta that pond for at leasht three years." Even if the Corps of Engineers restocked it today, it would be another three years before catfish would be eatin' size. And right now thersh so mutch scum on the surface, you couldn't catsh a turtle without gettin' hung up."

"Are you calling me a liar?" Red fumed, "I'm telling you I pulled out a twelve-pound catfish yesterday. Right now, its in my deep-freeze, dressed and cut into steaks. Come over to the house and I'll prove it to you."

"That pond ish a stinkin' hole, an I wouldn't eat nothin' that came out of it."

Junior drained his bottle, and motioned to the bartender for another. "How long has this been going on?" he asked him.

As he delivered the ice-cold brew, the bartender nodded toward Doug and Red, then rolled his eyes and shook his head, disclaiming any camaraderie with either of them. Then, knowing Junior's love for Kansas City football, asked, "How about them Chiefs?"

"They're going all the way this year, Buddy. Vermeil's the man!" His immediate thirst quenched, Junior took smaller gulps from the second bottle. He really didn't want to go home yet to begin another boring evening sleeping in his recliner in front of the TV, but on the other hand, spending the evening in the bar didn't excite him either. His evenings hadn't always been so tedious.

Closing his eyes, he reminisced about the time he had his own family, remembering going home after work, puttering about in the garage, or curling up with Betty on the couch, or playing with Karen. Karen loved for him to throw her up in the air and catch her, or push her in the high swing in the Maple Tree until she sailed over the garage. But the good memories also brought ones that pierced him to the heart: Karen wedged between two boughs in an apple tree in Frazier's Orchard, her long fawn-colored hair blowing about her pale face, and her immobile blue eyes starring in horror. His mother, at the time, had insisted Karen was not his child, and convinced his confused mind that Betty had betrayed him. But as time passed, he dismissed her hateful assertion, longed for his wife, and confirmed in his heart the undeniable bond between himself and his lost child. It was true Karen had not favored him. He was dark, big-boned and muscular, she was slight-built and fair. He had called her "chicken-bones" when he playfully tossed her around because she seemed lighter than air.

Suddenly, he was startled from his depressed thinking as Doug's awkward backhand swiped his beer bottle and spilled the brew over the countertop and onto his lap. "Junior, I'm sawry buddy," he slurred, "but thish guy ish a damned liar."

Junior, who had jumped to his feet with an oath when the cold beer penetrated his underwear, decided a bad day was getting worse and he might as well go home for a good meal. Pulling five bucks from his jeans pocket and leaving it on the counter, he snorted to Doug, "I hope you swallow your tongue and die!"

U-turning his S-10 in front of the tavern, Junior headed home. In his rear-view mirror, he noticed Betty and a black woman crossing the street. "It's Wednesday night," he thought, "I guess they're going to church." He hadn't "darkened the door" of the church for years, even though Pastor Sharpe visited him at home in the evenings occasionally and invited him to return to the fold. The pastor insisted everyone missed him and would welcome him with open arms.

"Yeah, right," Junior muttered under his breath.

* * *

A brown grocery sack in her arms, Sarah Frazier hurried on stiff legs into the bright and cheery kitchen. Spying her muscular husband springing across the hall toward their bedroom wrapped in a towel, she announced that dinner must consist of microwave TV dinners in order to get them to church on time.

James shouted from the bedroom, "I'm too tired to go to church tonight!" Then in irritation, added, "And you know I hate TV dinners! I'll eat at the tavern tonight."

Sarah's heart fell as she realized her lateness had inspired James to go to the tavern instead of church. "I'm sorry I'm late, Jim, dear, but I have just spent an hour talking to a poor lady who moved into town a couple of days ago. Her face is covered with horrible looking scars she received in a fire."

James stopped, frozen in his tracks, his heart racing.

"She lives all alone," Sarah continued, walking toward the bedroom, "and, apparently, has just left her husband. She says she has no family. I just can't figure out why she came to our little town; it doesn't make sense." Sarah looked directly at her husband. "Have you ever heard of a woman named Rose Findley?"

"Is that the mystery woman's name? How would I have ever heard of her?" he scoffed defensively, as he buttoned his shirt. Later, dressed in a clean pair of jeans and a pressed blue denim shirt, he entered the kitchen, kissed his wife on the cheek, and then left the house.

* * *

Young, serious-minded Pastor Jonathan Sharpe flipped on the sanctuary lights, raised the furnace thermostat to seventy degrees, and set out a few typed prayer requests on the table inside the door. His dark brown hair was prematurely streaked with gray, and his wrinkled brow told of concentrated spiritual battle. Tonight, he expected only a handful of the flock for the six thirty prayer meeting, and maybe an additional twenty for the seven o'clock service. The entire congregation of the Cramer Creek Baptist Church numbered less than one hundred twenty-five, and while most members attended the ten-thirty Sunday morning service, the Wednesday night prayer meeting was attended by fewer in number each week. This fact worried the good pastor because he knew by experience that prayer was not only the backbone of the church, but the greatest supernatural force available to God's people, and a church with little emphasis on prayer was in big spiritual trouble. He thanked God for the few dedicated prayer-warriors entreating God to enact miracles of healing, reconciliation, and intercession in the lives of individuals, as well as in the affairs of government. He believed they were the only reason the church was still viable. In his heart he recognized the lukewarm tendency of most of the members, and admitted and confessed to God that they closely resembled the Church of Laodicea: "neither cold nor hot."

With these thoughts, he quickly knelt at the altar, and began to beseech God. "Dear Lord," he prayed, "blessed be Your name, and may all glory be Yours. Father, I confess we desperately need Your forgiveness and Your power. It seems we call on Your name only to satisfy our own desires. We ignore You six days out of seven, and don't recognize Your presence in our lives. Our conscience is seared with our continual and unrepented sin. For the most part, we have closed the church doors and not invited You in. Oh, God Almighty, I ask You to rain down Your Holy Spirit on this place, to open the stagnant pools of our hearts, and bring Your living water into our midst...." At six twenty he arose from his knees and waited for his flock.

Geneva was the first to arrive, and immediately arrested the pastor's attention with the latest gossip, carefully steeped in platitudes "God blesses" and "we need to pray fors." The usual small group arrived in the next five minutes: Betty Bryson, who brought her friend, Emma Cleates, for the first time; John Lacey, and his daughter, Elizabeth. Brian Bentley, Aunt Lucy Kirby, Sarah Frazier, Sheriff Roy Gilmore and his wife, Lori, completed the group. Jonathan's wife, Ruth, a quiet, dark-haired beauty, and their two children, Gregory, 2, and Dorcas, 4, arrived a few minutes later. Ruth was holding Dorcas's hand and carrying Gregory, as well as various Golden storybooks, and a Fischer Price barn with several barnyard animals. She unloaded her arms on the back pew and sat with her squirming children, waiting for seven o'clock when the nursery would be available.

Geneva continued to monopolize the conversation. "Pastor, you need to get over there, I wouldn't be surprised if she was gonna kill herself. Why else would she move here where nobody knows her? I'd want to kill myself too if I had all those ugly scars, and I can tell you she's sure 'nough depressed!"

Jonathan, systematically screening out most of Geneva's viper-like rhetoric, as was his practice, now turned his attention to her narrative, and vowed to visit the newcomer, Rose Findley, in the morning.

Aunt Lucy, who cared deeply for other people and kept a long prayer list, also determined to visit her new renter in the morning. Never having met Rose, as all the arrangements to let the house had been done by mail, she had already planned to stop by and introduce herself sometime this week. "If Geneva's assertion is correct, and Mrs. Findley is suicidal," Aunt Lucy ruminated, "I will pray for her right now and get over there before school in the morning."

"Are there any other concerns to add to our prayer list this evening?" asked Pastor Sharpe.

Brian spoke up, "Yes, everyone please pray for Edie, she's sick tonight. She said she'd be all right in the morning, but she didn't look very good." Several pens wrote Edie's name on the printed prayer lists.

"Pastor Sharpe, everyone," Betty announced. "I'd like you to meet my friend, Emma Cleates. She's a new teacher in town."

Everyone nodded and greeted the young woman. "Hello," echoed the pastor. "It's nice to meet you, Emma. What do you teach?"

"Thank you," she smiled, "I am the new Language Arts teacher at the high school."

"Is that a lovely English accent I hear?" he asked.

Betty broke in, "It gives our little town a touch of class, don't you think, Pastor?"

"Definitely!" he smiled warmly at Emma, then checking his watch, said,

"Well, let's get started, there are a lot of things to pray about tonight. As you can see the prayer list is full. Aunt Lucy, would you begin, and then anyone pray as you feel led, and I'll close."

* * *

Spirited laughter and boisterous talking emanated from the Drinking Trough Tavern as James rounded his pickup and walked toward the worn front door. Inside, the volume crescendoed, and James felt his tense muscles relax immediately as merry, carefree compatriots greeted him. He often thought if the church had even a small percentage of the excitement and merriment as the crowd at the tavern, it wouldn't be such a bad place. After several drinks, he began to think about Rose and the past affair. It had been physically satisfying for him, and had for the most part kept him from his other perversion. Using a feigned interest in the "Feeling Wonderful" seminars had provided the perfect cover for their relationship. The last night they spent together had been in the Kansas City hotel room the night of the fire. And the last time he had seen her was early the next morning, when zipping his jeans on the way out the door, he had left her sleeping peacefully, and left a cigarette burning in the ashtray beside the bed. Still angry at her for phoning him at home, but driven by an overwhelming physical desire to be with her, he paid at the counter and sauntered out the door.

CHAPTER 5

She and Junior were lovers walking hand in hand over hilly terrain. They smiled and kissed standing next to the rocky creek. Small pebbles to huge gray boulders dotted the landscape, beautiful lush tufts of dark green grass grew between the rocks, and scattered sunny wildflowers waved their small brightly-colored heads. Occasionally, a larger boulder blocked their upward path and they dropped hands to go around or climb over it. As time passed, the inclined grade became progressively steep and difficult, and the two climbers had to assist each other continually. Junior, however, appeared to lose strength with each obstacle, so much so, she had to support much of his weight. "You can do it, dear, don't give up, keep trying," she pleaded. On and on she struggled, pulling and pushing him up what had become a sheer rock wall with few footholds. But she was determined not to give up; they would reach the ragged pinnacle. Looking above, she saw they had almost reached the summit, just a few more hand holds and they would be safe on the plateau. Suddenly, however, a dark shadow loomed directly over them from the peak of the cliff and made loud raucous terrifying shrieks. It was an eagle, huge and ferocious, its wing span great and talons poised to strike. Fear paralyzed her body as she now held an unconscious Junior. As she stared into the threatening eyes of the bird of prey, the vision of the eagle melted into the cruel face of Geneva Bryson, who continued to shriek at them. Together, they fell backward and the lovers descended into the open abyss.

Betty screamed herself awake. As she opened her eyes, the darkness of the bedroom perpetuated the frightening atmosphere of the dream and she imagined shadowy talons reaching for her.

* * *

The brassy alarm rang at precisely five a.m.; one hour earlier than Aunt Lucy usually set it. Her cat, Carman, sleeping at the foot of her bed was greatly put out with this change in routine, and protested with an arched back, a loud "yowl," and high steps, raising the surface of the thick comforter with each step as her claws caught the wool material. Carman was a female domestic black and gray tiger, with white socks and a pink nose that Aunt Lucy had rescued from the Humane Society eight years ago. She had never regretted bringing Carman home, as the cat had a sweet disposition interspersed with a playful nature she had not yet outgrown. Aunt Lucy threw back the comforter over Carman, sat on the side of the bed and silenced the alarm. Under the cover, Carman pretended to be a whirling Dervish until Aunt Lucy peeked in at her, prompting a new game entitled, "attack." Deciding all this was too much activity before coffee, Aunt Lucy scuffed to the kitchen.

Getting up an hour early would allow her to check on Edie's well being, and to visit her new renter, Rose Findley. She had been troubled by Geneva's assessment of Rose's state of mind and chided herself for not visiting her earlier. Not that she put any credence into Geneva's poisonous spewings, but until she could assess Rose herself, would not discount them entirely. Her uncharitable thoughts regarding Geneva occurred often and were a source of Christian rebuke to herself, but thus far had been unable to eradicate them. Amazingly, Geneva had first become an irritant to her when she was a young and idealistic teacher, and Geneva, only a five-year-old in kindergarten. The young child's first victim had been Marcy Jones, a poor, but sweet classmate. She could still see little Marcy on the first day of school, jumping up and down, so excited to be in school, so full of smiles. She was, however, dressed shabbily with her older sister's hand-me-down dress and shoes, along with socks that had lost their elastic, and she immediately drew little Geneva's scorn. After only a week, the little girl had become the scapegoat of the class in spite of Aunt Lucy's protective devises and scathing sermons. Thereafter, Marcy's head remained bowed in the classroom, never raising her hand. And on the playground, when treated as an outcast by the other students, she cursed them with barroom language. Through the years, Aunt Lucy's initial irritation of Geneva had disintegrated into revulsion as she witnessed too many lives maimed by her unrestrained, malicious gossip.

Aunt Lucy, dressed in her long-sleeved green and purple printed polyester dress and warm black sweater, two cups of coffee drunk, having fed Carman, and two plastic bags in her arms, headed for Edie and Brian's house.

Brian answered her early morning knock, yawning and still dressed in pajamas. Edie, looking as if she had slept in her clothes, came up behind him, and greeted her at the door. "Morning, Aunt Lucy, you're up early." Her monotone greeting sounded accusative.

Aunt Lucy smiled at the young girl. "Well, I just wanted to check on you this morning; Brian said you weren't feeling well last night. You do look a bit under the weather, Edie." Not attempting to enter the house, she handed Edie one of the plastic bags, and said, "There's Vitamin C, Echinacea, and some chicken soup in there. I hope they'll help you feel better."

Edie answered without expression, "Thank you, Aunt Lucy."

"You're welcome, dear. Now, you better get back to bed," she commanded, smiling again. Aunt Lucy felt grandmotherly toward Edie and Brian, especially since their parents' death, and even though Edie was a young woman of twenty now, she seemed even younger and more vulnerable than her age indicated.

Turning right at the sidewalk, Aunt Lucy walked around the block to her rental house. She hoped she wouldn't awaken Rose at this early hour, but had felt driven to talk to her since last night's prayer meeting. As she approached the front door, she was relieved to see movement through the leaded glass into the lighted doorway of the kitchen. Turning the antique ringer beside the door, she waited as Rose walked toward her clothed in a warm fleecy pink robe with a coffee cup in her hand. Aunt Lucy was shocked at the ravaged face Rose presented, but not averting her eyes, smiled benignly at her.

Rose, eyes red and puffy, opened the door a crack, and ventured a subdued greeting, "Yes?"

"I'm sorry to come by so early," Aunt Lucy said amiably, "but I wanted to introduce myself. I'm Miss Kirby, your landlady, but please call me Aunt Lucy, everybody does."

"Please come in, uh, Aunt Lucy, would you like some coffee?" Rose backed into the living room, allowing her to enter.

"No thank you, dear, I've already had my two cup allotment today. Any more and I start bouncing off the walls." She followed Rose into the kitchen where they sat on upholstered red plastic and metal chairs that surrounded a matching oval chrome and red Formica table. "Another reason I came by this morning was to see if you were alright. Your next-door neighbor, Mrs. Bryson, mentioned at church last night you might not be feeling well."

"I just have a cold, and have been staying inside since I came to town, but it's getting better, I think. This must be a very friendly town because I've had a lot of visitors. Mrs. Bryson brought me some beef stew, and a sweet young lady selling cosmetics visited with me yesterday. I felt so sorry for her; she has experienced so much tragedy in her young life!"

"Yes, that was Edie Bentley."

"Bentley? Did you say Bentley?" Rose queried, breathlessly.

"Yes, I wonder what 'stories' did she tell you?" queried Aunt Lucy, with a knowing smile and rolling eyes. Then, sensing Rose's immediate negative reaction to her intimation regarding Edie, she rebuked herself for the flippant attitude regarding Edie's character. She really did care a great deal for Edie in spite of her tall tales, and to expose Edie to skepticism and ridicule had not been her intention. More than that, she had unintentionally alienated this troubled woman, whom she expressly wanted to help.

Rose considered Aunt Lucy's question that cast doubt on the authenticity of the young girl's stories, and determined not to confide in Aunt Lucy, Edie's obviously malevolent detractor. "Oh, nothing really specific, she just seemed to have suffered a lot in her young life." Then, abruptly changing the subject, she explained to her visitor she was very tired, needed to rest in bed, would she excuse her, and then promptly ushered Aunt Lucy to the door.

Aunt Lucy cursed her own bluntness. Her heart was in the right place, but being a plainspoken woman she sometimes left the wrong impression. "I'm so sorry you're not feeling well, Mrs. Findley." Then handing her the remaining plastic bag, she entreated, "Please accept my little care package of Vitamin C, Echinacea, and Chicken Soup. I hope you feel better soon." Then, in a gloomy spirit she left the house and headed toward her office.

Alone again, Rose returned to the kitchen, sat the plastic bag on the cabinet, then buried her face in her hands and sobbed. Each visitor, it seemed, had driven her to further despair: the young tragic girl, two spiteful women, James Frazier, his wife, and her own angry husband. Worse than the visitor this morning was her relentless self-accusation regarding her behavior last night. Edie had given her a small ray of hope for understanding and redemption, but with her new knowledge that was gone now.

* * *

Aunt Lucy stared out her second floor office window. None of the children and only a few teachers were in the building this early, and the resulting solitude was healing to her spirit. She knelt down beside her old oak swivel desk chair and asked the Lord for forgiveness of her many sins. Many years ago she had thought proudly that she sinned very little. She rarely broke the Ten Commandments, including the two she considered the least important, coveting and "little white lies." However, as time passed, she discovered the sins of omission, uncharitable thoughts, occasional gluttony, an uncontrolled tongue, and the pride of knowledge and education, especially pride of Biblical knowledge. For, in the Bible, even St. Paul was given a "thorn in the flesh" that he might not be filled with pride for the great revelations he had received from God. She supposed once her current list of sins were conquered, more insidious ones would appear. Perhaps her sins, she mused, were similar to the clumps of underwater muck that rose slowly to the surface of Cramer Creek's pond and floated there for a season until it inevitably disappeared, leaving clear, reflective beauty, like a mirror of Heaven. With this revelation, she joyfully praised and thanked God for His son, Jesus, who died for all of her sins, past, present, and future, clearing away all the clumps of muck in her life, and giving her eternal life. Unlike the pond, whose depths contained the refuse that would eventually rise again, Jesus promised her sins were buried in the depths of the sea never to rise again. She knew she was fully forgiven for slurring Edie's reputation earlier, and, thus, erasing her opportunity to help Rose, but prayed that God would send someone to minister to Rose in her place.

* * *

Across the hall, in her Social Studies classroom, Sarah Frazier busied herself with the day's lesson plans, arranging the worksheets in order of the day's five class periods. There was very little to organize today or any day for that matter, for Sarah had taught the same subjects of Civics, World History, and American History for thirty-five years and they remained basically the same, with the addition of new legislation and names of current incumbents. The recently purchased textbooks filled with revisionist, politically correct history remained on the shelves as her students were provided with the old lap-eared pages and taped bindings of the older textbooks printed in the fifties and sixties. Sarah didn't consider herself political in any way, she was not a conservative, or a liberal, but she was old enough to have observed the remaking of history by post-modern political activists, and she chose to teach the truth. Her current problem, however, was not related to teaching, but to time management. Specifically, the problem of how to design her third hour free period in a such a way that would enable her to go to the bank and also canvass her assigned area for Chili Supper donations. She was determined not to make the mistake of getting home late and not having dinner on time again, and thus, giving James an excuse to go to the tavern. Last night, unable to sleep until she heard his truck approaching the house at three-fifteen in the morning, she had decided to try harder.

* * *

On the way to school, after relating her scary dream to Emma, Betty felt much better. As a matter of fact, early morning grocery shoppers noticed both women bent almost double with laughter, as they crossed the street in front of the market.

"Can you picture her as an eagle, shrieking and flapping her wings at eligible young maidens drawing too near the princely Junior?" Emma chortled happily, visualizing a comical Geneva outfitted with talons and a sharp beak.

"Yes, it would be entirely in character. The more I think about it, my dream was very realistic," Betty replied, laughing. Then holding her sides, she rasped, "Oh, I just had another vision of Geneva perched on the chimney over her house keeping her eagle eye on every move Junior makes, and swooping down for the kill when she spies a predatory female."

"Seriously, though," Emma asserted, as they entered the double doors of school, "I think she could be a very dangerous woman."

* * *

Geneva finished washing the breakfast dishes, wiped her hands on the hanging hand towel/pot holder combination purchased at the school craft bazaar last year, and stared out the kitchen door at Aunt Lucy's rental house. She wondered suspiciously what Rose Findley was up to. Why had she come to Cramer Creek? There had been a steady stream of visitors next door for the past two days, all but one Geneva had recognized. The man who arrived in a dark four-door sedan last evening around nine o'clock was definitely a stranger. The great surprise, however, was the tall muscular frame of James Frazier who entered Rose's house just after the dark sedan raced away, squealing tires. Determined to uncover more about her mysterious neighbor, Geneva prepared to visit Rose, using the retrieval of her stew pot as an excuse. Just as she descended her back porch steps, however, she saw Pastor Sharpe, his Bible under his arm, approaching Rose's house. Not wanting a third party, especially the pastor, present at her planned interrogation, she returned to her house.

CHAPTER 6

At 3:45 p.m., every resident of Cramer Creek heard the siren of Sheriff Roy Gilmore's cruiser. Ten minutes earlier, the 911 information had been transferred to the powerfully built and handsome sheriff from the dispatch center located in the county courthouse fifteen miles away. Amazingly, the originator of the call, Lucy Kirby, Cramer Creek School principal, had reported a murder, and was waiting for him at her rental house, the scene of the crime. His thoughts returned to Geneva Bryson's ranting at church the previous evening regarding Aunt Lucy's new renter. He couldn't recall her name, but remembered Geneva's description of her disfigurement and her possible suicidal intentions. He had taken Geneva's assertions with a grain of salt, knowing her tendency to exaggerate well beyond the limits of reality. One example being her libelous gossip concerning her quite respectable ex-daughter in law, Betty Bryson. At any rate, the emergency call had definitely said murder, not suicide, and Aunt Lucy wasn't one to confuse the two. If she said murder, it was murder.

There had been few serious crimes since he had been elected sheriff: a few fights to break up at the tavern, an occasional domestic dispute to settle between spouses, a couple of runaway teenagers he had returned to their families, two alleged rapes, and an occasional break-in and petty theft, and he felt totally unprepared to investigate a murder. Of course, he remembered the sensation-causing murder of little Karen Bryson, but that was two years before he had become sheriff. Karen, he recalled, was a slight, colorless little girl with strawberry blonde hair. Her complexion had been milky with a small smattering of freckles across the bridge of her nose. At the time of the murder he had been attending the Missouri Technological Institute in St. Louis, working on his associates degree.

It was in St. Louis he had met his wife, Lori, a large framed, blue-eyed blonde, now the Cramer Creek High School art teacher. She was the reason he rushed home after work, not stopping to hobnob with other men at the tavern. After six years of marriage he still looked forward to curling up with

Lori on the couch after dinner, as well as wrapping himself around her in their bed at night. Their greatest disappointment was her inability to have children, but Lori had compensated by lavishing her love on him, as well as a motherly love for her students, resulting in his contentment at home, and her great popularity at school. Her classroom was always full of loitering, jocular students before and after the school day.

In addition to their two incomes, he worked part time out of their basement fixing anything electronic, updating computer systems, and keeping the church's and school's computers in upgrades and working order. Not needing the extra money, he charged little for his services, but continued to work for enjoyment as well as to keep up with the field.

As he pulled next to the curb at the scene of the crime, volunteer First Responder, Doug Patton, had already arrived and was talking to Aunt Lucy on the front porch. The temporary blue emergency light held by a strong magnet over the cab of Doug's pickup truck was still flashing, and alerting the curious citizens of Cramer Creek. Spotting Geneva Bryson coming toward them from her back door, Sheriff Gilmore realized in a matter of minutes most of the town's residents would be lining the yard. Consequently, to protect the integrity of the scene, he shouted to the volunteer, "Doug, don't let anyone set foot on the property!" He noticed a withering scowl appeared on Geneva's face as Doug approached her in the yard. He added, "And see if you can radio for some Highway Department barriers and flashing lights until we can get the area taped off. They had never used barriers, flashing lights or crime scene tape during his tenure, but he considered the action movies he loved to watch on television, while curled up with Lori, more instructive than his few hours of training. As Doug hastened to obey orders, Sheriff Gilmore climbed the steps to the porch where Aunt Lucy stood waiting for him, her head cocked slightly to the right as if listening to something. Pausing, he listened for whatever sound she might be hearing, but heard only the confused questions of a few spectators on the sidewalk, and something else, the unique shattering sound of the wind through the paper-like leaves of the nearby Poplar tree.

"Are you okay?" he asked her. She looked calm enough, but if her heart was racing like his, she wasn't.

"I think I'm alright, but my old legs are shaking. I've just never encountered a situation like this before, Roy. That poor woman, it just breaks my heart." Aunt Lucy gripped the porch banister and shook her head.

Noticing an increasing crowd gathering on the sidewalk, and hearing distant sirens on the way, the sheriff opened the front door and motioned for Aunt Lucy to follow him inside. A sickeningly sweet odor reached their nostrils as they entered the living room, where, centered between them and the couch on the far wall was Rose's body. She was lying on her stomach, her blemished right cheek against the floor and her arms out-stretched toward the kitchen doorway. A seemingly ordinary kitchen carving knife rose perpendicular from a large bloodied and ragged-edged circle on the back of her pink chenille robe. Between Rose's opened hands lay an empty perfume bottle and cap with its now dried contents soaked into the area rug beneath her body.

"Was she holding an opened perfume bottle and struck from behind?" he thought, "or did she open the bottle as she lay dying in order to somehow identify the killer? Did the murder weapon belong to the murderer indicating a premeditated crime, or belong to the victim perhaps indicating an unpremeditated crime?" he asked himself.

Trying to remember the procedures outlined in the training manuals, and finding it easier to remember examples seen on detective shows, the sheriff squatted next to the body. He knew the first rule was not to disrupt or contaminate the crime scene by touching or moving anything. He asked Aunt Lucy, "Is everything exactly as you first saw it, have you touched anything? Tell me everything that happened, how did you happen to find the body?" He knew his questions were rushed and didn't sound very professional, and he felt wholly inadequate in his investigative role, but Aunt Lucy didn't seem to notice.

"Well…Roy," she paused, and draped her hands on each side of her head, "I think I must still be in shock, my brain seems to be taking a vacation."

"That makes two of us, Aunt Lucy," Sheriff Gilmore admitted.

Just then, the sirens of two Highway Patrol cars and the coroner's van interrupted them. Standing up, the sheriff noticed Doug Patton enlisting the officer's help securing the scene, and county coroner, Doctor Bill Judd, making his way toward the house.

He turned toward Aunt Lucy and said, "Let's take it slowly." Then, ushering her into the kitchen, he pulled a chair out from the table, which she gratefully sat upon. "Excuse me for just a moment," he begged, "while I have a word with the coroner."

Doctor Judd had already come through the front door and was staring down at the pink chenille robe. He lifted his eyes and nodded to the sheriff. Nodding back, it passed through the sheriff's mind that Bill had not much experience with murder either. "What's the procedure, Bill? I'm in the kitchen about to question Aunt Lucy, who discovered the body, Doug Patton is attempting to secure the scene, can you think of anything else I should be doing?"

The coroner looked exasperated. "Have you called the crime lab? I can't touch the body until we get some photographs and forensics collected," he snapped, "and you can't touch anything until they go over every inch of this place."

Rebuked, Sheriff Gilmore lowered his head and made the necessary call, as the coroner went back to his car to await the lab team. Then, fearing he had left Aunt Lucy alone too long, he reentered the kitchen. In spite of the coroner's admonition, he looked for and found a glass in the cabinet, filled it with water from the sink and handed it to Aunt Lucy. "Now," he smiled rebelliously, "just tell me what you can remember right now. Later, we will go over it again with more precision." He pulled up another chair for himself, and removed a small notebook and pen from his shirt pocket.

"Thank you, Roy, I feel much better. You have always been such a considerate boy," she said, remembering him as a student in school, and patted his knee. "Now, let me think. Oh, yes, I was so upset with myself by something I said to Mrs. Findley this morning, I came back here immediately after school to apologize."

Not wanting to distract Aunt Lucy, he made a note to ask later what she had said to the victim to make an apology necessary. "Go on," he encouraged her.

Aunt Lucy continued. "Well, when I first got to the front door, I didn't see Mrs. Findley on the floor, but after knocking and receiving no answer, I looked through the glass and saw her lying there. The sun was coming through the south window and made a bright patch of light over her body. At first I didn't take it all in, because the sunlight made a pattern that seemed to be vacillating, and shaking violently. I guess it was just the sun shining and the breeze blowing through the old Poplar tree that caused a sort of strobe light effect on her body. So, even though I saw the knife in her back it didn't look real to me." Aunt Lucy's narrative was spoken matter of factly and she appeared to be recovering from the shock and weakness experienced earlier. She continued, carefully selecting her words, "I thought she might have fallen, so I opened the door. It was unlocked. Once inside, the reality of what had happened was forced upon me. I found myself frozen, unable to move or think, and my heart seemed to stop when it finally dawned on me she had been murdered. I touched her arm and shook her, but it was obvious she was quite dead." A shudder went through the old woman. "Then I dialed 911 and spoke to the county dispatcher. She told me to go outside and wait for you, so I did. I don't think I touched anything except her shoulder when I shook her, and of course the telephone, and then, the door. I may have touched something else, Roy, I just don't remember."

"That's okay, Aunt Lucy, the lab team will figure it out. Now, you mentioned being here early this morning, about what time was that?"

Aunt Lucy thought back to her morning's activities. "Well, I went over to Edie's to check on her around seven. You remember Brian telling us last night at church that Edie was sick. I brought her some chicken soup and some vitamins. I didn't stay long at Edie's. Then, because of what Geneva Bryson told us last night about Mrs. Findley, I brought a similar care package to her. It must have been about fifteen after seven. I should have visited her earlier in the week because I hadn't met her in person yet. She had rented the house from me sight unseen after answering my classified ad in the paper. She mailed the first and last month's rent and I sent her a receipt and the key by return mail."

Sheriff Gilmore interrupted by asking, "Do you remember off hand Mrs. Findley's previous address? Do you know if she has any family?"

She shrugged her small shoulders. "No, I don't recall the exact address, but I have it at home. I do remember it was Marshall, Missouri. I have no idea if she has a family."

After making a note, he asked, "You said earlier something you had said to Mrs. Findley upset you this morning. Would you tell me about it?"

"Well, I hate to tell you, Roy," she confided with downcast eyes, "but I was very un-Christ-like. I came with the best of intentions, hoping to cheer her up and offer my friendship. I knew if what Geneva Bryson said was true, she was depressed and might be suicidal, and I wanted to help her if I could. As I said, I did bring her some chicken soup and vitamins. But, then," she shook her head woefully, "I failed miserably and made a very uncharitable remark, a hint really, about Edie's lack of integrity. Then she, Mrs. Findley, that is, immediately clammed up," she groaned, "and proceeded to march me to the door. You see, Roy, I guess Edie befriended her and, of course, told her at least part of her 'so-called' life story." Shaking her white head sorrowfully, she cried, "Oh mercy, there I go again, I'm so ashamed of myself."

Sheriff Gilmore put his arm around her fragile shoulders. "Don't be so down on yourself," he said, and smiled down at her. "Yours was a pretty normal reaction, don't you think? That is, for anyone around here who really knows Edie?"

Aunt Lucy objected, "That's no excuse, and you know it, Roy!"

Sudden activity in the living room alerted them that the lab team had arrived with their equipment. Sheriff Gilmore stepped into the room and watched the professionals set up shop. Photographs of the body were taken from every conceivable angle. The knife, that had made three discernable wounds, was discovered to have no fingerprints and was bagged. Then, a hand-held vacuum was swept over the victim's skin, hair, and clothing. Only then did Dr. Judd, the coroner, approach the body in order to determine rigor mortis.

Using a small gauge to discern the temperature of the room and a pointed digital thermometer in her ear, and noting the body's beginning stiffness, he calculated silently, then announced, "Looks like she's been dead approximately three to six hours."

"Is the time for sure?" queried Sheriff Gilmore.

Dr. Judd narrowed his eyes, frowned, and looked at the ceiling. "Well, that's a guesstimate right now," he said slowly, "I might be able to narrow it down after the autopsy." He then prepared to move the body to the regional hospital, which also housed the county morgue, fifteen miles away, where he would perform the autopsy. After the contents of the vacuum were bagged, sealed, and labeled, it was run again over the various other surfaces in the room and bagged accordingly. As the crew and small vacuum moved into the kitchen, the sheriff and Aunt Lucy moved toward the front door.

The lab technician, Tom Gray, halted them. "We need the lady's fingerprints before you leave, sheriff. I'm sure yours are in the data bank."

"That's fine, what do I do?" asked Aunt Lucy.

As he watched her ten fingerprints being applied to the card, the sheriff asked Tom, "How are you fellows getting along? Anything you can tell me yet?"

"One thing, but it won't help you. There were lots of fingerprints, but none on the knife. Other than that, you'll have to wait until the state lab reports the findings and I make a report. Give me a call tomorrow, if I know anymore I'll let you know."

A few minutes later, after walking through a crowd of inquisitive spectators and the press gathered beyond the roped off sidewalk, and answering minimal questions, Sheriff Gilmore drove Aunt Lucy home.

"Will you be okay?" he asked, as he walked her to the door. "I can call someone to stay with you for awhile." He thought Lori would be a perfect evening companion for her.

But Aunt Lucy declined. "Oh, no, thank you, dear. I have Carman to commiserate with. She's very sympathetic you know, and quite understanding for a cat. She seems to always know how I'm feeling." Bluffing slightly, not really wanting company, she added, "I'll be just fine, don't worry about me!" After closing the door and watching Sheriff Gilmore walk toward his car, she fell into the nearest chair. Carman, jumping from her blanket-covered personal shelf in the front window, walked regally toward her, head and tail held high. Then squinting her green eyes at the old lady, leaped into her lap, purring. As Aunt Lucy stroked the cat's back, she closed her eyes, and prayed collectively for everyone involved with the murder: perpetrator, investigator, and the victim's friends and family members. She prayed fervently that Rose had known the Lord before her death and most of all, that God's perfect will would be done. When she finally opened her eyes, Carman was asleep on her lap and dusk had come. She arose, sending the cat, instantly awake, to the floor on all four pads, then bustled her small frame into the kitchen to fix a little supper for the two of them.

* * *

At every dinner table in Cramer Creek, the discussion centered on the murder. In the Bryson household, Geneva complained bitterly to Junior that Sheriff Gilmore had not returned her calls, even though she had spoken, clearly, several times into his answering machine stating that she had incriminating evidence about the murder, and would he call her immediately.

"What could you know about it?" Junior asked sarcastically, not really wanting her to answer his question. Any question from him excited her and elicited a thorough answer, which experience told him could take all evening. He did, however, want to hear more about the murder than the five o'clock local news had reported: that a woman had been murdered in the small town of Cramer Creek, committed by a person or persons unknown, and the victim's name was being withheld until the family could be notified.

"Well, I jest know'd the last person to see her alive, or dead," she retorted. "And I know'd a strange man visited her late last night, that was jest before your big boss snuck up to her door."

"What?"

Satisfied, Geneva crowed, "I waited a couple of hours to see him leave, but he never did, so I fin'ly went to bed."

"You are talking about my boss, Mr. James Frazier?"

"You bet I am. Mr. High and Mighty, hisself."

"Mother," he said, clipping his words, "you can't tell that to the sheriff, if you're wrong you could ruin Frazier's life, his marriage, not to mention, my job! What time did you see all this? If it was dark," he reasoned, "you were probably mistaken."

"No, sir, I am not mistaken, anybody half blind could've told it was him. Him with his broad shoulders and little rear end, and besides, her porch light was on." She summed up, with self-satisfaction, "It was him!"

Junior sighed and started eating the crispy fried chicken just as the phone rang.

Geneva threw back her chair and ran to kitchen wall phone. "Hello," she shouted, and then nodded her head vigorously at Junior and pointed to the phone. "Yes, sheriff, I seed about twelve people go in that house in two days. The last one was Aunt Lucy. Yes. Yes, I know that. Well, what do you think you're accusing me of? Well of course I'm sure. Huh?" Her voice changed from a high-pitched petulance to a musical purr. "Yes, I'll be here. Eight o'clock? Alright, Roy, I'll be waitin." She quietly placed the phone on the hook, hiked up her dress to expose her upper thighs, walked demurely back to the table and smirked at Junior.

Junior glared at her white, bony legs. "He's coming in the morning?"

"Sure he is, and don't look so worried. I'll tell Roy not to tell anybody I told him about Frazier so you won't lose your job. Then speculating further, she added, "If'n he didn't kill her, he was sure nough doin' something else a married man shouldn't be doin'. If'n he did kill her, then he most likely killed Karen too!"

Instantly livid, Junior jumped to his feet and threw the chicken leg he was eating on the table. "You've gone too far this time, Mother!" he shouted, and banged the back door on his way outside.

* * *

Dinner at the Gilmore home was later than usual, as the sheriff had decided to stop by his office at the county jail before coming home. He caught Nancy Armstrong, deputy, cum file clerk, leaving for the day and asked if she could stay a little longer to do a background check on the victim, Rose Findley. Promising to fax the information to his computer at home, Nancy returned to the computer and began the task. Then, after checking his messages, and making needed phone calls, the sheriff headed home to Lori.

* * *

After a healthy dinner of baked chicken, spinach Mirabella, and a cup of consommé, Betty decided to make her favorite comfort food, her special brownies recipe. It was really her mother's recipe, and the ingredients were the best: real butter, Mexican vanilla and four country brown eggs. "Too bad I always turn to food for comfort," she thought, "but it could be worse, right?" To Betty, comfort was a memory of a warm red robe and soft blue slippers curled up on the couch with a good book to read and a plate of warm chocolate brownies to eat. "That's my formula for 'well-being.'" She thought it would be interesting to compare her formula of comfort to other people's. "What was comfort to Junior, I wonder? Oh, I know. It was cuddling up with me watching the Chiefs play football."

Betty jumped as someone knocked lightly on the back door. "Who in the world could that be?" she wondered, and peeked through the short Venetian blinds of the kitchen window. The murder today had made her more cautious than usual. She and Emma had been walking home after school when they heard the emergency sirens and followed them to Aunt Lucy's rental house. They had stood on the sidewalk with the quickly gathering crowd and watched the confused, but serious professionals as they proceeded with their work. Then, after listening to a multitude of speculations from the bystanders, the only certainty, announced by Sheriff Gilmore to the press, was a murder had been committed. Stunned, she and Emma had watched the five o'clock news together, but afterward had more questions than answers.

Seeing Junior waiting at the door, she hurried to open it. "Hello, Junior, what are you doing here?"

He stood silently on the stoop, trying to formulate an answer until she said, "Well, come on in."

Looking around the familiar kitchen he murmured, "Uh, well, I guess you heard about the murder. I just wanted to see if you were okay. Are you okay?"

"Actually, I am a little jumpy. When you knocked on the door I was afraid to open it. Do they know who killed her? Who was she? I heard about her for the first time at church last night. She rented Aunt Lucy's house. Your mother told everyone at church the lady might be suicidal. Oh, I'm sorry," she apologized, "let me slow down and give you time to answer."

Junior looked at the mixture on the countertop. "Are you making my favorite brownies?"

"No." She laughed. "I'm making my favorite brownies, but if you are here when they come out of the oven you can have some." Then with a more serious tone, she asked, "What have you heard about the murder?"

"Everything I've heard, except for the little bit they had on the news, comes from Mother. You know her," he fumed, "ever since the lady moved next door she's had her eyes glued to the window and her mouth running. Now, she's fixin' to tell the sheriff who killed her."

Betty gasped. "Does she really know?"

"I don't know, she thinks she does. Right now she's probably making a list of everybody who went in and out of the house for the past two days, about twelve people according to her. To my mind, the murderer must be a stranger, because anybody that knows my mother, would never murder someone that lived next door, unless they wanted to get caught."

Betty nodded, and laughed. "You're joking, but you're right! It seems I've had a lot of laughs lately at Geneva's expense."

"What do you mean by that?" he asked.

"Oh, just a crazy dream I had. I might tell you about it some day," she added.

"You used to tell me your dreams all the time," he said wistfully, and looked steadily into her calm gray eyes. When she didn't look away, he kissed her softly.

* * *

For Brian, last night's suppertime repeated itself. Edie was still in bed, so he baked a pizza for the two of them. She did, however, come out of her room when he called her to the table. Entering the kitchen with her head down, she only partly concealed her bloodshot and swollen eyes.

CHAPTER 7

The next morning, instead of fixing Brian a hot breakfast as usual before he went to school, Edie was still in her bedroom behind a closed door.

"Edie, Sis?" Brian called lowly, and rapped softly at her door.

Hearing no sound, except the radio, he returned to the kitchen, dropped two pieces of bread into the toaster and poured a large glass of milk. PFR, his favorite Christian rock group, was singing on KLTE:

> *Though this world will hand me my fair share of pain,*
> *leave me broken and bruised,*
> *I know there's a Father and His Son who know my name,*
> *and they will see me through. Oh, yeah.*

Brian was really worried about his sister. Last night, after Brian had baked the frozen pizza, Edie had eaten only a small piece and had been uncommunicative during the meal, answering Brian's questions with monosyllables, and even neglecting to talk about the murder, which was extremely unusual behavior for his sister.

> *I believe He paid the price, a sacrifice,*
> *so we could be together, forever.*

In the past, she would have been talking excitedly non-stop about the lurid murder to anyone who would listen. Brian didn't know what to think about his sister's weird behavior. She didn't seem to be what he would call sick anymore, but something was definitely wrong with her. After a hasty breakfast, he listened at the door, then knocked softly. "Edie, are you awake?" After waiting a few seconds with no reply, he tried the door, but it was locked. Shrugging his shoulders, he grabbed his backpack and left for school.

* * *

Junior and his crew had been working on a row of Jonathans an hour before the boss, James Frazier, arrived. The collar of the older man's rawhide jacket was pulled up over his ears, and a cup of hot coffee was cradled in both gloved hands.

"Oversleep?" Junior yelled down good-naturedly.

"Nah, just lazy this morning. Couldn't make one step follow the other. I think I'm getting old!"

"Never happen," Junior bantered, but then remembering what his mother had told him about Frazier's late night visit to Rose Findley, he added, "maybe you've been staying out too late at night." Receiving no rejoinder, he changed the subject. "What do you think about the murder?"

"Pretty gruesome. It brings back bad memories, doesn't it," he acknowledged in a sympathetic manner, thinking of Karen. He continued, "Sometimes I wonder, Junior, how you can work in the orchard every day."

Junior agreed, "Yeah, I try not to think about it." Then, he changed the subject away from the private sorrow he was not willing to discuss. He had not revealed to anyone that he refused to allow his eyes to linger on the tree where he and Betty had found Karen. Leaving that devastating memory in a secret, private place in his mind, he returned to the current murder of Rose Findley. "Were you acquainted with the lady that got killed?" he asked, and then added, "Mom met her a couple of times."

James looked Junior in the eye and smiled laconically. "Nope, never met her. New in town, wasn't she?"

Junior agreed, "Yeah, she was. Mom said she was sick, or depressed, or something, and she had ugly scars on one side of her face. I guess nobody can figure out why she happened to settle here, being a stranger and all." Junior watched Frazier's face as he added, "But I guess Sheriff Gilmore's investigation will turn up something."

James's lips formed a ready smile. "I expect so, he's a good man," he said, and without another word he turned away and headed for the packing area.

* * *

Geneva's heart fluttered when she watched Sheriff Gilmore leave his cruiser and start up the sidewalk. This was the most important thing that had happened to her for years, maybe in all her 68 years. She visualized herself as a star witness for the prosecution, pointing a manicured finger, yes, she would have a professional manicure, at the unrepentant evildoer, declaring, "That's the man, or, that's the woman." She would have known the gender if only she had not taken a short nap yesterday morning after observing Pastor Sharpe going to the murdered woman's door, thus delaying her own visit. After the preacher, the next person she spied leaving the house just as Junior had finished eating the noon meal, was Edie. And finally, the last person she spied entering the house was Aunt Lucy, who supposedly discovered the body. It had to be Edie, she surmised; she must be the murderer.

"Come in, Sheriff," she said jubilantly, opening the door on his first knock.

"Good morning, Geneva. How are you today?" the sheriff said perfunctorily.

"I'm fine, just fine," she purred, "let me take your jacket."

Wanting to stop this nicety nice stuff and get down to business, he declined her offer and inquired, "What do you know about this business, Geneva? What did you see next door that makes you think you know who murdered Ms. Findley?"

Geneva, puffed up, began importantly, "Well, Sheriff, I seed at least a dozen people go into *that* woman's house fer the past two days. Jest think about it," she paused dramatically, "she claimed to be a stranger, but people was comin' and goin' out of that house like Grand Central Station. And she told me she din't know a soul in town. I could tell that was nothin' but a bald-faced lie, and it was proved a dozen times over. Why, two men, one a complete stranger to me, spent a long time in there after dark, and the other one, someone, I might add, we all know well," Geneva raised her eyebrows to accompany her innuendo, "probably stayed the night. I don't know when he left, because I couldn't keep my eyes open after midnight and finally had to go to bed."

"What an old cat," Sheriff Gilmore thought, then, said aloud, "Well, I am very interested in what you have to say, Geneva, but we need to be methodical as to who visited Mrs. Findley and the exact time each one arrived and departed." As he spoke, he reached for the pen in his pocket, and began to add new information to his notebook.

Smiling smugly, Geneva licked her lips, and invited the sheriff to ask his questions at the kitchen table, where she had prepared a braided yeast coffeecake for the interrogation.

"Not right now," he rejoined, "but I would like a cup of coffee if you have some made."

Geneva, miffed at his refusal of her offering that she had risen at four in the morning to prepare, she poured a cup of coffee for each of them. She looked askance, to which he replied, "Just black, please," and, "thank you."

After nearly two hours of exasperating hemming and hawing, and chasing several rabbits, the sheriff's finished timetable looked like this:

DATE	ARRIVED	NAME	LEFT
Wednesday	12 noon	Edie Bentley	2:00 p.m.
"	2:00 p.m.	Geneva	2:30 p.m.
"	4:15 p.m.	Sarah Frazier	5:15 p.m.
"	9:00 p.m.	? man	10:00 p.m.
"	10:05 p.m.	James Frazier	midnight+
Thursday	7:15 a.m.	Lucy Kirby	7:30 a.m.
"	10:00 a.m.	Pastor Sharpe	?
"	?	Edie Bentley	12:50 p.m.
"	3:35 p.m.	Lucy Kirby	

He wrote, "Mrs. Bryson affirms the above timetable to be correct, but reluctantly agrees she was not watching the neighbor's house consistently. She especially notes being away from the window and/or back kitchen door (which faces the victim's house) while preparing the breakfast, dinner and supper meals (approximately 6:30-7:00 a.m., 11:00 a.m.-12:00 noon, 4:15-5:15 p.m. respectively), and when taking a short nap from 10:30 a.m. to 11:00 a.m. Thursday."

Back in the car, Sheriff Gilmore radioed the county office and asked if the background check on Rose Findley was completed, and was informed by Deputy Armstrong the computer search had come up blank. "And, Nancy, I need a trained investigative female officer to assist me in the field, would you like to volunteer?"

"Would I? Yes sir! Thank you, sir." To make certain she had heard correctly, she asked happily, "You want me to work with you, on the murder, in the field?"

Hearing the exuberance in her voice, he smiled, "Yes, starting today if possible." Then, added, "I'll tell the others to pick up the slack for you in the office while we're on the case, and I'll pick you up in a couple of hours. We need to interrogate some witnesses." Then, after informing the staff coordinator to reorganize the clerical duties in his office, he drove the fifteen miles to Dr. Judd's office.

Besides being the county coroner, Dr. Judd also had a small medical practice in the neighboring city of Boonville. This morning, the waiting room was inhabited by a young mother and baby, and a middle-aged man with red, swollen eyes. The sheriff spoke to the receptionist, alias Mrs. Judd, requesting an immediate appointment regarding county business. She ushered him into her husband's private office and invited him to help himself to the coffeepot, then left him to wait. Within five minutes Dr. Judd appeared, and similar to his patient in the waiting room, had red, swollen eyes.

"You look terrible, Bill."

"Well, I might look better if the county wasn't so cheap and hired me full time. Maybe I wouldn't have to stay up all night doing county business and up all day tending my medical practice," the coroner ranted. "You must know what I'm talking about, I don't know how you get by on the pittance they pay you."

The sheriff agreed, "Yeah, but with Lori working and my part-time business we do all right. Anyway, Cramer Creek is an economical place to live, you should try it."

"No way! Me, live in the same town with those old biddies that know your business better than you do? Believe me, I know them; some of them are my patients. I know just what would happen if I lived in town and happened to fix the kitchen sink for a decent looking young woman, the grapevine would have us in a full-blown affair and a divorce in the works. No thank you!"

Anxious to hear results of the autopsy, Sheriff Gilmore retrieved his pen and notebook, and changed the subject, "Well, what did you find out last night?"

"If you had any patience, you would wait to read my report later today. However," he sighed, "the cause of death was asphyxiation caused by blood filling the lungs through perforations made by the murder weapon. She probably lived ten to fifteen minutes after she was stabbed."

"Was she conscious or unconscious during that time?"

"Well, she was conscious at least part of the time as witnessed by the spilled perfume. The lab tech said only her fingerprints were on the bottle, and none of the perfume was under the body, indicating she opened the bottle and emptied the contents on the floor as she lay dying."

"Why would she do something like that?" Sheriff Gilmore asked incredulously.

"The why is your problem, Buddy, not mine. Let's get this over with, I have patients waiting."

Persevering, the sheriff asked, "What about the weapon?"

"That's not my jurisdiction either, but it was obviously an ordinary kitchen butcher knife, but very sharp. The blade sliced the muscles of her back cleanly with one cut passing through the right lung and a second cut perforating the left lung. The third stab wound was peripheral and did no terminal damage. There was no extra tearing of tissue or turning of the knife in the wounds, which would indicate there was no struggle. Mrs. Findley must have been taken by surprise by her attacker. The lack of skin or blood under the victim's fingernails would substantiate that."

Sheriff Gilmore agreed with the hypothesis of the coroner. The no-struggle theory was further strengthened by the orderliness of the room. Of course, the murderer could have straightened the room afterward. He thought for a moment and asked, "What kind of person am I looking for, Bill? Tall or short, someone with a lot of strength?"

"Well," he paused, "by the slant of the wound someone a few inches taller than the victim, maybe five-eight or ten, but as far as strength goes, the knife was sharp enough that an average man or woman could have done it with moderate swiftness and force. Oh, one other thing, after getting some of the other organs' temperatures, I was able to narrow down the time of death to not earlier than 11:00 a.m. nor later than 1:45 p.m. My best guess would be noon. Now," he barked, "I'm getting back to my practice, if you don't mind. Anything else you want to know, you can wait for the report."

* * *

Emma and Betty entered the smoky teacher's lounge a second time in a week, a record. Curiosity was their motivating factor, as the murder would be the main topic of conversation. As they sat at the edge of the fray and opened their lunch sacks, the informal exchange of opinion was in progress.

Opal James, the short, plump second grade teacher, was saying, "I don't know what to say to the class, they are so curious and have the most outrageous ideas. Tommy Samp swears that Aunt Lucy murdered the poor woman."

"He knows better than that, he's still upset because she made him apologize to Mary Thomas," observed Mr. Warmbrough, "and, of course, Mary's been lording over him ever since."

Sarah Frazier chimed in, "Of course Aunt Lucy didn't do it, she would be the very last person anyone would ever suspect of murder."

"That goes without saying," Betty responded, "but who did murder this woman? I have to admit, I was afraid to answer the door after dark last night."

Her friend, Emma, gave her a knowing smile.

Lori spoke up, "I was scared last night too until Roy finally got home. I was alone in a quiet house listening to Geneva leave a dozen messages on the answering machine demanding Roy call her immediately because she knew who the murderer was. Well, you know I never answer the machine until I can tell if it's personal or county business, but it really freaked me out to hear her voice, over and over again, saying she knew who the killer was."

"That's our Geneva," Mr. Lacey chuckled, "she's probably had her binoculars glued to the house ever since the lady moved to town. That's why I never worry about our place, living across the street from her is like having a guard dog without having to feed it."

I probably shouldn't say anything, but Roy won't put much stock in what Geneva might tell him," Lori conceded, "he's waiting for the lab and coroner reports, and they still don't know about her family. She seems to be a total stranger to everyone, and it's a real mystery why she moved into town."

"Good point," Mrs. Patton affirmed, "why in the world would anyone move to this town!" Adding a grim personal note, she said, "Of course, I don't know why Doug and I are still here. As a matter of fact, I don't know why anybody lives here!"

An embarrassing silence ensued as the teachers sympathized with Cheryl Patton and her difficult marriage to a boisterous alcoholic. Then trying to amend, Lori spoke to her, "Roy said Doug was the first responder on the scene."

"Yes, he was," Cheryl said proudly, "he tried to calm Aunt Lucy down, and worked with the highway patrol to put up barriers to keep people away."

"Blimey, what do you think about that?" Emma exclaimed as they walked back to their classrooms. "Your ex-mother-in-law thinks she can identify the murderer."

"Yes," said Betty thoughtfully, "but if she really does know who killed that woman, I don't think Roy would approve of Lori announcing it to everyone."

* * *

Nancy Armstrong, the thirty-year-old excitable blonde (her father always told her she would get excited over a glass of water), bounced down the courthouse steps following the sheriff to his car. Although fully trained as an investigator, her usual duties were substitute 911 operator, miscellaneous file clerk, computer operator, coffee maker, and current office pool keeper. To escape those mundane jobs and actually take part in a murder investigation had made her lightheaded and giddy. She knew, but didn't care, the only reason the sheriff had chosen her was her gender, "female," and was because he was concerned about interrogating other "females" alone. This was true. However, the sheriff was concerned with only one particular female, Edie Bentley. He knew Nancy was better than liability insurance, and he was making sure he had a witness to corroborate he was not a new actor in a growing list of unfortunate players on the stage of Edie's imagination.

On the ride back to Cramer Creek, Sheriff Gilmore fully updated Nancy on the murder investigation, as well as the character of Edie Bentley, the subject of their first interrogation. "So, now you know everything I do, Nancy. Our first priority, since the computer came up zilch identifying Rose Findley, will be to search her house thoroughly and see if we can find out more about her, and her next of kin. Then, handing her his notebook, he concluded, "Afterward, we'll begin questioning everyone seen entering the victim's house on Wednesday and Thursday."

Nancy studied the extensive list constructed with Geneva's help. "Well, there is one thing I will agree with Mrs. Bryson about, I don't believe the victim was a stranger in town."

"I'm inclined to agree with you," admitted the sheriff, "but she was definitely a stranger to me. On the other hand, I've lived in this weird town most of my life and I know how the people think, and if there's one thing they can't abide, it's not appeasing their curiosity. Between the natural friendliness of some folks wanting to welcome a new neighbor, and the curious and prone to gossip others wanting to look for skeletons in the closet, it is possible she was a stranger here. Furthermore, the stories going around about the scars on her face and possibly being suicidal made her even more irresistible to the curious. Now that I think about it, I'm surprised she didn't have more visitors." Then, pulling to the curb in front of the Findley house, they got out, ducked beneath the yellow tape, and went inside, using Aunt Lucy's key.

"I've never seen so little of nothing," Nancy exclaimed, after examining the victim's nearly empty purse and every drawer and closet in the house. "No credit cards, no unpaid bills or receipts, no driver's license, not even a Social Security card. The murderer must have taken them."

"Yes, it is curious, but remember she has only been in town a few days.

Perhaps she hasn't moved the bulk of her stuff yet," the sheriff reasoned. "And, she came on a bus, so she might not have a driver's license. Well, I suppose we might as well leave." He banged the front door screen and headed down the steps.

"You didn't check the mailbox, did you, Sheriff?" Nancy shouted from behind him before he reached the car.

Turning toward her, he saw her waving a small brown box in the air. "What is it?"

"Checks, can I open them?"

A few minutes later they stared down at Rose's newly ordered checks that carried her name, address, and social security number.

"You're all right, deputy. I'd give you a raise," he paused and grinned, "if, I could. Anyway," he ordered, "enter her Social Security number into the system when you get back to the office, download a background check, and fax me the results at home, ASAP. Now, let's question Edie Bentley."

After the third knock on Edie's door, she answered and stared at the two officers.

When she didn't invite them in, Sheriff Gilmore began, "Edie, this is Deputy Armstrong, and we would like to ask you some questions about the lady who was murdered yesterday. Could we come in?"

Reluctantly, she opened the door wider and stepped back. "I've been sick, Sheriff, and I don't know anything about it."

"We won't stay long, Miss Bentley, I'm sorry you don't feel well," the deputy said sympathetically.

Sheriff Gilmore interceded impatiently, "Let's get right to the point, Edie, we know you visited Mrs. Rose Findley at least twice the last two days of her life, and we want you to tell us about those visits."

Not making eye contact, Edie protested shakily, "I swear, Sheriff, I don't know a thing about her. I just went over to see if I could sell her something. She didn't buy anything. The second time I went I took some foundation samples for her to try, but she wasn't at home. And that's all there is to it."

"We have a witness, Edie, who saw you coming out of the house around the time of the murder."

"That's a lie, I only knocked at the door, and left."

"You didn't have a conversation with her at all?" quizzed the sheriff skeptically.

She whined, "No, Sheriff. Now can I go back to bed?"

"Sure, Edie, but we will be back!"

Walking back to the car, he said, "She's lying through her teeth."

"After what you've told me about her, I believe you."

"If you knew her, Nancy, you would know exactly what I mean. First of all, sick or not, she would never miss a chance to tell a customer some tall tales, like the story of her life, for instance, and that goes double for a stranger in town. I promise you, the mousy little person you just met was not Edie. She's lying, and we are going to find out why!"

CHAPTER 8

"Roy, good to see you," Pastor Sharpe said warmly.

"Good afternoon, brother Jonathan, same to you." Sheriff Gilmore turned toward his deputy, and said, "Nancy, I'd like you to meet Pastor Jonathan Sharpe. Pastor, this is my deputy, Nancy Armstrong."

Shaking her hand, the pastor smiled broadly. "Very nice to meet you." Then turning to the sheriff, he shook his head. "Well, I guess I know why you're here, very sad. How can I help you?"

"To get right to the point, Brother Jonathan, Geneva has given us a list of everyone she saw going into and out of Rose Findley's house the past couple of days and you are on the list. Would you tell us about your visit?"

"Of course. And by the way, her maiden name was Findley, her married name was Vanhuss."

"You must be the only person in town who knows that," Deputy Armstrong declared. "The sheriff and I have been spinning our wheels trying to find information about her background under the name, Findley."

The sheriff added, "What else can you tell us about her, Pastor? I assume you went to see her because of what Geneva told us at Wednesday night prayer meeting."

"That's right, Roy," the young minister agreed. "I was very concerned about her after Geneva led us to believe she was suicidal. After spending a few minutes with her, I had to concur with that assessment. She was obviously distraught and tearful. At first she tried to pass off her disheveled appearance as the result of a cold, but soon afterward began to confide in me. Ordinarily, I wouldn't disclose a private conversation, but I consider the restraints of confidentiality to be moot after her murder." Then he made eye contact alternately with his visitors, and cautioned, "However, I just want you both to understand, in respect for Mrs. Vanhuss, her indiscretions must not become public knowledge unless absolutely necessary. Do I have your word?"

Both officers nodded assent.

"Well, then," he motioned them to sit in two mint green arm chairs on the opposite side of his desk, "let's get comfortable, shall we, this may take a little while. Would you like a cup of coffee?" With their consent, he poured three cups, and then began his narrative.

"As I said, she appeared to be quite upset, and, naturally, I asked if there was anything I could do. Her words to me were, 'There's nothing anyone can do, pastor. I've reached the end of myself, and have nothing worth holding on to.' My thought at the time was this was an admission of her intent to take her life, so I tried to assure her if she had eternal salvation in God she could look at her problems with a new perspective. If she would trust in Jesus, no matter what her circumstances, He would never leave or forsake her, and would forgive all her sins, no matter what she might have done. Then I asked if she would like to share her troubles with me, and it appeared she was grateful to have someone in whom to confide. She confessed she had separated from her husband and come to Cramer Creek attempting to renew a relationship with a local man, Mr. James Frazier, as a matter of fact."

"James Frazier?" Sheriff Gilmore asked incredulously.

"Yes, and according to her story, she succeeded, for he spent most of Wednesday night with her. However, she awakened Thursday morning overcome with guilt. You see, she had actually met James's wife, Sarah, earlier in the day on Wednesday. Sarah had come to ask for desserts for the chili supper next month. Well, the two women got acquainted, and, Sarah, not knowing about the relationship between her husband and Rose Findley, the name the lady was using, attempted to make Mrs. Vanhuss feel welcome in town. She actually invited her to dinner, and volunteered to bring her to church, introduce her around, that sort of thing." Pastor Sharpe paused, taking a sip of coffee.

"So let me understand," Nancy interjected, "she was suicidal because of the guilt she felt about the affair with Mr. Frazier?"

"Not really, that's only one part of a larger picture." Pastor Sharpe sighed and continued. "A greater guilt had plagued her for the last two years. I suppose you remember the hotel fire in Kansas City that took the lives of several people, including David and Edith Bentley from Cramer Creek?" Observing their nods, he continued, "Well, this unfortunate woman was the cause of that fire. She and James had been together at the hotel that night. The two had used the 'Feeling Wonderful' seminars as a front to cover up their relationship."

Making a face, Deputy Armstrong asked, "'Feeling Wonderful?' I don't remember that."

"Yes," the pastor answered, "it's actually a thinly disguised pyramid scheme based on greed, one's sense of personal inadequacy, and a lack of true Biblical knowledge by the participants, but that's another story. Anyway, to continue, Mrs. Vanhuss had apparently fallen asleep leaving a cigarette burning which caused the fire. Later, she awakened to find James gone and her room ablaze. She barely escaped with her life. That night, she confessed to me, was the last time she and James were together until last Wednesday night."

Astonished, the sheriff considered the several possibilities the pastor's narrative suggested.

Deputy Armstrong was also given to furious thinking. "Tell me, Sheriff, and I'm afraid of the answer," she interposed. "Is the Edie Bentley on our list related to the Bentley couple that died in the fire?"

Pastor Sharpe answered for him, "Edie is the daughter of those Bentleys, Nancy, and I'm afraid I have even more of Mrs. Vanhuss' story to relate." When no one spoke, he proceeded, "She told me when Edie first introduced herself, she didn't catch her last name. You know how Edie chirps like a bird and always two seconds ahead of you. Anyway, Edie was giving her spiel selling her cosmetics, and in addition, told her the story of the fictitious fire in which she supposedly saved the life of her brother. However, Edie hadn't gotten to the true story of her parents' death in the hotel fire. Consequently, Mrs. Vanhuss didn't realize she was talking to the daughter of the Bentleys, and proceeded to relate the horrible account of the hotel fire and how she was personally responsible for the people who died. At that point in her story, Mrs. Vanhuss related to me that a look of utter shock and dismay had suddenly come over Edie's face. At the time, she thought the look was in commiseration, since they had supposedly survived similar experiences. It wasn't until Aunt Lucy visited the woman Thursday morning and spoke of Edie, that Mrs. Vanhuss suddenly realized to whom she had told her story."

The three sat silently for a moment, then Sheriff Gilmore shook his head and started to rise. "Thank you, Pastor, you've given us a lot to chew on."

Pastor Sharpe, however, wasn't finished. "Roy, I can't let you go until I tell you the good news."

"Pastor, I already know the good news," the sheriff said with a twinkle in his eye. "I don't know about Deputy Armstrong though. Nancy have you been born again?"

Smiling at them, Jonathan said, "You are joking, but I really was referring to that 'good news.' You see, Rose accepted Jesus' free gift of eternal life

Thursday morning, only a few hours before she was murdered. Praise God, she was at peace when I left her and wanted to begin a new life with the Lord. Her first step was going to be an attempt to reconcile with her husband."

"That's wonderful news, Brother Jonathan! You deprived Satan of another soul."

The men were instantly aware of the deputy's wary silence, and a moment of understanding passed between them.

Then, breaking her silence, the deputy asked, "So, what time did you leave the victim's house, Pastor? Geneva was taking a nap or fixing lunch for her son and didn't see you leave."

"Oh, does this mean I'm a suspect?" He smiled. "Let's see, I probably left about 11:05 to 11:15, and then, having a grocery list from Ruth, I picked up a few things at the market before going home for lunch."

As they left the church, the sheriff told the deputy to call the state lab, and put a rush on their report.

* * *

"Yuk," pretty Elizabeth Lacey snorted, as she looked at today's cafeteria offering, tuna casserole. "I'd like to know why we can't have a few choices for lunch like other schools. Some schools even have salad bars. And tell me, why do they call this a cafeteria, huh? Doesn't that mean we have choices?"

"You wouldn't be so picky, if you had eaten microwave pizza the last two nights like I have," complained Brian. "If Edie doesn't get it together pretty soon, I just want you to know I'm available for adoption." Brian lowered his head close to her chest, put on his abandoned puppy dog face, whimpered, and looked up at her with sad eyes.

Elizabeth laughed and pet his head. "I don't think Zippy would share his doghouse with you, and Dad says we can't have an indoor pet. So, sorry." Then, noticing the lunchroom monitor looking in their direction, Elizabeth straightened in her chair and asked, "So, what is wrong with Edie? She isn't still sick, is she?"

"Yeah, I guess she's sick. She's sure not herself, she cries a lot and she doesn't talk to me. She won't even talk about the murder!"

Their discussion was forgotten as all eyes spotted Sheriff Gilmore, a woman officer in uniform, and Aunt Lucy entering the dining room together and walking to the front of the cafeteria line where they received the day's lunch offering for $1.25, and sat with their trays at the corner table reserved for teachers. As they ate, the officers and Aunt Lucy kept their heads close together in serious conversation. If Brian had been able to overhear, he would have been surprised that Edie was the main topic.

Aunt Lucy appealed in a low voice, "Roy, I just can't believe Edie is mixed up in this murder. As I said before, the only unusual thing I've seen her do lately was on Wednesday afternoon when I saw her racing toward home at breakneck speed hugging her sales kit. Now that you've told me where she had just come from and what Rose Findley, I mean, Vanhuss, unintentionally revealed to her, it makes sense. She must have been devastated to meet the woman who caused her parents' death."

Apologetically, Sheriff Gilmore said, "Yes, I'm sure she was. However, and I'm sorry, Aunt Lucy, but I'm afraid we're going to have to bring her to the county jail for questioning. You have to be aware of the facts. She has motive, and opportunity. She was identified at the scene at the time of the murder."

"Well, there doesn't seem to be anything I can do about it, is there, Roy?" Her voice faltered. "I just feel so sorry for that girl. Would it be all right if I come to your office after school to be with her?"

"Not during the questioning period, but afterward if you want," he acquiesced. "Then, if she's allowed to leave, you can take her home. As long as you're coming to the office, I'd like you to make an official statement regarding your finding the body."

* * *

Junior walked through the back door just as Geneva put the final touches of his lunch together. Today, she had outdone herself with smoked country ham, mashed potatoes, red-eye gravy, and macaroni and cheese. "That will stick to his ribs a few hours," she thought with satisfaction. After filling his plate, she sat beside him with thinly-veiled anger filling her face. Junior, knowing his mother and her moods, hoped he could eat quickly and get out the door before her obvious venom exploded in speech.

"Great meal. Where did you get the country ham?"

Pleased by his compliment, but not enough to erase what Betty's neighbor had revealed this morning, she answered his question, "The Mennonites were sellin' them this morning. They come into town with a wagonload. I couldn't wait to fry it up for you."

Keep her talking, he thought to himself. "It sure is good, and that red-eye gravy…umm."

Knowing her son as well as he knew her, she decided to cut to the chase. "You'd never guess such nonsense I heard this morning from one of Betty Abbott's neighbors." Not waiting for his guess, she continued, "She said she seed you visitin' that woman las night. She said she was sure it was you." Geneva's voice rose to a crescendo, then exploded, "Now, tell me the truth!" Her face flushed with emotion, she demanded. "You tell me if you had the gall to visit that harlot!"

Both bristling with anger, mother and son stared each other down. Then Junior shouted, "Yeah, I certainly did visit Betty Abbott Bryson, and I plan to do it again! If you don't like it, you know what you can do about it!" Grabbing his jacket, he slammed out the door for the second time in a week.

Geneva looked over the uneaten dinner she had slavishly prepared for her beloved son and felt rage fill her heart. "She won't get away with this!" she hissed.

* * *

Putting off picking Edie up until later in the day, the sheriff and deputy stopped by his house to check the fax. As expected, the background check on the victim using her social security number found on her newly printed checks had arrived. However, not a great deal of new information was added to their knowledge received earlier from Pastor Sharpe. It did contain Mrs. Vanhuss' prior address in Marshall, her husband's name, their credit history, her implication in the hotel fire, and a blank "prior arrests" report. "What we need now, Nancy, is a complete list of area residents that attended that 'Feeling Wonderful' seminar in Kansas City, as well as those staying in the hotel that burned. I am not completely sold on Edie Bentley being our murderer, even though she had plenty of motive and opportunity. James Frazier's name comes readily to mind. By owning his own business he is free to come and go as he pleases which gives him opportunity. His motive could be Mrs. Vanhuss had threatened to tell his wife about their affair and he decided to shut her up. So, we don't quit investigating until we uncover every possibility, right?"

"Yes," the deputy agreed, "Mr. Frazier should receive an equal amount of attention. And, remember, his wife, Sarah, is also on our list of the victim's visitors. If she was aware of the relationship between her husband and Mrs. Vanhuss, she has a pretty strong motive too."

"If she knew about it, and if she had the opportunity. Two big 'ifs.' Unless she played sick from school yesterday, she had no opportunity. Better check on that. And don't forget Mrs. Vanhuss' husband, who possibly had the same motive and perhaps, opportunity."

"I wonder if he was the mysterious visitor Geneva spotted Wednesday night before James Frazier showed up," she pondered. "And by the way, who is going to inform him about his wife's death?"

"I think I'll do that personally instead of letting the local cops break it to him. I'd like to see the look on his face when he finds out. Right now is as good a time as any. While I'm gone to Marshall, you check on alibis. Make sure Sarah Frazier was at school all day; and see if you can get that information on the 'Feeling Wonderful' seminars and all the participants who stayed in that hotel in Kansas City the night of the fire. Instead of me taking you back to the office, why don't you work in my office at home until I get back, then we'll pick Edie up."

* * *

Sheriff Gilmore found Donald Vanhuss at the ReMax Real Estate office taking his turn manning the phones at the front desk, a duty he disliked. He preferred the more active and lucrative business of showing homes to prospective clients. The rule of thumb, though, instituted by the company, was everyone had to serve time at the front desk. It was also mandated for the person taking phone calls to match likely prospects to agents in a prearranged order. "Which means I'm working for someone else's paycheck," he grumbled. He looked up from the desk as the sheriff entered the office, and a look of fear passed over his face. He waited until the sheriff introduced himself and specifically asked for him before he blurted out, "It was Rose then, it was my wife that was murdered in Cramer Creek?"

"Yes, it was Mr. Vanhuss. I'm very sorry to bring you such sad news."

"When I first heard about the murder, I thought it couldn't be her. I had just seen her the evening before." His lips quivering, he implored the sheriff, "I wanted her to come back home and try to work things out."

"I'm very sorry, Mr. Vanhuss," said the sheriff sympathetically. "And believe me, I do sympathize with you, but I'm afraid I must ask you some questions."

"Yes, I understand," he nodded, and fought for control, "believe me, I want you to find the bastard that killed her. I'll help you in any way I can!" he sobbed.

"You just mentioned you saw her Wednesday night," the sheriff began. "Can you tell me what time you visited her, and what else you talked about?"

"I got to the house about eight thirty, I guess, and stayed about forty-five minutes. I went to talk her into coming back home. Told her I would try harder to make her happy, but she wasn't buying it. I'll tell you the truth, Sheriff, we've never had a real happy home, but a couple of years ago, things got ten times worse when she accidentally started a fire at a hotel in Kansas City that killed some people. It was just too much on her conscience, I guess. I don't think she ever had another peaceful day, and if you want to know the truth, she never gave me one either. I'm sure you saw her face. Well, after three operations it looks good compared to what it looked like after the fire, and there are more skin grafts to come...or were," he corrected. "Anyway," he summed up, "she told me plain and clear, she wasn't going to come back."

Sheriff Gilmore put a kind hand on his shoulder. "Mr. Vanhuss, that is not quite true. Our pastor, Jonathan Sharpe, visited with your wife just a few hours before she died, and according to him, she did find peace, and her first desire was to reconcile with you. I hope you'll find some consolation in that. I'm sure the pastor would be glad to share her experience with you."

Having left Mr. Donald Vanhuss calling friends and relatives, and making funeral arrangements, the sheriff, perhaps too hastily, crossed him off his personal suspect list, and returned to Cramer Creek. He was anxious to find out what his deputy had learned. As he passed the school and noticed the buses ready to roll, not wanting Brian to get home before they brought Edie in for questioning, he hurried home. "Nancy," he called, as he crossed the threshold of the front door, "we need to rock and roll!"

"Give me a minute," she called back, "I just need to get my notes together and grab my jacket." Grinning at him as she entered the living room, she said, "Do you realize how exciting this job is for me after being stuck in the office for so long? Am I ghoulish for enjoying it so much, when someone is dead and a murderer is on the loose?"

"Yes, to both questions." He smiled. "But this is just your first day, give reality some time to sink in. Now, let's pick up Edie."

The Bentley home was only a few yards from the Gilmores' and in a matter of seconds they were knocking on the door. On the third knock, Edie answered, looking much as she had earlier in the day, with her hair disheveled, no makeup, and wrinkled clothing.

The sheriff spoke dispassionately, "Edie, we have to take you in for questioning in the matter of the Rose Findley Vanhuss murder."

Edie looked shocked. "No! No, Sheriff, believe me, I don't know anything about it. I told you when I knocked yesterday, nobody was home."

"I know what you said, Edie," he agreed, "but we have information that you know more than you've told us. Get your coat," he said gruffly, "and whatever else you might need and come with us."

"Brian won't know where I am."

"Leave him a note if you like."

Twenty minutes later, facing Sheriff Gilmore across his desk with tears in her eyes, Edie listened to the recital of her rights under the Miranda law and was informed their conversation would be recorded. Then, as she had earlier in the day, denied having anything to do with the murder.

Deputy Armstrong spoke, "That may be, Edie, but until you tell us the truth, in detail, about your two visits with the murdered lady, you will stay here and answer questions. Are you sure you don't want a lawyer?"

"I didn't do anything wrong so I don't need a lawyer." She whined tearfully. "You need to look for a real creep, like the one who raped me, the one who killed my best friend."

"Sure," he answered sarcastically, then leaning toward the non-directional microphone, stated, "Let the record show Miss Bentley has refused legal counsel. Okay, Edie, just tell us again exactly what happened when you visited Rose Vanhuss."

"She told me her name was Findley, she lied to me. If she had told me her real name…."

"Then you would have known what, Edie?" Deputy Armstrong fired back.

Edie shook her head crossed her arms, and sat without speaking.

The sheriff spit out, "Then you would have known she was responsible for your parents' deaths! You would have known it was her cigarette that caused the fire that killed them!"

Her face turned white. "Yes, yes, yes," she cried. "I wish I had killed her. I wanted to, I was going to. But when I went to her house to do it, I couldn't, she was already dead." Sobbing uncontrollably, Edie continued, "I'm glad she's dead. I need my mommy and daddy and she took them away. I don't have anybody. I hate her. I'm glad she's dead." Her body shaking, Edie lowered her head to the table and continued to cry.

Motioning the deputy outside the room, the sheriff whispered, "I'm going to see if Aunt Lucy is here, and, if she is, I'll ask her to wait until you call her in. After that, I'm going home for dinner. You get the particulars out of Edie, and make sure everything is on tape. Get her to describe in detail the victim when she found her, narrow down the time she arrived and left, did she see anyone leaving when she arrived, help her remember every moment of her second visit to the house. Ask her how she planned to kill her, and did she bring along a weapon?"

"Okay, Sheriff. What should I do afterward?"

"First, send her home with Aunt Lucy, then give the tape of Edie's testimony to the night clerk and have her type it, save it, print it out and leave a copy on my desk. After dinner, I intend to pay a friendly visit to the Fraziers, there's no need for you to come. Go home and have a good evening."

"If you're sure you don't need me." Nancy looked wistful, as she pondered another dull evening at home. Her nights had been uneventful since she had broken up with her boyfriend a month ago, and was still hoping they would get back together again, but so far she hadn't heard from him. "I don't mind meeting you over there."

"No, you'll be busy here for quite a while, then go on home. I'll see you first thing in the morning, at my house. Check out a squad car."

When the sheriff left to find Aunt Lucy, Deputy Armstrong returned to question Edie. Handing her a box of Kleenex and sympathetically patting the young girl's shoulder, she said, "Thank you, Edie, for telling us the truth, and now we need to know everything you can tell us about your second visit to the victim's house."

The sheriff found Aunt Lucy giving her deposition to the secretary and waited at his desk until she finished. Then he spoke to her, "Edie will need you in there, Aunt Lucy, when she finishes her statement. I've got enough circumstantial evidence to hold her but I don't think she murdered the woman. She says Mrs. Vanhuss was dead when she arrived yesterday, ostensibly to murder her. Whether she would have, I don't know, but it's a moot point. As soon as she finishes giving her statement I want you to take her home. You might call the pastor to be with her too. I've got enough evidence to hold her," he repeated, mostly to himself, "but I don't think she did it."

CHAPTER 9

Sarah stood at the kitchen sink and slowly washed the few supper dishes she and James had dirtied. Tiredness swept over her as she stared out the darkened window over the dishwater, seeing nothing but the outside dusk to dawn light and the small area of the back yard it illuminated. Her thoughts centered on her married life that had begun with visions of "happily forever after." She had been twenty-two, had graduated from the State Teacher's College in Kirksville, and was teaching social studies in Cramer Creek when James begged her to marry him. Years earlier, as teenage classmates in high school, he had not appeared to notice her. She had been termed a bookworm, and was quiet and plain, while he was intelligent, gregarious, goodlooking and wildly popular with both sexes. He had a "devil may care" attitude that endeared him to his peers while his egotism drew the distain of his teachers. When he began showering her with attention in her final year of college, Sarah couldn't believe her good fortune. He would drive the ninety miles to Kirksville once a week and take her to dinner and a movie, and afterward would pressure her to allow him to take her to a motel room for the night, but she always refused. He punished her refusals by not coming to see her the following weekend, but would always return the next. They were married in the Baptist Church before a large crowd who had known them all their lives. Sarah, inexperienced and naïve, so much in love, and confidant love would conquer any problem that materialized was totally unprepared for the harsh reality that followed.

In what seemed to her a very short time, a vague sense of James's dissatisfaction in the relationship developed into definite coldness in his manner toward her. On the surface, all the niceties were in place. They visited friends, attended church, and hosted small dinner parties, but when they were alone, she found he had no need of her, except in the bedroom. He remained aloof and always busy and had no time to talk or listen. During their intimate moments, she felt an object of lust rather than love. And when they ventured together outside Cramer Creek, he habitually established sexually provocative eye contact with other women, even in her presence. In a restaurant, if even a passably nice-looking young lady waited their table, James's longing eyes would follow her throughout the evening, obviously undressing her as she took orders, scooped up dirty dishes and made trips to and from the kitchen. Sarah noticed the younger the girl and the more James had to drink greatly acerbated his behavior. Within a year following their wedding, she sat alone too many nights waiting for his truck lights to turn into the driveway, and her tentative self-esteem quickly deteriorated into despair and inadequacy. Now, after thirty-five years of marriage, they remained childless and she half believed his bitter accusation it was her fault because she couldn't satisfy him. Deep inside, however, as she hit rock-bottom again, she knew no one could ever satisfy his lusts, his search for wholeness, perhaps absolution. For years she had ceased to try. But, he would continue to be her husband, and nothing and no one would ever separate them. He belonged to her in spite of his weaknesses she dared not name, even to herself. And now, as she listened to his movements from the bathroom to the bedroom, then back to the bathroom, and smelled the Old Spice wafting through the hallway to the kitchen, she waited for the announcement that he was going out.

* * *

"Edie, where have you been?" Brian commanded angrily, as she and Aunt Lucy walked into the house. "You know, Sis, your note didn't say anything except, 'I'm going out.'"

"Oh, Brian, stop being such a worry wart!" Edie protested. "You're my brother, not my keeper!"

Gently, Aunt Lucy interrupted, "Edie, I really think Brian has been worried about you, especially because of the way you've been acting around here. I think he should know everything that has happened, about who the murdered woman was and where you have been, and he should hear it from you, not the kids at school."

Immediately, Edie's face sobered as her bravado disappeared and tears began to slide down her cheeks. "Alright, Aunt Lucy, I will." She lunged awkwardly toward her tall brother and held him around the waist. "Oh, Brian, it's been so awful! I wanted to tell you everything, but I didn't want you to know the truth; I didn't want to hurt you, to suffer like I have, it's so terrible, I just couldn't."

"Brian, before Edie explains," Aunt Lucy inserted gently, "I want you to know, Brian, that your sister has been hurting and has probably been in shock the past few days by circumstances she couldn't control," she looked kindly at Edie, and added, "and also very stupid not to confide in you. You two need each other, now more than ever." Then, she asked Edie, "Do you want me to stay with you while you tell Brian, or would you rather be alone?"

"I'd rather tell him alone," Edie said soberly, "if you don't mind?"

"I don't mind, but be certain you tell the whole truth and nothing but the truth," the ancient schoolteacher admonished.

"I will," she promised.

* * *

Lori, twirling her long golden hair around her finger, smiled invitingly at her husband. "I've been waiting for you."

"Don't you dare entice me like that," he whined longingly, "I still have to go out tonight."

"No you don't, I won't let you." Even more determinedly, she said, "I have plans for you."

"Well, you just keep that thought," he grinned, "and I'll be back before you know it!" Then taking her in his muscular arms, he kissed her long and passionately. Afterward, he patted her bottom and demanded, "What's for dinner?"

"Men!" she scolded. "Always thinking about your stomachs."

"Well, that's where you're wrong," he winked, and headed for the bathroom to wash up.

"By the way," Lori called, "just who was that good-looking female officer I hear you've been running around with? You were the talk of the teacher's lounge." Lori never admitted to jealousy, but she always expressed curiosity about any women within a specific age range that happened to enter her husband's life in any capacity.

"I love it when you're jealous," he teased. "But since you asked, she is my acting deputy on the case. She's smart and a pretty good investigator too, but she's not my type."

"Oh, well, what do you mean by 'your type'?"

"By that I mean someone whose name is Lori Gilmore and signed the same marriage license I did."

She smiled. "Pretty good answer, Bubba."

After a friendly but quick dinner, he reluctantly drove to the Fraziers' house.

* * *

Unlike the Gilmores', tension filled the Bryson home. Geneva's lips formed a grim tight line as she stomped around the kitchen slamming cabinet doors and dropping bowls and silverware on the table. Dinner, itself, consisting of leftover beef stew and Jell-O, was thrown carelessly together. Junior, keeping his anger in check, ate the meal in silence, then flopped on the recliner, grabbed the remote control and started watching the Fox Network, which boasted less media bias in their programming than the others.

After dinner, in the kitchen, Geneva continued her seething, stomping and slamming as she cleaned countertops and washed dirty dishes. Her angry resolve had solidified during the early evening as she waited for Junior to come home, and now she was adamantly determined to visit the harlot and demand she leave her son alone. She had only to wait for the inevitable, when Junior began to snore in the recliner, usually between eight and nine o'clock, then she would secretly leave the house and have it out with her.

* * *

"Roy, this is a surprise," Sarah exclaimed, tying her robe over her pajamas. Her gray hair was brushed and shiny in the lamplight, and her face appeared to be scrubbed clean and was shiny as well. She looked younger and softer somehow. "Do come in. I am sorry, but James is out. I'm not sure when he'll be back."

Removing his hat and stepping inside, the sheriff was pleased to find her alone, wanting to question the two of them separately, if possible. He apologized, "I'm sorry to disturb you, Sarah. I do need to talk to both of you, but if you're ready for bed I can come back tomorrow."

"No, that's fine. I wasn't really going to bed. I just like to get comfortable in the evening and read, usually." She pointed to the beige corduroy recliner and a book entitled, *Secret of the Villa Mimosa*, spine up, on the oak end table beside it. "How can I help you, Roy?"

"Well, I'm checking out some information we've received about the murder yesterday, just routine, and I have a witness that claims you and James visited the murder victim. Can you tell me about your visit?"

"Of course, Roy, but James wasn't with me, your report is wrong about that." Sarah, knowing from the gossip in the teacher's lounge that Geneva was the source of the sheriff's report, continued, "I stopped by, I think it was Wednesday after school. Yes, I'm sure that's when it was. You know, the chili supper is coming up next month, and I had to canvass the area behind the market for desserts. First, I went to the Brysons' and while I was there Geneva mentioned her new neighbor, so I decided to stop there too."

"I see," the sheriff said, and wrote in his notebook. "Can you tell me what time that was and how long you were there?"

"I know it was after four because we had a teacher's meeting after school, and I went to the Brysons' first. Just guessing I would say 4:15 to 5:15. Yes, that's probably right because I had to stop at the market before coming home and I was rushed to fix dinner and get to prayer meeting on time."

"So, you visited there over an hour?"

"Yes, I did, Roy. I shouldn't have stayed so long, like I said, it made dinner late, and James was put out about that, but I felt sorry for that lady. She had those terrible scars on her face and seemed so lonely. I invited her to come to dinner here this weekend and meet some other people in town. I hadn't invited anyone else yet, but I planned to invite some people from church so she could get acquainted."

The sheriff finished writing in his notebook. "Just one more thing, Sarah," he said plaintively, "and I'm telling you this because you have a right to know. I knew James didn't accompany you to the victim's house on Wednesday afternoon. The report we have claims James visited the victim Wednesday evening late, around ten o'clock, and stayed for several hours. I just thought you should know," he repeated.

"That's ridiculous, Roy! Wednesday night, James ate at the tavern because I was late and did not have time to fix a decent dinner. He hates frozen dinners, which was what I was going to fix. Anyway, he was back home in bed by ten. Whoever thought they saw my husband is mistaken!" she pronounced. Inside, Sarah's anger burned against the gossiping Geneva.

The sheriff considered the alibi Sarah had just given her husband and was skeptical. Although he disparaged Geneva's character, he was fairly confident in the accuracy of her eyewitness accounts of visits to the murdered lady. "Well, I won't keep you," he muttered, "but I'll still have to check with James in the morning. Sorry to have bothered you," he said, as he replaced his hat.

"That's fine, it was good to see you, Roy. Goodnight."

On the way down the long driveway to the main street, the sheriff decided to drop by the tavern before going home, where he suspected he would find James. However, when he scanned the poolroom, bar and the few tables, James was nowhere to be seen, so the sheriff headed home to his wife and what promised to be a thrilling evening.

* * *

In a closed video booth with the curtain drawn, James sat alone watching naked images of young children and adult men and women on the screen. After cultivating the friendship of the owner of a sordid "adult" book and video shop, he had been introduced to this illicit material in a special backroom. For James, the days had long past when soft pornography satisfied him and he demanded and paid top dollar for progressively harder core material. Even so, it didn't satisfy him for long, as his craving multiplied and accelerated with the passing of time.

* * *

Junior slept noisily in his chair with his mouth open, as Geneva, smiling grimly to herself, slipped out the back door. She had turned out the light and closed the door of her bedroom knowing if Junior did awaken, he would think she had already gone to bed. Just in case he might peek in at her, she had designed a sleeping body under the covers with an extra blanket and pillow.

It was a cool evening, and low dark clouds were blowing in from the southwest. Still, the moon remained uncovered, and Geneva could see her way clearly. Avoiding the streetlight at the corner, she kept close to the trees lining the jogging path and the dry creek bank. The enemy's house was only a few yards away, and she could see light shining around the edges of the front room curtains. Steeled for the confrontation, she went back over the speech she had rehearsed in her mind all afternoon, the adjectives having grown more bitter and condemning with each rehearsal. She paused for a moment at the front door, preparing herself, then, full of self-righteous fury, she rang the doorbell.

"Geneva?" Betty's voice was full of shock and surprise, and immediately surmised Geneva could only be at her door with malevolent intentions. Blocking the doorway with her body, she determined not to invite her into the house. "What are you doing here?"

"For just one thing, missy," Geneva screeched. "I'm warning you to stay away from my son. You got your hooks into him once, but you ain't gonna do it again. I'll do whatever I have to do, you scheming Jezebel. You're a dirty slut; you've always been a slut. And I'm warning you, if you ever come near him again, I'll kill you!"

Unable to control her laughter, Betty howled, "Oh, Geneva, you're too much!"

Geneva, furious that she was being ridiculed, lashed out at Betty with a scream, striking her twice on the face, drawing blood with her fingernails.

"You crazy old woman!" Betty gasped, as she felt blood trickling down her face, and quickly slammed the door in Geneva's face. Trembling, she leaned against the shut door and waited for her heart to stop pounding. "She's crazier than I thought!"

Geneva, both stimulated and frightened by her own daring, wheezed and stumbled toward the sidewalk. "She'll think twice before she has anything to do with my boy again." Holding her heart, she continued toward her house, becoming more pleased with herself with each step. In all her rehearsed scenarios she had never planned to actually strike the harlot, but now that she had done it she felt exhilarated. She was sure now her troubles were over. Thinking furiously, and so proud of her daring, she failed to notice the shadowy figure aiming an upraised object over her head. After the third strike of the sickle, Geneva drew her last confused breath.

* * *

As Aunt Lucy maneuvered her minivan away from the curb in front of Edie and Brian's house, she glanced at the digital clock on the dashboard. "Nine-twenty," she murmured, "not too late to call Pastor Jonathan and ask him to visit Edie and Brian."

In the old woman's eyes, the quiet town took on a quaint aura with its darkened streets and lighted lampposts. The golden glow of lamps inside houses spilled softly onto well-manicured lawns, late flowers and picketed fences. It reminded Aunt Lucy of the beautiful pictures by Thomas Kinkade, the "painter of light." Her old eyes, with their cataracts, intensified the effect as each light was surrounded by a large golden halo. This idyllic scene brought thoughts of the pond to her in the seasons when the surface was calm and clear, and the unsightly muck of the depths hidden. She turned the car left at the city limits sign, and drove the two blocks to her home. Pulling into the driveway, the headlights picked up the large poplar trees and the scruff willows that lined the now dry creek bank, and she caught the surreptitious movement of a human figure ducking behind an ancient tree.

"Teenagers?" she questioned under her breath, aware that the cedar chip trail and the sandy creek bottom were favored by young people as a contemporary "lover's lane."

* * *

The Ryrie Study Bible on his lap, and a pen and blank sheet of paper beside him on the bedside table, Pastor Sharpe sat in bed and wondered what his Sunday morning sermon would be about. The Lord had laid nothing on his heart as yet and since it was already Friday night he was concerned. Ruth was lying beside him, sound asleep still wearing her reading glasses with the book she had been reading face down on her chest. Although it was early, he decided to sleep too, and slid off his side of the bed to his knees for his final prayer of the day. Before he had finished, the phone rang.

Listening carefully to Aunt Lucy explain Edie's earlier questioning at the sheriff's office, of her confessed, but providentially waylaid plan to kill Rose, and how, at this moment, Edie was telling the entire story to her brother, Pastor Sharpe's good heart was anxious to help. Aunt Lucy asked if he could visit with them tonight, even though it was getting a little late. In full agreement, he hung up the phone, woke Ruth to repeat Edie and Brian's circumstances and prepared to leave the house.

Ruth drowsily kissed her husband goodbye, rolled onto her side, and was immediately asleep again. He gazed down tenderly at her lovely black shiny hair fanning the white pillowcase and thanked God again for the wife he had been blessed with. She was not only a beautiful woman but also a good mother to their children and a loving soul mate to him. He knew it was difficult for any woman, no matter how devoted or stoic, to be a pastor's wife. He remembered too well occasions when fellow ministers would unload the burden of their congregation's disapproving and gossip-mongering attitude toward their wives, and sometimes confess the resultant disharmony of their home. Within his own church, Jonathan was cognizant of uncharitable remarks about Ruth comparing her unfavorably to her more active and gregarious predecessors. He knew it was generally felt she should take a greater role in the many activities of the church. The very qualities that had first drawn him to her, her innate shyness and quiet nature, was misunderstood by too many members. Ruth, too, was acutely aware of her detractors, but to her credit, and his relief, she declined to change her behavior to appease them, and concentrated her efforts into maintaining a stable and loving home.

As he drove to Edie and Brian's, his thoughts switched to their tragic situation and he was shortly found knocking on their door. Brian, towering a full head above the good pastor, opened the door and peered down at him.

"Brother Jonathan," he exclaimed, "I'm glad you're here! Come in."

"Thank you, Brian," he nodded, "I hope it's not too late for a visit. Aunt Lucy called and thought maybe you could use me."

"Yes, I...."

Edie interrupted, unhappily. "What did she tell you?"

"I think she told me everything, Edie," the pastor acceded, then asked kindly, "I don't know anyone who has been through more than you two, are you okay?"

His heartfelt concern was apparent and touched Edie's heart causing tears once again to glisten in her eyes. "I'm not okay," she confessed quietly, "I don't know about Brian."

"Yeah, I'm okay," Brian answered unconvincingly. "Edie's the one that got hurt. I guess I'm glad I didn't meet that lady that killed Mom and Dad. I would have wanted to kill her too."

"I can imagine feeling that way," Jonathan agreed.

"I never felt such hatred for anyone in my life," Edie admitted tearfully, "except for when I was raped. And I've hated that man for a long time!"

"Edie!" Brian spit out her name angrily. "Everybody knows that's a lie. Nobody ever raped you!"

"Yes, he did, Brian!" she screamed at the top of her voice. "Nobody ever believes me! And nobody ever protected me, even Mom and Dad. Why did they let that happen to me? Why didn't they believe me?" Edie was sobbing so violently, her entire body was shaking. "There was nobody to save me. Nobody! I was all alone!"

As she continued to sob, Jonathan cradled her in his arms and patted her head lying against his chest. "I believe you, Edie," he said kindly. "It will be all right. I believe you."

* * *

Suddenly, Junior awakened, startled to find himself still on the recliner.

Pat Robertson was praying on the Family channel, the movie, whatever it was he had been watching, something with Bronson in it, was over. "What time is it?" he wondered. With difficulty, he straightened the chair, stood up, and checked the wall clock in the kitchen. "Ten thirty," he mused aloud. Then noticing the back door unchained, he locked and chained it, and went upstairs to bed.

CHAPTER 10

"Who could be ringing the doorbell at this hour?" Lori looked at her watch. "It's only six fifteen, and on Saturday, too!"

"It could be my new deputy." The sheriff glanced out the window observing the early morning light. "I asked her to meet me here first thing this morning, but I was thinking around eight o'clock. I guess she took me literally."

The bell rang again. "You get the door, Sweetheart, I'll butter the toast," suggested Lori as she took the butter knife from her husband's hand.

After combing his hair with his fingers and tying his robe, he opened the door just as the insistent bell rang the third time. The young woman in the black spandex shorts and lavender t-shirt looked familiar, but he couldn't quite place her. She was a thin and attractive African-American with short straightened hair and a wide nose. At the moment, however, her face was pinched and worried, and she was out of breath.

"May I help you?" he asked.

"Sheriff, I'm Emma Cleates," she panted. "I met you at church…last Wednesday night; I came with Betty Bryson."

"Oh, yes, I remember. How can I…."

"You've got to come right bloody now," she said hysterically. "A dead body… I found…jogging."

Emma's entire body was shaking and it appeared to the sheriff she might be going into shock. "Come inside, Miss Cleates, could you sit here while I run upstairs and get dressed?" He motioned her onto a sofa in the living room, and closed the front door where a chilly wind had been cooling the house. Sticking his head in the kitchen, he whispered, "Lori, bring the lady some orange juice and stay with her while I get some clothes on." He bounded upstairs to their bedroom two steps at a time, dressed hurriedly, then consulted the phone book, and dialed a number.

When she answered, he said urgently, "Betty, this is Roy. Your friend, Emma, is at my house, and I think she needs you. Could I bring her to your house in a few minutes?"

"Sure, Roy, what's wrong?"

"I'm not sure myself. We'll be right over." Grabbing his jacket and hat, he bounded down the stairs again; only three minutes after he had raced up them.

Emma was slowly drinking orange juice with a shaking hand, but a little calm had returned to her face. Lori was sitting beside her on the sofa with an arm around her shoulders. "Now Emma," he asked kindly, "do you feel like showing me what you found this morning?"

"I found a dead body, Sheriff," she said, gritting her teeth, holding back hysteria. "I think it's Geneva Bryson, but I might be wrong. I only met her at church the other night. She is next to the old creek bank near the jogging trail." Emma stood up. "Please hurry," she pleaded.

The sheriff pecked his wife on the cheek. "I'll be back soon or give you a call, honey. If my deputy gets here before I get back, tell her to wait here until she hears from me." Then holding Emma's arm, he guided her out the door.

"It would be faster to walk," Emma said, as he drew her toward his official car. "It is just over there." She pointed to the southeast.

"Just the same, we'll take the cruiser," he commanded and opened the passenger door for her. "I might need to use the radio," he explained, wondering if he could trust Emma's judgment regarding a dead body. Flashing through his mind was the evening a widowed neighbor had called, frantic because a huge rat was lying on a rug in her entryway. They were both embarrassed later, when the "rat" turned out to be a large darkened rubber plant leaf that had fallen off the plant. No doubt, this summons would turn out similarly.

They drove around the long block and stopped at the end of the Bryson property, got out of the car and walked the few yards to the jogging trail. There, just off the cedar chip trail to the south, was Geneva Bryson's skinny body. Sheriff Gilmore knelt to feel for a pulse though it was obvious she had been dead for hours. Her back had been striated with three long red groves of blood, the scalp featured a gaping elongated hole at the crown of her head, and clotted blood was matted in her short gray hair. The sheriff noticed Emma hyperventilating and immediately walked her back to the car. As he radioed the county dispatcher, and for the second time in a week, set the investigative machinery into place, he drove Emma the short distance to Betty's house. She was waiting for them on the front porch having observed their activity near the jogging trail from a distance. As they pulled to the curb, Betty loped to the car and opened Emma's door and helped her into the house. The raw scratches on Betty's face were noted by Emma and the sheriff, but he made no mention of them, saying only that he would return shortly. He then u-turned on the short street and stopped in front of Geneva and Junior's house.

He had to knock several times before Junior, groggy, answered the front door. Junior liked to sleep late on Saturday mornings, and expecting his mother to answer the door, had waited until the third knock before grumpily demanding her to "get the door!" On the fourth knock he had struggled out of bed, thrown on his heavy black terry-cloth robe, and thundered downstairs. Looking irritably at the sheriff after jerking open the door, he grumbled, "What do you want?"

The sheriff alternated between suspicion and sympathy as he formed the answer in his mind. "Junior, I think you'd better sit down."

It was Junior's turn to look suspiciously at the sheriff. "What's wrong?" He stayed in the doorway, and demanded, "What's going on?"

"There is no easy way to tell you, Junior. Your mother is dead." He paused to let the words sink in. "She's been murdered."

"Have you been sniffing glue, sheriff? Mother's around here someplace. There's nothing wrong with her."

As he turned, shouting for her, the sheriff caught his arm and spoke in measured, unhurried words, "Junior, you Mother is dead. She is lying a few yards away, near the dry creek bank. I just came from there. I'm sorry to have to bring you the news like this, but someone found her just a few minutes ago." As if to add an exclamation point to his words, blaring sounds of the first sirens were heard as emergency vehicles again neared the small town.

Junior started down the steps. "I don't believe you. If it's true, take me to her then, now," he pleaded.

"No, Junior," the sheriff stopped him once more with his arm. "Hold on. I can't let you walk all over the crime scene just now." Then more gently, he said, "Go, get dressed, and we'll walk over together." Soberly, now, Junior acquiesced and went back inside to dress, the sheriff went out to the street to speak to the first responder, Doug Patton, whose blue truck had just screeched to a stop at the curb.

"What's up?" he yelled out of the cab.

"Looks like another murder, Doug," Sheriff Gilmore answered unhappily, walking toward the pickup. "Geneva Bryson's over there," he pointed, "in the brush on the other side of the trail. The sheriff got down to business. "Doug, same as last time, your job is to keep curious people out of the way, and set up the barriers." The sheriff thought back to the Vanhuss murder, and remembered how Geneva had scowled at him when he ordered Doug to keep people away from the first murder scene. Now she was lying dead just three days later. "Is she dead because she saw the murderer enter the Vanhuss house?" he wondered. "Did she know more than she told me? Is everyone who went into that house on the list, or might the murderer be someone she didn't see?" Then aloud, he called to Doug, "Put barriers and tape all the way from the street, and around the Bryson house, to the creek, okay?"

"What's going on, Sheriff?" called Nancy Armstrong, walking up behind them. "I heard the sirens."

"Geneva Bryson's been murdered," he explained to the deputy. "And I'm waiting for her son, Junior, to get dressed. He wants to see his mother. I don't think he'll believe it's her unless he sees for himself."

"Geneva Bryson, our eyewitness?" She pondered the meaning of the new murder. "Sheriff, this opens up all sorts of possibilities, doesn't it?"

"Just what I was thinking, but a can of worms would be more like it."

Junior, overhearing their conversation, joined them at the curb. "What do you mean by that?" he asked.

"Well, Junior," the sheriff mused, "it's a possibility your mother had become a threat to whoever murdered Mrs. Vanhuss." Then, deliberately changing the subject, he patted him on the back and asked, "Are you sure you want to see her now? We can't get very close anyway until the coroner and the lab people are finished."

"I want to see her," he said stubbornly, still denying the truth of the sheriff's assertion, unwilling to accept his mother's death.

As they approached the coroner squatting next to the corpse, he waved them back. "I'll be with you in a moment, Sheriff," he called.

Junior stared at the body in a familiar dress that was obviously his mother, and he broke down, his face knotted with grief. "I don't understand it. The doors were still chained this morning, how could she be here without unchaining a door?" Then, the truth hit him just as the sheriff answered.

"My guess is she's been out here all night," he judged.

The deputy added, "So, you must have locked up last night after she left the house."

"Did you lock up last night, Junior?" the sheriff asked him.

"Yes, I guess I did. I thought she was already in bed. It was about ten thirty." He wiped his eyes with his shirtsleeve. "She never goes out late at night. I never figured she wasn't in the house."

"So you didn't see her leave," ruminated the sheriff. "Do you have any idea why she went out last night or where she might have gone?"

A frightening possibility entered Junior's mind, which he declined to express. "No! No! I have no idea!" he stated forcefully.

* * *

Emma was quiet now and breathing normally. Now, Betty was shocked and unbelieving. "No! Who would have done such a thing?" she cried, and then panicked. "They will probably think I did it, especially after the fight I had with Geneva last night."

"What do you mean? You had a fight with your ex-mother-in-law last night?"

"Did I ever! Look at my face." Betty lifted the hair on the left side of her face for full effect.

Emma was astonished. "Geneva did that to you? I thought she was just a bad joke. I know I said she might be dangerous, but I had no idea she was really dangerous."

"I never thought she was physically dangerous," she agreed, "but, believe me, she has been morally and emotionally dangerous to others for years. Last night, she showed up at my front door and attacked me, demanding that I stay away from her precious son! She must have found out about Junior's visit Thursday night, probably from one of my nosy neighbors."

"Betty," Emma pleaded, "you didn't hit her back. Did you?"

"Of course not. You don't think I killed her, do you, Emma? However, I mean, it's true, if I wanted to kill anybody, it would be Geneva!"

"No, of course you didn't, Betty. I didn't mean that."

"Unless, well, maybe I could kill someone, if it was to save someone else, or to protect my child," she said fiercely, thinking about Karen. "But, I must confess, there was a time, when Junior and I were married, that I fantasized about killing Geneva." Grimacing, she added, "Actually, my fiendish plan was to grind up yew berries from the bushes out front and mix them with ground coffee, make a pot and serve it to her. But, I'm way past that. Now, I just feel sorry for her. Listen to me, talking about her as if she were still alive. The fact that she is dead, murdered in fact, doesn't seem real."

"Believe me, she's dead, all right. Finding her like that will give me nightmares the rest of my life. It was horrible. You can't imagine."

"Actually, I can imagine." Betty sighed heavily, remembering the day she and Junior had found Karen. "I've not talked much about my daughter, Karen, have I?"

Emma shook her dark head.

"She was only eleven years old when she died," Betty continued. "And even though the Lord has given me peace about it, and I know she is with Him in heaven, the pain of living without her will never go away until I can be with her again."

"Betty, you know I don't believe the same way you do, but I'm your friend, and I'm here for you if you want to talk about it."

"Thanks, Emma." She sighed. "I think I do. It hurts so much to think about her murder, but everything that has happened the last few days has brought it back with a vengeance. It's probably crazy, but I've been wondering if the same person who murdered Karen could have murdered the lady that lived next door to Geneva, and now, maybe even Geneva, herself."

"I guess anything is possible, but it doesn't seem very likely. How many years ago was Karen killed?"

"A little over eight years."

"And they never caught the person who did it? Who were the suspects?"

"No, they never charged anyone. Most people assumed a stranger passing through raped and killed her."

Betty lowered her voice and looked at the floor. Tearfully, she began to tell Emma of the worst day of her life. "When Karen didn't come home for dinner that night, I started to worry about her, but I wasn't worried too badly, at first. She loved to be outdoors, and it was a warm summer day, so I thought she was enjoying herself and had probably lost track of time. When it started getting dark, though, I was frantic. She was always home by dark. Junior was beginning to worry too, so he drove all over town looking for her, while I started telephoning our neighbors and her friends. One of our friends had seen her and Edie Bentley walking west toward Frazier's Orchard. This didn't surprise me because those two were regular tomboys and loved to climb those apple trees in the orchard, even knowing they would get in trouble if caught. Junior had been working with the apple trees that day, putting supports under the boughs that were heavy with apples, and he hadn't noticed the girls around. Another of their favorite destinations in that direction was a swimming hole in the creek, and since it had been a hot summer day, we thought they might have decided to cool off wading in the water. So, anyway, I called the Bentley house and talked to Edith, and she told me Edie had come home before four o'clock because she had a piano lesson. Then, Edie came to the phone, and said the last time she saw Karen, Karen was wading at the pond. She didn't wait for her because she thought she would be late for her lesson."

"So, Edie was the last person to see her alive?"

"Yes, we think so, except for the murderer. When Junior came back with no sign of her, we drove as close to the pond as we could and then walked around it with flashlights. I think both of us were afraid she might have decided to swim, gotten a cramp or something, and drowned. But we didn't see any sign of her, not even her clothing on the bank, so we gratefully discounted drowning. Then, we retraced her probable steps toward home, and walked through Frazier's orchard, and…and, well," she sobbed, "that's where we found her, wedged between forked branches of an apple tree. We saw at once she was dead, but didn't realize she had been murdered until Junior lifted her to the ground and we saw the back of her shirt slashed and covered with blood." Her hair was still wet from swimming and her Nikes were untied. Later, the authorities told us she had been raped. So, somehow, before she was killed, but after she was raped, she managed to put her clothes back on. Tears continued to flow down Betty's cheeks, as her friend moved closer, putting her arm around her shoulders. They sat in silence for a few moments, until the doorbell rang.

On the porch, waiting to enter, were Sheriff Gilmore, Deputy Armstrong, and Junior. Wiping her eyes, Betty greeted them quietly, then looking sympathetically at Junior, said, "Oh, Junior, I'm so sorry."

Noticing the scratches on Betty's face, Junior took her in his arms. "What did she do to you?" he asked sadly.

Betty looked up into his face, and said simply, "She wanted me to stay away from you."

During this startling exchange, the sheriff and deputy exchanged glances, and the sheriff looked directly at Betty and demanded, "I think you had better tell me everything that happened between you and Geneva last night."

Betty returned to the couch, and the others found seats around her in the living room. Junior perched above her on the couch arm on one side and Emma sat beside her on the other. "Geneva rang my doorbell around nine last night," Betty began. "She basically just called me names and ordered me to stay away from Junior. I don't know what came over me." She shrugged. "I guess being called a harlot and a Jezebel struck me as so ridiculous and ludicrous, I started laughing. I couldn't help myself, even though I could see it was making her really angry. Then, I really don't think she could help herself, she was in such a rage, she clawed my face." Betty touched the several soft red scabs that had formed long lines on her face. "At that point, I truly believe she wanted to kill me, but I managed to close the door on her, before she could strike me again. And that's all there is to tell." Betty leaned back against the sofa and closed her eyes. "That's the last I saw of her. After she left I don't know what happened to her."

The sheriff looked at the dowdy woman thoughtfully, scrutinizing her through half-closed lids. "What time did she leave your house?"

"It couldn't have been later than 9:15 or 9:20."

"Betty," the sheriff commanded, "I want you to go with Deputy Armstrong to my office at the county jail and make an official statement. While you are there, with your permission, I want to search your house. If you refuse permission, I will get an official search warrant." He continued to watch her closely as he spoke, and observed the color drain from her face.

Emma defended her friend. "Sheriff, you can't believe Betty had anything to do with Geneva's death!"

Junior put a protective arm around Betty, and stared belligerently at both officers. "You're out of your mind, if you think Betty killed my mother!"

"I believe anybody can kill anyone if given the right provocation, Junior. Anybody," he repeated, looking pointedly at Betty. "And, without a doubt, provocation was there!" Then, to Betty, he asked again, "Do I have permission to search your house?"

"Yes...s," she stammered. Her eyes wide and frightened turned toward Junior, and then Emma.

Deputy Armstrong opened the front door and motioned for Betty to accompany her. "Let's go, Ms. Bryson," she commanded.

"I'm going with you," Emma cried.

"I'm going too," echoed Junior.

"Good idea," agreed the sheriff, "both of you go. I want depositions from each of you regarding your movements last night, and this morning. And, Nancy, as soon as you deposit them in the right hands, get right back here."

"Yes sir," she said.

As the four left in the cruiser, the sheriff walked back toward the murder scene full of purpose. He felt put upon. He was tired of being putty in the hands of people he called his friends and acquaintances. He had been too soft on Edie yesterday. No longer would he base his judgment on what he loosely termed, character, so-called character that was probably skin deep. It had come home to him, with undeniable certainty that he was dealing with a murderer probably well known to himself. Someone who was seemingly above reproach, someone he knew on a first name basis, someone perhaps who sat beside him in church, a pretender, not what they seemed like on the outside, an insidious personality with a façade that defied casual detection. "A trap," he thought, "I need to set a trap!"

He greeted the coroner, who was watching the proceedings of the lab team. "Bill, what have you got?"

"Not much, yet, Roy. As you know, lots of people use the track, not only for jogging, but for cutting through town without having to go around the block."

The sheriff agreed, "That's right, then add the kids who play in the dry creek bed, and the teenagers who use it as a 'lover's lane,' and you've got zilch."

"No sign of a murder weapon either, whoever did it took it with them."

"What do you suppose it was?"

"Something he or she could swing, not a knife this time, but more like a sickle. The indentation of the scalp would be conducive to the shape of a sickle. I haven't had a chance yet to check the wounds on her back, but the long deep strokes we're looking at rule out a lot of weapons. When the lab team are finished I can tell you more."

"Do you have a guess about the time of death, Bill? And don't tell me to wait for the report."

"Well, if you want to deal with facts, you'll have to wait for my report, but an educated guess is she's been dead at least six to eight hours."

"She left Betty Bryson's house last night around 9:15 or 9:20, according to Betty. If she were killed immediately after she left, that would be," checking his watch, he continued, "about ten hours ago."

"That would work," Doctor Judd affirmed.

"Looks like she never knew what hit her."

"Right, all the blows, three of them, were well placed behind the head and between the shoulders. It looks as though she didn't suspect a thing. However, I don't want to second guess at this point because it looks like she has blood and skin under her fingernails."

"Yeah, and it will match the scratches on Betty Bryson's face."

"Doctor Judd, you can remove the body now," shouted Tom Gray, the lab team leader. As the coroner moved to the corpse, Tom walked toward the sheriff. "By the way, Sheriff, I grabbed this report on the Vanhuss murder as we were leaving the lab. Sorry it took so long, but the state boys take their time." Then, nodding back at the new crime scene, he added, "The report on this one shouldn't take long. We have the skin under her fingernails to examine, but otherwise, there are no obvious clues, no fingerprints, nothing else to look at. We collected the leaves and debris around the body, and will save the soil under the body, but whatever we find could have been left last night or last month. That's all we can do."

"Maybe not," said the sheriff, taking the offered report, "I want your team to search two houses before you go. That one," he pointed to the victim's house, "and a possible suspect's, the house facing us at the end of the block. Geneva was supposedly only on the porch at the door, but I would like to know that as a fact. That's where I'll be," he added, as he turned his back to Tom Grey's grimace and walked back to Betty's house.

* * *

In the shower again, James coldly considered his actions over the past few days. He had always known it was strange not to feel anything, no remorse, no guilt, no pleasure, and no pain. These emotions he had feigned for years. The only rush he experienced anymore was momentary, disappearing before he could fully ravish it. Yet, he had to have those moments, fleeting as they were, they were the only occasions he felt alive. Wrapping a thirsty green towel around his waist, he hurried into the bedroom to dress and encountered his wife sitting at the foot of their bed.

"James, I need to talk to you," she began, even as she noticed the look of resignation on his face. "Don't look at me like that, this is serious. Sheriff Gilmore came to the house last night looking for you," she said accusingly. "Where were you? No doubt, he will be back this morning. He said Geneva Bryson saw you go into that murdered woman's house Wednesday night. That was the night you were gone until dawn, if you remember. Were you with that woman all night? Who was she to you? Tell me, James," she demanded, "I have to know. For now, I've given you an alibi. I told the sheriff you were home and in bed by ten o'clock that night." Her voice rose with determination. "I insist you tell me the truth if I'm going to lie for you. I want to know about your relationship to that woman!"

James continued to stand in front of his wife; coldly his eyes swept over her. "Geneva Bryson is a crazy old lady, Sarah, you know that as well as I do! Nobody is going to believe anything she says. Now, listen to me, I swear I was not in that lady's house. I have no idea who she was. Last Wednesday night I went drinking with some good ol' boys in Moberly, and slept it off at this guy's house, that's all. Just let the sheriff believe I was home all night, I wouldn't want to embarrass you by telling him the truth. You do believe me, don't you?" He dropped the towel, leaned over and held his wife intimately to himself, and began kissing her neck and shoulders.

Sarah tried to relax her body, and let him lift her back onto the pillow.

CHAPTER 11

"Enough work for Saturday," he thought, "murder or no murder." It was afternoon by the time his deputy, the lab team, coroner, and press had left to do business elsewhere. The lab team found nothing of an incriminating nature during the search of the two houses. Geneva's prints were found on the door and doorframe but nowhere inside Betty's house. Roy knew there were lots of loose ends he and his deputy should be working on, but when Nancy returned to Cramer Creek after leaving Betty, Emma, and Junior to make statements, he had sent her back home while asking her to keep her beeper handy. What he needed most of all was time to think. Actually, too many thoughts were whirling about in his mind right now, some unimportant, and some, probably, very important. If only he could figure out which were which. There were two murders to solve now, a handful of suspects, and lots of circumstantial evidence. How did everything fit together? With the unread lab report in his hand, the sheriff walked inside his house.

Lori, sitting at the kitchen table, was bent over her first hour students' sketches when he entered the room. She jumped up and hurried toward him, a look of concern on her face. "Hey, you're finally home. What has been going on? I heard Geneva was murdered last night, is that right?"

"I guess the grapevine is in good working order," he grumbled.

"Who needs a grapevine, with sirens blaring all over town. Do you know who did it?" she questioned.

"No, I don't, sweetheart," he grimaced. "Now, I know you want to talk, but I need to be by myself for awhile." He opened the refrigerator door and stared inside.

"No problem, Sweetie, I'll fix you a quick sandwich," Lori offered, "then you can barricade yourself in the office for the rest of the afternoon."

"You're the best." He smiled and pecked her cheek, wanting to do more. Then, as she fixed lunch, he went to his office and opened the blue folder that contained the lab report. Several findings recorded in the report, while not totally unexpected, were potential nails in the murderer's coffin. The spilled perfume bottle found around Rose's head area, but not under her body, was identified as Vision Cosmetic's newest scent, Mirage, which added to the evidence incriminating Edie. Most of the fingerprints found at the scene were accounted for, including those of James Frazier, except for one set probably belonging to Mr. VanHuss, Geneva's mystery man. The story Rose had told Pastor Sharpe and Geneva's eyewitness account had already discounted Sarah's assertion that James had been home Wednesday night at ten. The fingerprints found by the lab were further proof that he knew the victim and had been in her house. Semen samples from the bed sheets were taken and would be DNA tested. And, finally, as previously assumed, the murder weapon was an ordinary, but very sharp kitchen butcher knife. "But whose knife was it?" he wondered. In general, Rose's kitchen, like the rest of the house, was sparse in furnishings. "Would a very sharp butcher knife be one of the few items she brought with her to the rental house? Or was a very sharp knife something the murderer had brought." He made a note to have Mr. Vanhuss attempt to identify the knife, and to check the other suspects' homes for knives of the same brand, possibly with a matching pattern.

Lori interrupted her husband's thoughts as she delivered grilled pastrami and Swiss cheese on rye, and a large glass of milk. Setting the lab report aside, he pulled her onto his lap and wrapped her in his arms.

"None of that, young man," she chided in her best schoolteacher voice. "Get to work and find that horrible murderer, before he finds his next victim!"

Roy tightened his grip around her waist, and rested his head on her breast. "He might not be that horrible, you know," he said seriously. "I sincerely believe he, or she, is someone we know, perhaps even a friend."

"Do you really think so? Who could it be?" Lori questioned, then spoke vehemently, "No, I think I would know intuitively if someone close to me were a murderer. I don't think anyone I know could hide something like that."

"You're wrong, Lori. I would bet you there are plenty of black hearts in this little town that are safely hidden under friendly handshakes and sunny smiles."

"Well, I hope you're wrong," she said quietly, then left him with his thoughts, and returned to grade artwork.

Alone again, the sheriff took a bite of sandwich, and began to think about Geneva's murder. Occurring in the evening opened up the suspects as far as opportunity was concerned, but the motive seemed much more obvious than in the Vanhuss murder. The killer had somehow discovered Geneva's boast of being able to identify Rose's killer, and had shut her up. If that motive was the correct one, it worked. His one and only witness had been eliminated, which made the list she gave him only hearsay in court. An alternative theory was Betty murdered Geneva in a fit of rage after Geneva attacked her. He really didn't think Betty was the type to kill someone in a passion, but as he told her earlier, "Anybody can kill under the right circumstances." He sincerely believed that. But he didn't think these particular circumstances would incite Betty to kill. On the other hand, maybe she left something out of her story. Had she really laughed at Geneva's libelous name-calling? Moreover, if Betty killed Geneva, did that mean she murdered Rose, or were the two crimes totally unconnected? To date, there had been no evidence that irretrievably pointed to one person. The obvious similarity between the two crimes was the attack with a sharp weapon that had come from behind the victims. The search of Betty's and Geneva's houses had turned up nothing incriminating. In Geneva's case, the sharp curved blade that had sliced Geneva to death had not been recovered. And since her death, no new witness had come forward who could testify about Rose Vanhuss' visitors. Indeed, no one was likely to, as each house surrounding Rose's was empty during the critical time on Thursday. Of the two houses directly across the street, one belonged to Mr. Lacey and Elizabeth, both at school during the day; and in the other, both husband and wife worked during the daytime hours. He and Lori lived behind both Rose and Geneva, and the neighbors on each side of him were elderly couples who claimed to have seen nothing. He wished he could question Geneva again about Rose's visitors in more detail, but whatever else she could have been added to her previous information was lost forever. Suddenly remembering he had forgotten to ask Nancy what she had learned concerning alibis yesterday while he had been talking to Mr. Vanhuss in Marshall, he reached for the telephone.

Nancy, doing her best thinking while cleaning house, was furiously dusting furniture in her two-bedroom apartment when the phone rang. She had been miffed because the sheriff had not allowed her to accompany him when he visited Sarah Frazier last night. She definitely wanted to be with him when he questioned Mr. Frazier, which had been their plan this morning until Geneva had been found.

"Hello?" she answered.

"Nancy?"

"Yes, Sheriff. I was just thinking about the murders. What's up?"

"Well, I forgot to ask what you found out yesterday while you were working here at the house. Anything important?" he asked.

"Just a minute, let me grab my notes." He heard her drop the phone and sprint away, then return after a few seconds. "Right, okay, here it is. A couple of things…alibis…I checked the Fraziers' alibis. Sarah left school Thursday during her free hour to run errands; that would be between 10:30 and 11:15. I verified her statement that she went to the bank and canvassed two homes for Chili Supper dessert donations. She stayed and visited at both houses for a few minutes. It's unlikely she could have also committed murder during that forty-five minutes, plus, the time she was out coincides with Pastor Sharpe's visit to the victim when she was very alive," she concluded.

"So, Sarah is cleared," the sheriff added.

"Right. Next, I spoke to Mr. Frazier on the phone. He claims he didn't leave the orchard all day and his secretary verified it. However, I think that would be difficult to verify absolutely because the operation is so spread out and the secretary says he is always on the go. For instance, he goes outside to check on the pickers, to the barn to check on the sorters and packers, spends time in his office, and even runs to the house at no set time for lunch every day. Nobody would notice if he decided to slip away for a half hour."

"I'm beginning to think he is entirely too slippery in a lot of ways," the sheriff concurred. "But I also think if he did come into town Thursday, someone would have noticed his truck. I don't think Geneva could have missed that even when she was cooking Junior's lunch. What else have you got?"

"Mr. Vanhuss, we can't discount him. Being a real estate salesperson, he is free to come and go anytime. We should check his movements more closely."

"But, there again," Roy objected, "someone would surely have seen him come into town." Then he added, "By the way, Rose's funeral is tomorrow afternoon in Marshall. Mr. Vanhuss has asked Pastor Sharpe to officiate. We can talk to Mr. Vanhuss afterward, if you want to go to the funeral with me and my wife."

"Sure. I hate to be left out of anything, even if it is a funeral. You know, Sheriff, I really wanted to go with you to the Fraziers' last night."

Surprised, the sheriff apologized, "I'm sorry, I just figured you would rather go home and have a nice evening watching the tube or something. Don't you have a boyfriend?"

"Don't be so personal," she chided. "But, actually, no I don't, right now anyway. But honestly, sheriff, I would rather work on the case than sit at home."

"You got it. From now on, I won't leave you out of it. Actually, maybe you can work the case alone and I'll stay home with my wife."

"You're not serious."

"Yes, I am!" he answered wholeheartedly, "but unfortunately, duty calls."

Changing the subject, Nancy summed up, "Anyway, as far as I can tell, in addition to Sarah Frazier, only Betty Bryson, Aunt Lucy and Brian Bentley have air-tight alibis for Rose's death. They were at school all day."

The sheriff was thoughtful. "Okay, so who's left on our list? Let's see, there's Edie Bentley, James Frazier, Mr. Vanhuss, or a mystery guest."

Nancy piped up, "Don't forget Pastor Sharpe."

"Very funny."

" Hey, don't you pay attention to the news, don't you watch movies?" Nancy declared hotly, "The cloth is not sacred, you know, it's a cover for everything from fleecing the flock to sexual abuse."

"That is true, unfortunately, for a few ministers. However, don't believe everything the media hypes, the vast majority of pastors are out there living on meager wages, counseling, marrying and burying, visiting hospitals and their congregation, saving the lost, preparing and preaching sermons, and of course, praying. Pastor Sharpe is one of the most dedicated men I know."

"Well, he's still on my list," she retorted.

Changing the subject again, Sheriff Gilmore asked, "What did you find out about the 'Feeling Wonderful' seminars? Who else was involved in them from Cramer Creek?"

"Pastor Sharpe was right about one thing," she said grudgingly, "those seminars were nothing but a get rich quick scheme for the few at the top of the pyramid, while offering a lot of psycho-garbage to those on the bottom rung. An initial ten thousand dollars was required for each person to get into the program. The State Prosecuting Attorney is sending more information. There were several people attending the seminar from this area the weekend of the fire in Kansas City, but only six from Cramer Creek proper. They were David and Edith Bentley, James and Sarah Frazier, and Doug and Cheryl Patton."

"Weren't there other people killed in that fire besides the Bentleys?" the sheriff asked.

"Yes, there were three others who died, and twenty-four more injured with burns and smoke inhalation. Of the three that died, two were a couple from Arizona, and the other one was from St. Joe. The injured were from all over, and sooner or later, all recovered. For right now, that's all I have in my notes," she concluded.

"All right, thanks, Nancy. Let's spend the rest of the day contemplating this thing, and tomorrow afternoon I'll pick you up at two o'clock and we'll attend the Vanhuss funeral. On second thought, why don't you go to church with Lori and me in the morning and come for dinner before we go to the funeral? Lori would love that; she wants to get to know you. And, even if you aren't interested in Pastor Sharpe's sermon you might spend your time observing some of the suspects."

The deputy frowned to herself, thinking he might have an ulterior motive for inviting her to church, but she had asked him not to leave her out of anything. "All right, Sheriff, I'll meet you at church."

* * *

After signing statements, Betty, Emma, and Junior were driven back to Cramer Creek. It was lunchtime and Betty offered to fix a light lunch for the three of them. They gathered in the cozy kitchen as Betty brought the makings of bologna sandwiches from the refrigerator and poured large glasses of iced tea. She glanced at Junior's face knowing this was hardly the gargantuan meal he usually consumed at lunchtime. "Are you doing okay?" she asked him gently.

"Yeah, I'll be alright, I guess." He reached for the mayonnaise and began spreading it on two slices of whole wheat bread. "It's hard to think of Mother dead and laying out in the open all night while I slept," he said with self-incrimination, "I should have checked on her before I went to bed to make sure she was okay!"

Betty covered his hand with her own. "Junior, there wasn't anything you could have done. Your mother made sure you were asleep before she left the house. There's no way you could have known she was gone. Don't blame yourself."

Emma agreed, "Betty's right, Junior."

"I know you are right with my head, but my gut tells me I'm to blame. We had been fighting just about all week. This murder of the lady next door had her hepped up, feeling important, you know. I should have known she was in trouble and had made herself a target with all her boasting. She probably told everybody in town she could identify the killer. I don't think she really knew who it was myself, but maybe she did."

"Do you know what your mother's final wishes were? I mean where she wanted to be buried and funeral arrangements?" Betty gently asked.

"Yeah, I think she wrote everything down and put it in a box on the shelf of her bedroom closet. She told me if anything ever happened to her everything was taken care of. I better go get it and see what needs to be done." He stood and walked toward the front door, leaving most of his sandwich on the plate, then turned to Betty as though he wanted to say something. "Betty, would you mind…uh…."

"What, Junior? Do you want me to go with you?"

"Yeah, I would like that. If you want to, not a very pleasant thing to do, but would you?" At that moment, he looked to the women more like a lost schoolboy than a middle-aged man.

Emma spoke hastily before evaluating the content of her words. "Junior, don't you have another name besides Junior? It makes me want to check you for bruised knees, or something."

Betty ignored her friend. "Sure." Getting up from the table, she said, "Let's go," and followed Junior toward the door. She then yelled back to the lone person at the table, "Emma, hold down the fort, okay?"

"No problem," Emma yelled back, and then taking a deep breath, she continued to sit at the table slowly sipping her iced tea. So much had happened since her early morning jog and the horrible discovery. Her emotions had been swinging erratically since then, from near shock at finding the body, to defending her friend from the sheriff's accusations, then having to re-live the finding of the body when she made her statement to the authorities. Now, she felt she had come to the point of sheer exhaustion.

* * *

Lori opened the door to her husband's office and stuck her head inside. "I'm sorry to bother you, dear, but Aunt Lucy would like to talk to you. She's sitting in the living room."

The sheriff rose and resignedly followed Lori to the living room. He gave a half-smile to the small figure on the couch, and Lori inquired if she would like some coffee or iced tea. When Aunt Lucy declined, Lori excused herself and returned to her schoolwork.

"Aunt Lucy," he said shortly. "How can I help you?"

Aunt Lucy felt distinctly uncomfortable. She should have called before dropping in unannounced. "I'm so sorry, Roy, I see I've come at a bad time. I'll just ask you to stop by when you get a minute."

"No, no, Aunt Lucy. Forgive me; I really am glad to see you. But there's been another murder, and I've been trying to get my thoughts together this afternoon."

"Oh, I know, Roy," she returned, "that's why I'm here. I may have seen the murderer on my way home from Edie's last night. My headlights picked up someone trying to hide behind an old poplar tree next to the trail. It was probably a teenager out with his girl, but I thought I should tell you."

"What time was that?"

"It was exactly nine-twenty. I had just noticed the time on the dash, and was wondering if it was too late to ring up Pastor Sharpe and ask him to visit with Edie and Brian."

"I see. So you thought it was a teenager?"

"Yes, I did, but I think I thought it must be a teenager because of the lateness of the hour. It was too far away to tell who it was, and my eyes are not as sharp as they used to be."

"Nine twenty?" he mused. "If it was the murderer, that would be exactly the right time to spot him." The sheriff stood and offered his arm to the old lady. "Could you show me exactly where you saw him?"

"Yes, of course," she responded as he helped her to her feet.

"Be right back, honey," he shouted to his wife, as he opened the front door for Aunt Lucy. "Where's your car?" he asked.

"I just cut across the jogging trail to your house, don't drive unless I have to," she answered.

As they walked back to Aunt Lucy's street, she explained how her cataracts had grown to the point that her vision was very poor, especially at night. Consequently, she could not identify the figure in the woods, except to say the person was, "lean and of medium height, and as to clothing, the trousers, jacket and hat were dark colored. Brown or gray, I think."

"Then, it could have been a woman?"

"It may have been, but the impression I had was of a male. Not at all graceful."

When they reached the dead-end next to the old creek area, Aunt Lucy led the sheriff directly to the large tree the mysterious figure had ducked behind. But, although they searched the area thoroughly, they found nothing but a few bent twigs in the brush behind the tree. Since there had been no rain in several weeks, and it was a highly frequented area, there were no telltale footprints to discover.

As he walked her back home, the sheriff thanked her for the information.

"We can't be sure you saw the murderer, Aunt Lucy, but if you did, it narrows down the area he was coming from."

"You're right, Roy, there are only few houses left on this side of town."

"On the other hand, if he wanted to escape detection, he might have left his vehicle on this side of town and actually lives somewhere else."

Aunt Lucy added, "Or the person I saw could have been my first impression, a teenager out with his girlfriend."

"Anything is possible at this point." Then opening her front door, he wished her good night and walked home thinking, "I think it was him. Perfect timing. If only Aunt Lucy's eyesight was better."

CHAPTER 12

The sanctuary of Cramer Creek Baptist Church was filled to capacity. The backbone of the congregation was present with the addition of Christmas and Easter Sunday only attendees, as well as the doting parent and grandparent crowd who attend only when their little ones perform in a play or choral program. The joint was humming with innuendo and speculation regarding the murders, and recently scrubbed necks were stretched this way and that perusing the pew occupants for possible suspects and sources of gossip.

Junior Bryson, attending church for the first time in years, sat uncomfortably beside Betty and Emma. "How did I let you talk me into this," he complained. "I feel like a sore thumb. Everybody's looking at me."

Emma added to his reproach, "I feel the same way. At least you aren't the only black person in the room."

Sitting between the two, Betty grimaced and shook her head. "Will you two relax. Church is a great place to be."

"Well, I do like Pastor Sharpe," agreed Emma. "He's a really sweet man. But look at all the bloody busybodies looking around for something to gossip about. Church is supposed to be better than the world, isn't it? I still can't get over listening to Geneva's evil tongue on my first visit here." Then realizing her gaffe, she apologized profusely. "Oh, Junior. I'm so sorry. I feel terrible. I really didn't know your mother that well and that was a terrible thing to say about her."

"It's okay. It hurts, but you said only what was true, Emma," Junior reflected sadly. "She was worse than you know. But, she was my mother, and there were good things about her, too."

"Yes," agreed Betty. "She was a very complex woman. I thought perhaps she had been abused as a child or something, and that had messed her up. One thing for sure, she made Junior her whole life, and was determined to hold tight to him, like he would run away if she didn't." She reached out and patted both their knees, and implored, "To go back to both of you feeling uncomfortable here, I just want to say, every church has plenty of hypocrites and sin. Worse, there are always people who act like they aren't and they don't. That will probably never change. The great wonder is why God chose to love us anyway and actually send his only son to die for our sins. His love is one thing I'll never understand. But I'll never be able to praise Him enough for it."

* * *

Nancy Armstrong, also out of her element, stood at the back and searched the backs of the many heads seated in the sanctuary, hoping to spot Sheriff Gilmore and his wife. Never having met Lori, she focused on close-cropped brown hair belonging to relatively tall men with slightly protruding ears. In the right front quadrant, she spied Betty, Junior and Emma conspiring with their heads together, and in the left center was Aunt Lucy, Edie and probably Edie's teenage brother, Brian. A pretty girl sitting next to Brian was flirting with him outrageously.

"You made it," the sheriff exclaimed, touching her shoulder. We've been watching for you. See, over there," he pointed toward a large pretty blond, "that's Lori. We've saved a seat for you."

Nancy allowed herself to be squired to the second row pew in the center of the sanctuary. "I had no idea it would be so crowded," she murmured, then with a gleam in her eyes, added, "Pastor Sharpe must be raking it in, huh?"

He smiled down at her. "You can't get away with that, I see right through you. You're not half as cynical as you pretend."

"You wanna bet?" Nancy was about to say more, but the organ and piano duet began, playing, "He Touched Me," and the choir members, robed in black and purple, filed in and remained standing behind dark and satiny walnut posts and railing.

Reaching the second row, Sheriff Gilmore introduced his wife to Nancy. Lori held out her hand to the deputy, and whispered, "Nice to meet you." Their exchange was cut short by the choir's call to worship.

Afterward, the congregation sang two hymns, "Victory in Jesus," and "It is Well with My Soul," with gusto. Then a particularly boisterous time of welcoming visitors took place as the regular folks tried to smile at and shake hands with each of the many newcomers. Junior and Emma were inundated with "welcomes" and "nice to meet yous." Eventually, the friendly crowd returned to their pews and became circumspect once more.

Pastor Sharpe walked quickly to the pulpit. His dilemma last Friday night of choosing the sermon had disappeared after his nighttime visit with Brian and Edie. The Lord had spoken with clarity and the pastor's fingers had flown across the computer keyboard late that evening as the sermon took shape on the screen. Momentarily scanning the faces of his diverse audience he began to speak boldly.

"Who is guarding the front door of your house?" he asked with fervor, and paused, letting the question sink in. "I would suggest to you, the answer is: 'nobody!' There is a thief that has free access to your home and is not stopped by dead bolts and security systems. He enters unhindered to rob your entire family of what you hold most dear: high moral principles, godly character, biblical truth, and your children's innocence." Brother Jonathan's words were spoken slowly emphasizing each word.

"This filthy, violent, sadistic, lewd, immoral and corrupt thief has the ability to cross your threshold every day. He enters through sitcoms on primetime television where promiscuity, adultery and homosexuality are the usual fare, through advertising in which sex sells everything from cars to perfume. You will also find him in popular music videos glorifying sex, violence and degradation of women, and in unsolicited e-mails and net sites that bring the vilest acts and images to you in virtual reality. Moreover, not only are your homes vulnerable to this thief, but, also your children's schools. Only a few years ago, parents could trust public schools to adhere to the same basic moral values they held. But, now, we hear educators tout lax sexual attitudes as okay (just use a condom), anti-religious values (to hold to one reality is bigoted), homosexuality as a legitimate optional lifestyle (it's an inborn trait rather than perversion), and evolution as fact (not a theory). Today, the Word of God is often banned in the public arena, while every perverse and ungodly subject is allowed. Most public libraries refuse to protect young children from pornography, thus making it readily available on their many on-line computers, and openly displayed on their bookshelves. I repeat, NO ONE IS GUARDING YOUR HOUSE!"

The earlier freewheeling, somewhat electric carnival atmosphere turned quickly into a subdued, but expectant, dread. Each negligent parent who thought policing their children's Internet access and television watching was too much trouble, or had procrastinated learning about and buying the V-chip, or other protective software, felt panic welling in their chests. Every wife who suspected her husband was secretly addicted to pornography felt despair, if not terror. Many of the families who habitually spent night after night in front of their televisions laughing at sexual situations and lewd jokes, lusting after nude figures, and allowing Christ's name to be cursed without thinking twice lowered their heads in shame. However, in other minds, the prevalent emotion was self-righteous anger, and they inwardly cursed the young preacher for crossing the line of their personal business. Sarah, with burning pink spots on each cheekbone, sat rigidly, looking straight ahead, while her husband, slouching casually beside her, looked bored.

The pastor then charged the church to be the instrument of change in the world for their family's protection as well as society's. His sermon ended with a quote gathered from psychologist James Dobson's interview of Ted Bundy, in which the serial rapist and murderer blamed his early access to pornography as the initial spark that ignited his subsequent addiction and obsession, and led to the rape and murder of so many young women.

After the service, it seemed the congregation mimed the parting of the Red Sea as they separated into two distinct groups: the haughty and annoyed who couldn't wait to escape by the nearest door never to return, and the shocked and sorrowful wanting to express their gratitude to Brother Jonathan for his faithful and uncompromising message.

Sheriff Gilmore made his way through the crowded aisle until he reached James and Sarah Frazier. After pleasantries were exchanged, he asked if he and his deputy might visit with them in the afternoon on their return from the Vanhuss funeral. With the Fraziers' agreement, he made his way back to his wife and deputy, moving slowly with the crowd toward the front door.

"What was that all about?" his deputy queried.

"I just made an appointment to meet with the Fraziers' at their house after the funeral," he replied.

"Good," agreed Nancy, "its about time Mr. Frazier answered some questions."

Lori asked her husband, "Do you think the Fraziers' are hiding something? I mean, are they the people you were talking about yesterday, people we think we know, but really don't?"

"Yeah, I think you can definitely include James in that category." Then he warned her, "But, Lori, don't repeat that to anyone."

Reaching the double doors where Pastor Sharpe was shaking hands and exchanging greetings with the congregation, the sheriff and Lori voiced their approval of the sermon. Although Nancy was silent on that point, she drew the pastor aside and asked if she might schedule an appointment with him to discuss his knowledge of the "Feeling Wonderful" seminars, and the people who attend them.

"Of course, Nancy. I am generally in my office in the mornings. My office hours are eight to noon Monday through Friday." Changing the subject, he spoke to the three of them, "Could you wait a few minutes and meet me in the office? There is something I need to discuss with you."

"Sure," the sheriff answered. Then the three walked out into the September sunshine, where several small groups were scattered on the front lawn. Today, they could almost believe that Cramer Creek was the picture perfect town it looked to be. Nothing could be hidden, or evil, or stagnant here. Under the sparkling periwinkle blue sky the sweet country air was crisp and invigorating, a herald of the approaching season, witnessed by the ancient maples on the grounds turning gorgeous hues of russet, orange and yellow.

"I'm definitely going to have to dig out the wool skirts and sweaters," commented Nancy, shivering.

Just then, they observed Junior, Betty and Emma approaching them purposefully. Junior was the first to speak.

"Roy, we've been talking a lot about Mom's and that other lady's murder and we were wondering if you would consider opening up Karen's case again? We believe there is a possibility the same man might be involved in all of them."

"I don't know, Junior. What makes you think that?"

Betty spoke up, "Roy, you know Karen's murderer was never caught. And, when it happened, I think everyone just assumed he wasn't from around here. But, now, since the other murders, we think it's just too coincidental there could be multiple murderers in such a small town."

"But, it's been years, Betty."

Emma echoed their conclusion, "I know I'm an outsider, Sheriff, and I don't know much about the people here, but, I agree, it does rather stretch the imagination. Three persons have been murdered in a town with less than 300 people."

Sheriff Gilmore considered their words and the unspoken emotion behind them. "All right, then," he promised. "I will look into it. There is nothing I'd rather do than find whoever murdered your little girl!"

"Thank you, Roy, I know you mean that," Junior conceded, then added. "By the way, Mother's funeral is Tuesday afternoon at two at the Mayan Funeral Home."

"We'll be there, Junior," Lori responded sympathetically. "Let us know if we can do anything."

The crowd was thinning as the three edged toward the side door to wait for the pastor.

Lori said, "Well it's a good thing our lunch is in the oven. When we get home all I have to do is put it on the table, and then we can eat and hurry to the funeral. Nancy, I hope you like roast beef. What time is the funeral again?"

"Three o'clock," her husband answered. "Don't worry, we won't be late. Remember, Brother Jonathan is preaching it, so he won't keep us long."

* * *

Determined to spend time alone, Brian and Elizabeth found a secluded spot out of the wind on the west side of the church.

"You are acting so strangely today, Brian," Elizabeth pouted, her blue eyes searching his familiar face. "I felt like an idiot trying to get your attention earlier. It seems like you're in another world."

"First thing's first," he implored urgently and captured her in his arms. He kissed her cheek, and then as she turned her head toward him, kissed her partly opened lips. Then checking the corner of the building to make sure they were not observed, he kissed her briefly again.

Elizabeth smiled coyly, and leaned against the brick wall of the church. "Brian, you are so sweet. But, returning to my question, what is wrong with you? You've been acting really different today."

"I know," he agreed. "It's Edie, well, it's me, too. You know, Edie wasn't really sick last week...." Brian related the entire ordeal Edie had lived through the past few days, and that the murdered woman was the careless smoker who caused their parents' death. "I don't blame Edie," he confessed, "I might have thought about killing her myself."

"Oh, Brian, I don't blame you for feeling that way," Elizabeth commiserated. "You have had too much hurt in your life already. I love you." She kissed his cheek, and then began to walk backward toward the front lawn of the church. "I don't want to go, but I've got to find Dad before he finds me," she said, then turned and ran. "You know he's got to be looking for me. Bye, Brian."

He waved and followed a short distance behind, feeling much lighter after sharing his burden with her.

* * *

"Come in, come in," motioned Pastor Sharpe from the doorway. "I don't have a lot of time before I must leave for the funeral, but there's something on my chest I need to tell you about. Before I begin, I know you'll probably think I've been taken in, by Edie no less, but, when I visited her and Brian Friday night, I left their house absolutely convinced her story of being raped several years ago is true. I feel in my spirit she was telling the truth, although no one seems to believe her. I admit, a man wearing a ski mask holding a knife to Edie's throat and raping her while her parents slept in the next bedroom is difficult to believe, and even more so when you consider all her other manufactured tales. But, like I say, I believe she's telling the truth about this. Also, she believes the same man must have raped her little friend, Karen Bryson. Of course, Karen and Edie were unable to compare notes since Karen was killed after she was raped, but the two incidents did occur around the same time. I'd like to think I'm a pretty good judge of character, Roy, and I can't say I believe all of Edie's stories, but this may be the case of calling 'wolf' too many times. If she hadn't already had the reputation of a liar, she would have been taken at her word about being raped. When I was with her the other night, Edie's emotions were stripped bare and she was truly suffering, I would stake my life on it."

"Well, Brother Jonathan, I have a lot of respect for your discernment, and I intend to take what you've said very seriously. However, I have to admit, part of me has difficulty believing her story. Let us do some checking into the reported rapes in the area around that time, and I'll get back to you."

"Roy," Lori interrupted her husband, "remember Mary Jane Oglesby claimed to be raped a year or two ago?"

"Yes, I investigated it, but there was no evidence. By the time she and her mother came forward, a week had already passed, and all the evidence had been destroyed. There were no fingerprints unaccounted for, and she couldn't identify the man." He scratched his head and tried to recall the details of the case. You know, I remember she claimed the man was wearing a ski mask!"

"Maybe Edie is telling the truth," observed Nancy.

The sheriff started for the door. "Well, we'd better get going if we're going to make the funeral on time. Thanks for your input, Brother Jonathan. I'll get back to you." He held the door open for the women as they said their good-byes, and then rushed home to eat.

Over dinner, the three ate quickly while reviewing the progress of the investigation and began planning their next moves.

"We've talked to everyone on Geneva's list except James Frazier, and we'll get to him today," the sheriff pledged.

"Maybe we should visit everyone in the neighborhood again," Nancy offered.

"No, it wouldn't do any good. Everyone in direct view of Rose's house was working, except Geneva and Rose. Even Geneva took a short nap during the key time. Besides, if anyone knew anything they would have come forward."

"I guess you're right," Nancy acknowledged. "Well, I checked the murder weapon out of storage as you asked, for Mr. Vanhuss to identify. And we want to check his alibi, if he has one, right? Anything else to talk to him about?"

"Only if he was aware of his wife's affair with James," the sheriff concluded.

Lori listened carefully to their conversation, puzzled by the various trails that seemed to go nowhere. "I don't understand it," she protested. "Do you two even have a clue who murdered Mrs. Vanhuss or Geneva? Do you think Junior and Betty are right, that the same person murdered Karen Bryson too? And where do the rapes come in, do they have anything to do with the murders? Do you even know if Edie Bentley was really raped?"

Nancy, feeling attacked, answered defensively, "All the pieces are coming together."

Sheriff Gilmore smiled indulgently at his wife. "No, you're right, honey," he admitted. "We've got a lot of loose ends, and not one of them tell us the identity of the murderer. We don't even know the gender of the murderer." He closed his eyes and pondered the situation. Then, after a few moments, he hazarded to put forward the plan that had been teasing his brain since yesterday morning. "What if," he ventured, " we set a trap for the murderer by insinuating that we know more than we actually do, and then watch the behavior of our suspects? Today, for example, when we question both Mr. Vanhuss, and James Frazier, let's lay every incriminating card we have on the table, and hint that we have another one or two held back. Let's push both of them hard, let them think they are our prime suspect. What do you think?"

Considering his plan, both women cautiously nodded their heads.

* * *

On Sunday afternoons, Aunt Lucy didn't change into more comfortable clothes after church. Hers was the generation that expected Sunday visitors to call, everyone dressed in their Sunday best, and she always prepared a little refreshment beforehand. Today, an angel food cake sat inside the pedestal glass cake holder. Yesterday, after Sheriff Gilmore delivered her home, she had made the cake from scratch, beating twelve egg whites in her old Mixmaster she had purchased in the forties. These days she had few Sunday visitors but was prepared "just in case." She often thought how lonely her life would be if she retired from the school system, or became disabled. Would anyone think about her or visit her? She shook her old head in disgust. "No, I will not indulge in self-pity!" she fumed, remembering her many blessings, and the continuous presence of her best Friend. Just when she had concluded there would be no visitors today, the doorbell rang. Carman jumped from her window perch and beat her to the door.

"Edie, Brian, how nice to see you." She gave them each a hug and invited them into the front room that her mother had called the parlor.

"I know we just saw you at church," Edie began.

"...But we didn't have anything to do, so we thought we might come over," Brian finished.

Edie frowned at her brother's poor choice of words, and added, "Are we disturbing you? You weren't taking a nap, were you?"

Aunt Lucy took no notice of Brian's implication that she was far down the list of things he would like to do today. She understood children of all ages, and truly appreciated the innocent faux pas of the young.

"No, I was sitting here wishing someone would come to see me. I made an angel food cake and I need some hungry young people to help me eat it. Let me get you a piece."

"Sounds great," Edie assented.

"Me too," piped Brian.

They followed her into the kitchen and watched Aunt Lucy slice very large wedges from the tall white cake with pink and blue swirls and confetti icing.

After Aunt Lucy's blessing, and the first bite, Brian complimented the cook. "This is yummy!" he said, and then returned to his plate, totally engrossed in the dessert.

"Aunt Lucy," began Edie, "I wanted to thank you for calling Brother Jonathan to come over the other night. He made us feel so much better, especially after he prayed for us. I think I'm almost back to normal again." She smiled, and then pronounced, "He must be the only one who believes I was really raped."

Aunt Lucy wanted to say she believed her too, but couldn't quite bring herself to do so. Again, her prayers would be full of contrition tonight. "Edie, would you mind telling me again what happened?" She promised herself this time she would keep an open mind.

* * *

Karen's rape and murder was one subject of conversation in the sheriff's cruiser as the passengers sped to Marshall for Rose Vanhuss' funeral. Lori and Roy had not been residents in the area at the time of the murder, and Nancy had been a child, but Roy tried to recount the infamous event from his memory of the newspaper reports.

"As you know, dear, I was in St. Louis attending Missouri Tech, and..." he squeezed her hand, "trying to talk you into marrying me at the time. But, I did read the newspaper accounts. The way I remember it, Karen didn't come in for dinner when she was expected, and Junior and Betty searched for her, and consequently, found her dead in Fraziers' orchard."

"Fraziers'?" Nancy and Lori echoed.

"That's right." He nodded. "She had been slashed in the back several times, and then her body was lodged in the limbs of an apple tree."

"Oh, poor Betty and Junior," Lori moaned. "How awful!"

"And Junior works in that orchard every day. How can he do that?" Nancy sighed.

"Anyway," the sheriff continued, "the coroner discovered Karen had been raped as well, this was before DNA testing was widely used. The murder weapon was thought to be a slightly rusty, but sharp enough sickle found in another area of the orchard, but it was void of fingerprints. Frazier claimed the tool was used by his workers occasionally to clear tall grass or brush away from the trees, but no one admitted having used it around the time of the murder. There were traces of rust in the wounds, and traces of Karen's blood type on the sickle. The crime was thought to be unpremeditated since the sickle had been lying around for some time."

Nancy reasoned, "Then the rapist hadn't decided to murder his victim until after he raped her. Or was the rape an unplanned event also?"

"If we are looking at a serial rapist, the common modis operandi is a well-thought-out event," answered the sheriff. "If he hadn't planned to murder her, only rape her, he would have kept his face hidden, so she could never identity him."

"I get it," chimed in Lori, "that is where the ski mask comes in!"

"So, what happened during the rape that changed it to murder?" Nancy asked.

No one spoke as each passenger attempted to visualize the event. Then the sheriff voiced the conclusion in all their thoughts. "The most likely answer is during the rape, Karen unmasked him, and that's when he decided to kill her."

Lori asked, "Roy, do you think it could be James?"

"What I think is, the only fact we have is that James is an adulterer, and an adulterer does not a rapist make, much less a murderer." Changing the subject, he began to dictate, "Nancy, I want you to dig up the police reports on Karen's murder. Find out if there were other rapes reported around that time frame. Being so long ago, I don't suppose there would be any DNA evidence, but find out, will you? Edie's words during questioning echoed in his mind: "...raped me and murdered my best friend."

* * *

Well attended by relatives and friends, Rose's funeral greatly surprised those who thought they had known her best. Rather than the somber event expected, her passing was observed as a celebration by the officiating pastor from Cramer Creek. Pastor Sharpe recounted Rose's salvation experience only hours before her life had been taken, and those listeners who knew the Lord rejoiced greatly along with the angels in heaven. The reverend then asked the mourners if they had personally taken the soul-changing step Rose had and did they know where they were going to spend eternity. Following that most important question, he gave the plan of salvation in simple terms that even a child could understand.

Sheriff Gilmore noticed Nancy was listening with rapt attention to Brother Jonathan, her body leaning slightly forward as he spoke. Lori had also noticed Nancy's body language and squeezed her husband's hand. They wondered if the young deputy's heart had just made a decision.

Later, at the graveside, the three stood a distance away, until the service was concluded and then approached Mr. Vanhuss.

"This is no doubt the wrong time, Mr. Vanhuss," the sheriff inquired, "but we would like to ask you some questions."

"Oh, Sheriff, sure, thanks for coming. Especially thanks for telling me about Pastor Sharpe, and, uh, about Rose, and everything." Then acknowledging the question, he acquiesced, "Yeah, I guess now is as good a time as any. They're waiting for me to ride back to the funeral home so all the cars behind us can get out of the cemetery. If you'll follow us why don't we talk there? There'll be too many people at my house." He added disjointedly, "A meal ready, you know. If that's okay with you."

"That's fine, we'll meet you there." Back in the cruiser, he speculated, "Mr. Vanhuss is acting a little weird, don't you think?"

"Dear, since he just buried his wife, I don't think you should be so critical," retorted Lori.

Back at the funeral home, they all sat comfortably in hunter green upholstered wingback chairs. The large painting of a pastoral scene repeated the color and supplied the rest of the room's color scheme of gold and fuchsia, picked up in the muted floral print of the couch, throw pillows and the gold accessories. Nancy carried the long narrow box that housed the murder weapon and setting it on the mahogany coffee table in front of Mr. Vanhuss, opened it suddenly, causing him to visibly pale.

"It's the murder weapon, Mr. Vanhuss," the sheriff said matter-of-factly. Then he spoke menacingly, "Do you recognize it? Does it belong to you? Did it belong to your wife?"

Collecting himself valiantly, the victim's husband reached for the weapon, "May I?" Then after the sheriff nodded, he took it from the deputy's hand and appraised it carefully.

"Be careful," the deputy cautioned, "it is extremely sharp."

"Well, that settles it, now I'm positive," he nodded, handing the knife back to the deputy. "This knife could not have belonged to Rose. She was scared to death of sharp knives." Pausing, he calculated their incredulity, then explained his assertion, "You see, when Rose was a little girl, her mother always used very sharp knives in the kitchen and invariably cut her own fingers so many times that Rose became almost traumatized by sharp knives. She told me once, when she thought of sharp knives all she remembered were bloody fingers under the coldwater tap and blood flowing down the drain of the kitchen sink. A child can be so impressionable, you know. Anyway, the sharpest knife Rose ever used was a serrated bread knife or a steak knife," he said convincingly.

"I get the picture," laughed the deputy.

The sheriff, not amused, asked curtly, "Were you aware, Mr. Vanhuss, of your wife's affair with Mr. James Frazier?"

"With who? James Frazier?" He stood and confronted the sheriff angrily,

"I don't know anyone by that name. How dare you accuse my wife of such a thing when she cannot defend herself."

Not believing his protestations, the sheriff immediately fired back, "Do you have an alibi for the time of your wife's death? Can anyone verify exactly where you were between the hours of eleven a.m. and one p.m. last Thursday?"

Mr. Vanhuss appeared to be ill, but answered positively, "Yes, I believe I can, Sheriff. You have a lot of nerve, distressing me, confronting me right after my wife's funeral. It's disgusting. It's inhumane. Who do you think you are? You obviously believe I murdered my wife, but you can think that all you want, because I do have an alibi." With indignant boldness, he proclaimed, "I was showing a farm east of Marshall to a young couple, Mr. and Mrs. Harold VanSkike. I'm sure they will inform you I was with them from mid-morning to early afternoon the day of my wife's murder!"

On the ride back to Cramer Creek, Lori was outraged at her husband, and let him know it. "Roy, the way you treated that poor man was terrible, and on the day of his wife's funeral. How could you?" Lori glanced in the back seat at Nancy and could tell she felt the same way.

"Don't put me in the doghouse alone," he answered hotly. "If you would both remember, that was precisely the tactic we agreed on driving over here. We hit him hard with our suspicion of his guilt, and then watch to see what he does next. I'm not going to take any flack from you two. We decided together, the three of us, to go after Mr. Vanhuss and Frazier hot and heavy. So, if you want to pretend you are innocent angels and I'm the bad guy, go ahead, I can take it!"

Lori and Nancy looked at each other and frowned. "I hate to admit it, but, he is right," Nancy acceded. "It just seems different when you actually carry it through."

"I know," agreed Lori. "I am such a person-pleaser and I cannot stand for people to dislike me. But, to hurt an innocent, unsuspecting man, grieving for his wife, and right after the funeral, that goes beyond, way beyond, inexcusable."

"Even if he's a murderer?" her husband asked.

"Yeah, I guess so."

"Well, you two had better get tougher, because we are about to repeat the process with Frazier. If you can't do it, I'll drop you both at home first."

"I'll go, you said you wouldn't leave me out of the case anymore," Nancy charged. "At least James hasn't just buried his wife!"

"As for me," Lori retorted, "you'd better take me home. I do have to work with Sarah every day at school and I don't need her mad at me."

The remaining drive to Cramer Creek was mostly silent; each occupied with his or her own thoughts. After leaving Lori at home, the remaining duo drove the short distance to the Fraziers'. Sarah welcomed them at the door still dressed in her church clothes and invited them inside. James was dressed casually sitting in a Windsor rocker reproduction in the living room when they joined him. Raised similarly to Aunt Lucy in regard to Sunday mores, Sarah had baked chocolate chip cookies and made coffee for her guests.

Nancy, eating a delicious cookie, was again feeling uncomfortable with their scheme, and glanced at Sheriff Gilmore, who appeared to be totally at ease. "I've got to control my feelings," she panicked, "or I'll blow the whole thing." In her mind she began repeating the phrase, "James Frazier is a cold-blooded murderer, James Frazier is a cold-blooded murderer," and it helped immensely. The sheriff, watching her more closely than she realized, was gratified by the harder jaw, and more professional countenance she turned toward the Fraziers.

When everyone was seated around the living room, James commented on Pastor Sharpe's sermon, laughingly making the observation, "It tended to rile some people up."

"Yes, especially, the ones who usually attend church only on Christmas and Easter. They have probably never heard any other messages," observed Sarah.

"Yes, I guess you could say they were blind-sided," chuckled the sheriff.

"Sarah tells me you're here because some nosy bitty-body told you I visited the murdered woman," James looked askance at the sheriff, "what was her name, Rose something?"

Sheriff Gilmore was waiting for just such a pronouncement from James and answered quickly, "Oh, we're far past that now. We know you not only knew Mrs. Rose Findley Vanhuss, but you had an affair with her, which you renewed last Wednesday night, a few hours before she was murdered."

"That's a lie," James pronounced forcefully, and in complete control of his emotions.

The sheriff was equally in control; his voice edged in steel. "No, my friend, it's the truth. Your fingerprints have been identified at the scene, and not only that, but you left your personal signature on the lady's bed sheets."

Nancy thought Sarah was going to have a stroke. Her face was pale and she looked as though she was fighting for breath. Forgetting her resolve to maintain composure, she touched Sarah's arm and asked if she would like to leave the room. But Sarah shook her head and glared at the two men, one with his chin thrust forward in a challenge, and the other petulant, but dropping all pretence.

Casually, James eyed the sheriff, and simpered, "Adultery isn't a crime, Sheriff, but what you are doing to my wife should be, you self-righteous, opinionated bigot!"

"You are right, James," Sheriff Gilmore acknowledged. "Adultery isn't criminally pursued in our century. However, rape and murder are fervently investigated. And just for the record, the night Geneva was killed I was in your home, but you weren't. I hope you have a good alibi for Friday evening!"

Sarah caught her breath and stood, glaring at the sheriff, and wringing her hands. "How can you come into our house, pretending to be our friends, our Christian friends, and say things like that?" Sarah cried. "James could never do anything like what you suggest."

James, tall and lanky, stood up and smiled wryly at the two officers. "If you're not planning to arrest me, Sheriff, I suggest you leave this house, immediately. You'll be hearing from our lawyer."

The sheriff and deputy rose, and walked in single file toward the entryway, but before leaving, the sheriff turned and admonished James, "I wouldn't be too premature with your lawyer. As soon as the DNA evidence comes back," he bluffed, "you may have a better use for him. Show up at my office tomorrow with names, addresses and times of your whereabouts Friday night." Having the final word, the sheriff forcefully closed the door behind them.

CHAPTER 13

Aunt Lucy sliced a small piece of leftover angel food cake for her breakfast and poured a cup of coffee. Just as she lowered her stiffened joints to sit at the table, Carman pounced on her lap and begged for a bite. "You wouldn't eat cake if I gave it to you," she avowed, scooting the plate a few inches away from her sniffing companion. "How about some coffee and milk instead?" she asked, and poured a little coffee from her cup into the saucer, and added a dash of milk. Carman began licking it greedily with ingratiating throat sounds, while Aunt Lucy petted her absently, and began her morning prayers

* * *

A cold wind whipped rain under Betty and Emma's umbrella as they quickly walked to school. Fall was definitely underway. Over the weekend, Betty performed an annual rite of autumn by moving her light summer clothes into the guestroom closet exchanging them for the warm winter ones stored there. Today, she had dressed in layers, making provision for whatever the capricious Missouri weather would throw her way. The moss green knit skirt, crew sweater, and cardigan were one of her favorite winter outfits because it fit comfortably and the color accented her eyes. Emma, too, was dressed appropriately for a cool and rainy autumn day in a gold suede skirt, long-sleeved white tailored shirt and black wool jacket. The weather reminded her of many cool damp days on the English coast where she had been raised. Today's benevolent weather, however, Betty had warned her, would change drastically in a couple of months when temperatures would nosedive below freezing.

Emma ventured to open the conversation. "It seems you and Junior are getting along fairly well."

"Yes, I guess we are. He's coming over tonight to watch Monday Night Football. One of our old-time favorite pastimes."

"Football, huh? Just think, only a week ago you shocked me by saying you would actually reconcile with him after all the years. And I must confess I was totally skeptical. Now, I'm not sure what to think."

"You probably think if it didn't work before, why would it work now. Am I right?"

Emma smiled crookedly and shook her head. "No, not exactly. I believe people can change, if they want to badly enough. But, Betty," she said cautiously, "I do think you and Junior have some issues you should explore before your relationship gets more serious."

Surprised, but not embarrassed, by Emma's brave assertion about a personal subject, Betty answered. "Yes, I know you're right. Before Karen died, we tried to work through some stuff. Neither of us were whole healthy persons, and we sometimes tried to control and manipulate each other in subtle, and not so subtle ways." She shrugged her ample shoulders. "We were considering counseling, but after Karen died, Junior left, and that was that."

"Betty, I think I understand how Karen's murder brought Junior's raw emotions to the surface, perhaps motivating him to run away instead of facing reality. You know, the old 'fight or flight' theory. In fact, I remember reading the divorce rate is extremely high after the death of a child."

Betty agreed, "Yes, that's true, and to make it even more attractive, Geneva was only too happy to indulge him with stress-free living when he moved back with her. Talk about unresolved issues, a textbook on co-dependency could use me and Junior, and Junior and Geneva as perfect examples."

"I really admire you, Betty. You are being brutally honest with yourself, but you know, that's what it takes in order to change."

Betty hardened her jaw with resolve. "You're right, Emma. Now, seeing it is one thing, but, and this is where the rubber meets the road, Junior and I need to work at getting psychologically healthy before we get serious again."

Gaining confidence by Betty's willingness to discuss the subject, Emma dove even deeper. "What I still don't understand, Betty, is after you were divorced for years, and putting your marriage back together again appeared impossible, why did you continue to hold on to the past? I feel like you should have moved on with your life. Blimey, a week ago I thought either you had lost your common sense, or, your relationship with Junior was so dysfunctional you couldn't let go of it. But now, I don't know, I seem to be questioning what I believe as well."

"Well, if it's any consolation," Betty stated ruefully, "I'm sure your rationale is held by the majority of contemporary society."

"I know. But, what I'm confused about is why you think so differently?"

Betty frowned. "Think about it, fifty years ago my way of thinking was normal. You know what I mean, the honor code, 'a man's word is his bond.' and 'you made your bed, lie in it.' Back then most contracts were sealed with a handshake, and most marriages were sealed without the possibility of divorce as an option. So, call me old-fashioned, but I feel the same way. I promised something, Emma, I made a vow. You know the lines, 'for better or worse, for richer or poorer, in sickness or in health, until death we do part.'"

"Oh, yeah, I've heard of them," Emma mumbled as they entered the school's double doors, then, as her feminist mindset asserted itself, she snapped. "fortunately, I've never had to utter them!"

* * *

Alone all weekend, Cheryl Patton had not cooked a single meal and had slept until noon on Saturday. Monday morning, though, she awoke at seven to prepare for another school day. Blessed with a clear complexion she opted for a non-makeup day. Her long brown hair touched with a hint of gray was no problem either. She pulled it into a ponytail, turned it under and secured it with two long bobby pins. Then, searching her closet, she pulled out the one-piece that looked like a two-piece dress, slipped it over her head, and stuck her sockless feet into moccasin loafers. In less than fifteen minutes she was ready for work. Then, in an effort to maintain a residual semblance of her leisurely weekend, she lingered over instant French vanilla cappuccino, listened to news on the local radio station, and threw a sack lunch together consisting of a cold cut sandwich, small bag of potato chips and a Jonathan apple. She enjoyed her quiet weekends and evenings alone while Doug was on the road. And, for the past three years, their three children no longer demanded her time. The hours attending nonstop baseball, volleyball and football games, track events, and dance and music recitals were over.

The children had claimed possession of their own lives now and had moved to three different states. The oldest son had married a sweet girl he had met while attending SMU and subsequently settled in the Baton Rouge area. She hoped they would announce a new arrival soon because she was anxious for her first grandchild. Their younger son had not married and was a systems analyst for a large company in Dallas, and their youngest child was a very independent and unmarried daughter named Kate who lived in

Los Angeles. Regrettably, the three had endured a mixed, but mostly, unhappy childhood, and Cheryl speculated it was probably fear of a bad marriage that kept her younger son and daughter single. Though Doug had always loved the kids, like most alcoholics, his behavior had been erratic toward them, and he had doled out his time meagerly. Spending his days drinking had caused the children embarrassment, and consequently, they had seldom invited friends to the house. Each child had left home shortly after high school and put many miles and several states between themselves and their parents.

This trip, Doug was scheduled to be home on Wednesday afternoon, and for once Cheryl was anxious to see him. Last night's phone call from James Frazier and this morning's news on KWIX had brought home to her with a shock that she might have important information about last Thursday's murder. This, she had concluded when the morning news corrected the murdered woman's name from Findley to Vanhuss. With that insight, James's urgent call to Doug last night suddenly raised red flags. James had been adamant about reaching him immediately, not content to wait until Doug returned home on Wednesday, and had asked for phone numbers where he could reach him. She had given him numbers of two companies on Doug's route, but she doubted that he would be reached. She figured James wanted to ensure Doug's silence about his affair with the Vanhuss woman, and possibly ask for an alibi.

Cheryl's mind returned to the weekend of the fire in Kansas City when she and Doug, the Fraziers and the Bentleys had attended the "Feeling Wonderful" seminars. It was possibly the worse weekend of her life. The early Sunday morning fire had claimed the lives of her friends, Edith and Dave Bentley, and less important, but still devastating, was the knowledge of the affair between James Frazier and the Vanhuss woman conducted right under Sarah's nose. She and Sarah had simultaneously discovered the affair on Friday night when Sarah had come to their room looking for James, and Doug, drinking heavily, had let the cat out of the bag. Cheryl could still visualize the blood draining from Sarah's face when Doug slurred, "He'sh propley still gittin' it on wisth the blond!" The thunderbolt delivered, Doug accented it with grossly inappropriate gestures.

The following morning, Sarah was a no-show at breakfast and the scheduled meetings. Cheryl did notice, however, the obvious candidate of James's amorous attention in the dining room eating a healthy breakfast and gregariously engaging those around her. That Vanhuss was unquestionably the other woman was apparent to anyone at the conference even vaguely

121

interested in the adulterous co-mingling of others. The continuous eye contact and the sensed sexual energy reverberating between the two had been palpable at the Friday evening mixer and during the all-day Saturday events. Sarah remained in her room on Saturday, while James attended all the meetings, making excuses for his wife's absence.

"What should I do?" she wondered aloud. "Should I tell Sheriff Gilmore what I know, or wait to talk to Doug about it? Or should I talk to Sarah first? She's been hurt enough, maybe I'll just keep my mouth shut!"

* * *

Sheriff Gilmore, coffee thermos in hand, was first in the office Monday morning as he planned. He wanted an uninterrupted hour to organize his thoughts, as well as his desk. Glancing through several stacks of papers that had piled up rapidly since last Thursday's murder, he picked up Edie's deposition lying on top the nearest stack and began reading carefully.

Her description of the victim's body coincided with what he and Aunt Lucy witnessed three hours later on Thursday afternoon. She mentioned the stained robe, the knife perpendicular to the body, the spilled perfume (which she recognized as the sample bottle she had given Rose on her first visit), outstretched arms and the unblemished cheek turned upward in death, so similar to her attempt in life, to conceal her deformity from others. Edie was certain Rose was dead when she arrived and was reportedly shocked by the violence she witnessed, and yet, having premeditated doing the deed herself in a similar fashion, Edie had lingered over the body, and confessed that a part of her celebrated. Her enemy was dead without having lifted a finger against her; dead, murdered, and she wouldn't have to pay for the crime. She claimed to have been in the house no more than fifteen minutes, arriving at approximately 12:45 and leaving at 1:00 (the time confirmed by Geneva). As to her selected murder weapon, Edie had brought her father's somewhat sharp hunting knife, but had not removed it from her jacket pocket. She saw no one else near the victim's house.

"Well, that's that," he sighed, " no new information here." He would talk to Edie again, however, concerning her supposed rape eight or ten years ago. Taking out his small notebook, he listed his intention to question Edie again, and then added a second name Lori had mentioned, Mary Jane Oglesby, the possible victim of another unsubstantiated rape alleged to have been committed a little over a year ago. "If the two rapes actually occurred," he wondered, "were they connected to little Karen Bryson's rape and murder?"

Just then, a rap at the office door interrupted his reflections, and Nancy stuck her head in the door. "You're here early."

"Yeah, well, I thought I'd get a head start before the unpredictable begins."

"Good idea!" she agreed, "me too. What do you want me to start on?"

The sheriff was organized enough to fire out orders. "I think the first thing is to put a tail on Frazier. I want to know where he disappears at night. Second, search the computer for every reported rape in the county for the past ten years. I'm pretty sure Karen Bryson's rape was the only one that devolved into murder, but double check that, would you? Then, find out if we have a PERK on her. If we don't have any evidence saved with semen samples, get an order to exhume Karen's body for possible sperm residue for DNA testing and inform the coroner to that effect." He knew recovery of testable semen was a long shot because after four years semen samples usually deteriorate and cannot be tested, but if the PERK had been kept cool and dry, there was an outside chance. While you're down there, grab the bed sheet collected from the Vanhuss house with the semen sample and submit it for DNA testing. Also, I want to question the Oglesby girl today, as well as Edie Bentley again. So, call Mr. and Mrs. Oglesby for permission to talk to Mary Jane at school, and run the time past Aunt Lucy. I would like to use her office and want her to be present."

Nancy wrote furiously on the back of an envelope, then saluted her boss and asked with good humor, "Is that all, Sir?"

As his deputy began to back out of the office, the sheriff nodded with a grin. "For now!"

Nancy descended into the lower level of the county office building, heading for the cool air-dried vault room where the PERKs were stored. The deputy had learned during her training that a PERK was a physical evidence recovery kit used to collect evidence at every rape or murder scene. Each kit contained basic collection tools, such as a fine-toothed comb to use on pubic hair, a nail clipper to collect the victim's fingernails for possible skin or blood fragments of the perpetrator beneath them, rubber gloves for the investigator, sterile swabs to collect bodily fluids, and small plastic envelopes and labels. She had no problem locating the Bryson PERK with the semen sample inside and recovered the soiled bed sheet from the Vanhuss house. If the semen sample was testable Betty and Junior could be spared the trauma of exhuming their daughter's body.

After Nancy alerted Gencodes Forensic Science Lab in Jeff City, another deputy, Sam Taylor, personally took custody of the items to be hand delivered to them. Although the items had previously been analyzed for blood type and hair analysis at the state lab, the more recent forensic tool of DNA testing had not been used in the eight-year-old Bryson, or the newer Vanhuss case. Gencodes had informed the deputy a determination would be made in ten days if DNA typing were possible from the samples they received.

It was mid-morning before Nancy was able to schedule the sheriff's appointments to question the Oglesby girl and Edie. Afterward, she returned to her computer to search crime files for past sexual assaults in the area. She decided to increase the area of her search beyond the county level the sheriff had specified, and include all counties in a sixty mile radius of Cramer Creek, which would extend coverage to six moderately-sized towns, including the college towns of Columbia, Moberly, Fulton and Fayette. By lunchtime, she had completed the search and printed out every scrap of available information on past rapes. She carried the printout into the sheriff's office.

"You were right, Sheriff," she announced. "Karen Bryson's rape was the only one that culminated in murder in the past ten years."

"I thought so," he nodded, and then wondered aloud, "perhaps we should have traced the crimes back further in time, perhaps the past twenty years?"

"Sure. That would be no problem. Well, this is what we have so far," she confirmed, laying the printout on the desk. "As you can see, sexual assaults have radically increased in towns twenty to fifty miles from here, especially in college towns, but also in smaller ones. Cramer Creek has had only the three rapes of Karen Bryson, Edie Bentley, and Mary Jane Oglesby."

"I can't believe this!" he gasped, looking at the two-page report. "There must be thirty to thirty-five reported rapes here."

"At least, and they appear to have increased in number each subsequent year."

"Okay," he determinedly squared his jaw, relieved to have a new direction in the case, "you have another deputy coordinate the details of each rape on the list and look for similarities: the age of the girl, if a weapon was used, the time of day, how the perpetrator was dressed, the words he used, where the crimes occurred, you get the idea."

"Sure, sheriff, I'm on it. By the way, your appointment with the Oglesby girl is in half an hour, and her mother wants to be there. She asked if you could pick her up on the way to school. Aunt Lucy said you could use her office. Oh, and Edie said to come by anytime."

* * *

Running on automatic, Junior checked the pickers as they worked on the final rows of crisp Jonathan apples. The winesaps were at the perfect stage for picking also, and they would probably move to those trees within a couple of days. James had told him to take some time off, at least until after his mother's funeral, but Junior couldn't imagine knocking about the house for several days with nothing to do, so he opted to continue working. Twice during the day he saw his boss at a distance, but James mostly remained hidden within the confines of his office and the barn where sorting, packing and shipping was located. This suited Junior just fine, allowing him to continue his manual labor without interruption, and leaving his mind to roam freely, but pausing at the important markers of his life.

As he sifted through the past, Karen's murder was paramount. And it did not escape his awareness that his boss was a possible suspect in the murder of his precious child, as well as the Vanhuss woman and his mother. The more he thought about it, the more he believed the murders were all connected. After all, Karen had been killed in Fraziers' orchard, although neither he, nor Betty, had suspected James eight years ago. But, now, after the exposed affair with the Vanhuss woman, and the killer's subsequent need to silence the only witness, his mother, it all made sense. James had probably been his mother's favorite suspect of the next-door neighbor murder, and he knew she would not, or could not, keep her suspicions to herself. Consequently, her idle tongue precipitated her final downfall by starting a raging fire of gossip that reached the ears of her murderer.

"Maybe I should consider taking some time off," he thought, "because if he comes near me with these thoughts I've been having, I'll kill him myself!"

* * *

Mary Jane sat in Aunt Lucy's office, ill at ease, waiting for her mother and Sheriff Gilmore. Retelling the horrible thing that happened to her was the last thing she wanted to do. The nightmares were retreating slowly, but she had not recovered from the rape by any means. At fourteen, Mary Jane had an attractive face, mahogany brown hair and fern green eyes, and had had several chances to date like most of her friends, but had held back, being timid and uncomfortable around boys. She rarely made eye contact with boys or men. Even Mr. Lacey, her algebra teacher and her friend, Elizabeth's, father, had been unable to break through her cool, uncommitted reserve. A sharp rap on the principal's office door caused her to jump and was closely followed by the entrance of Aunt Lucy, her mother and Sheriff Gilmore. Mary Jane immediately lowered her head and stared at the old, fringed rug beneath her feet. She promised herself she would not cry.

"How do I tame this cowering creature?" Sheriff Gilmore wondered. She reminded him of the small woodland rabbit he had stumbled upon in the brush a few days earlier and how the small quivering piece of fur had frozen catatonically until he had bent down and nearly touched it. "If I reach out to touch Mary Jane she will blindly dart for cover just like that rabbit," he speculated.

Four chairs had been placed in a somewhat circular array in front of Aunt Lucy's desk. Mrs. Oglesby took the seat nearest her daughter and protectively encircled her shoulders with her arm. Aunt Lucy sat, after receiving assurance that her presence was desired, on the other side of Mary Jane. Sheriff Gilmore sat in the remaining and opposing chair, seeming to him as if he had been placed in the adversarial role of prosecutor facing the persecuted and her stanch protectors.

He began speaking slowly and quietly, "I'm so very sorry to have to ask you questions again concerning the assault you suffered about two years ago, Mary Jane." He wished she would give some indication that she was listening. "I know you don't want to talk about it, and I wish you didn't have to. But, I also know the man who hurt you might still be hurting other young girls the same way, and I want to lock him up and throw away the key so he can never hurt anyone else. Do you think you could answer some questions that might help me find him?"

Mary Jane nodded and spoke with a barely audible voice, "Yes."

"Okay, then," he sighed. "I've read the report you signed two years ago, so we don't have to go over everything. Just correct me if I say anything wrong, okay?" Mary Jane nodded. "As I understand it, you were riding your bicycle after dinner on a Tuesday evening. Then, as you were circling the pavement behind the school building a man caught you from behind, forcing you off your bike, and carried you into the janitor's workroom located in the basement of this building. Is that correct so far?"

Mary Jane nodded assent.

"All right. Then the first question I have is how did he get into the locked school?"

"He took me down the outside basement steps. The door wasn't locked.

He just opened the door and carried me in."

"It wasn't locked?" he asked, looking at Aunt Lucy.

"I don't know, it should have been locked. That particular door is the maintenance man's responsibility, but I don't remember when he was ever lax about keeping it locked."

"Do you ever check that door yourself to see if it's locked?"

"No, I guess I have always assumed it was."

"Well, let's go on. Mary Jane, what did the man say to you when he grabbed you?"

"Nothing until we were inside the room, then he showed me a big knife and said he would kill me if I didn't do what he said. He said he would kill me if I ever told anybody. He told me to quit crying. He told me he liked me and I was pretty. He said some nasty words."

"From the tone of his voice and the things he said, how old do you think he was?"

"I don't know. Older."

"Do you think he might have been as old as I am?"

"Maybe."

"Do you think it was a boy still in high school?"

"No."

"Did you see any hair on his head, arms, or anywhere else on his body?"

"He wore a ski mask. All I could see were his eyes, but his arms had mostly dark hair."

"Okay. That may help a lot. Now, did his eyes look like the eyes of a young man, a middle-aged man or an old man?"

"I don't know."

"I see in the report, you thought his eyes were dark, but couldn't tell exactly what color they were."

She nodded.

"Okay. I'm not going to make you describe what he did to you. Mrs. Swan, the social worker who asked you to replicate what he did to you on the doll she brought, submitted an excellent and thorough report. Now, I have just one last question. Was there anything at all about the man you remember that would help to identify him again?"

"He smelled. He must have put on a lot of cologne." She shuddered and closed her eyes. "I'll never forget the way he smelled."

Realizing this last statement of Mary Jane's had not been in the older report and might be instrumental in the capture of the rapist, he made a quick note to gather popular brands of men's cologne to see if the girl could identify the one she had depicted on the man.

"Okay, I think that will be all for now. Thank you, Mrs. Oglesby, for being here." Then, turning his attention to the girl, he apologized again and thanked her for her help.

As mother and daughter departed her office, Aunt Lucy instantly spoke with excitement, "Roy, I have something to show you." She turned and retrieved a somewhat dilapidated brown paper sack resting against the corner of her desk. Extracting from it a blackened metal sickle with a sharp curved blade, she asked, "What do you suppose that might be?"

The sheriff's eyes widened instantly as his body reacted to the object in her hands like it was electrically charged. He felt in his bones this was the missing weapon that had killed Geneva. The caked and spattered dark rust-like stains had to be blood; he would rush it himself to the lab in Jeff City to be sure. "Where did you find this, Aunt Lucy?" he asked excitedly, unable to contain his emotion.

"Well, you know Tommy Samp, of course." She sighed, remembering the many forays into the meaning of justice that she and Tommy had engaged. "The silly boy brought it to school this morning and was enjoying threatening Mary Thomas with it on the playground when Mrs. James confiscated it and brought Tommy and the implement into my office. He claims to have found it in the ditch adjacent to his back yard this weekend. When Mr. Samp came to take Toomy home (I suspended him for a week), he couldn't identify it and doesn't know who it could belong to." Then she pulled her glasses up from the gold chain around her neck, sat them on the end of her nose, and gazed fixedly at the sickle. "It is blood, isn't it?"

CHAPTER 14

"Good thing Frazier kept his distance today," Junior thought angrily. It was finally quitting time and he and his boss had not spoken one word to each other all day. They had not even been within speaking range. This fact spoke volumes to Junior's mind, since the two usually began each morning laying out the day's work schedule, and several times throughout the day would banter informally back and forth. Consequently, as far as Junior was concerned, this change in routine, alone, admitted James's guilt. "That arrogant pervert raped and killed my daughter; my only child," he alternately raved and grieved inwardly. It was obvious to him, after today, he would quit working at the orchard altogether, even though jobs were hard to find in Cramer Creek. Otherwise, he would probably end up killing James.

Junior forced himself to think of something else as his heavy frame climbed wearily into his truck to head home. He was cheered slightly by the prospect of spending the evening with Betty. At six-thirty, she had invited him for dinner at her place, and afterward they would watch Monday Night Football together, just like old times. He knew he had been intolerable toward Betty over the past eight years and wondered if she could ever forgive him. Looking back over those years, he felt as though part of him had not been functioning, as if his brain had disinherited any feeling. The result had been an emptiness in his soul that had made him feel hollow and barren like an arid desert wasteland, and he had survived, dry and thirsty, but had denied his parched existence by never allowing himself to think about it. If being a workaholic didn't block his emotions, he drank, if drinking didn't work, he would simply zone out watching mindless TV programs in the evening until he fell asleep. He wanted to change, and quench his soul again, he really did. Even now, though he was grieving his mother's death, he felt a stirring of life again when he was around Betty. And, for some reason impossible to fathom, Betty still seemed to want him. It made him think of the Mark Twain quip: "I wouldn't want to join a club that would have me as a member."

* * *

Sheriff Gilmore phoned his deputy to meet him at Edie Bentley's, and then walked with a bounce in his step the half block from school to Edie's house. He was pleased, and highly motivated, as new puzzle pieces had become visible. He still didn't know exactly how they fit into the big picture, but he was certain they would. The investigation had moved to a higher level today, almost taking on a life of its own. Finding the sickle was a Godsend, and he would take it to the forensic lab himself; and Mary Jane stating her ability to identify the unique scent of the rapist's cologne was icing on the cake. Moreover, he was optimistic the tail he had ordered on Frazier would bring rewards. James was an enigma he was determined to know more about.

He waited ten minutes outside the house for Deputy Armstrong, still gun-shy about visiting the imaginative Edie on his own. Upon seeing the deputy turn the corner at the market in a county patrol car, he stepped quickly onto the small porch and knocked.

Edie, who had been observing him through a lace curtain, answered immediately. "Hello, Sheriff." She spoke timidly, but minus the fear she had exhibited before. Also, Friday's bedraggled look was gone. Today, she wore makeup, her hair was styled and she was dressed neatly in jeans and a tailored pink blouse. "Come on in," she said with a grin.

With Deputy Armstrong close on his heels, he entered the living room cautiously, determined to give Edie the benefit of a doubt as she recounted the sexual assault that supposedly took place eight to ten years before.

After he settled comfortably on an overstuffed couch, and Nancy and Edie sat in two matching rose-colored rockers, Edie recited her well-worn tale. "It happened years ago, when I was eleven," she began. "I was sleeping soundly in my bed, so I don't know what time it was, and I didn't hear the man enter my bedroom. The first thing I knew I awoke with my mouth held shut forcefully by a man's hand. I struggled, trying to call out for my parents, but his grip was too tight. It was a bright night with a full moon and I could see his outline against the window, and could dimly see his face, but it was covered by a black ski mask with red knitted circles around his eyes and mouth. He held a knife in front of my face and whispered that he would take his hand off my mouth if I would not make a sound, and he told me he would kill me if I did. I nodded, agreeing to be silent. Then, he pulled my nightgown off and raped me. He hurt me so bad, and when I started crying, he held the knife against my throat again, and told me if I made any sound at all he would kill me. I tried to be quiet, but I couldn't hold back the sobs that were wracking my body. So, I guess to keep me quiet, he smothered the noise with a pillow over my face. I could barely breathe, but he held it there until he was finished. Mom, Dad and Brian were sleeping in their beds close by, but they never heard a thing. The next morning, Mom found blood on my sheet and thought I had started my period. I didn't tell anyone what happed to me until after Karen was raped and murdered, but nobody believed me. I knew it was the same man."

Sheriff Gilmore was startled by the similarity of Edie's story to Mary Jane's, even though the two assaults had occurred over six years apart and in different locations. The rapist had more carefully planned the more recent crime, basing the time of attack on the Oglesby girl's routine bicycle route and changing the location of the crime to a more secure one, leaving nothing to chance. Edie's assault, on the other hand, had the earmarks of an earlier, less secure crime by the perpetrator. Attempting to ascertain other points of congruity, he asked, "Edie, do you remember a scent associated with the rapist?"

"Yes," she answered, jumping immediately on the question, "I do. He wore a strong aftershave or cologne. Ever since that night, I haven't been able to stand the smell of Old Spice on a man. It always makes my stomach turn."

"Old Spice?" he cried. "Are you sure?"

"Oh, yeah. The first time I smelled it after it happened, I threw up. It was at church. Later, I asked the man what kind of cologne he used and found out the scent was Old Spice. I don't think very many men wear it anymore."

Nancy had been silent during this exchange, not having been present during the earlier meeting with Mary Jane and her mother. Therefore, she wasn't clear about Roy's line of questioning, but she picked up on his excitement. Having a question of her own, she asked, "Edie, could you describe anything else about the man, his size, for instance."

"No, not really," she considered carefully. "You see, I was so young and much smaller than he was; but, the man wasn't fat or skinny, and he wasn't short. I guess that's all I can tell you."

Because Edie and Mary Jane's stories matched so closely, the sheriff's doubt and suspicions of Edie's veracity was entirely assuaged. He believed Edie and felt more hopeful that they would soon nail this sickening deviant. Thanking Edie, the law officers returned to the office.

When they arrived, James was waiting in one of the uncomfortable molded plastic chairs in the wide hallway adjacent to the sheriff's office. Seeing him there brought a distasteful reaction to Sheriff Gilmore's gag reflex, and he felt as though he needed to expunge some lethal poison he had accidentally swallowed. Still, it was just a gut reaction, there was no ironclad evidence against James, at least anything that would stand up in court, and so, he forced himself to remain silent. Yet, his gut had taken over his mind and was lobbying to call the shots. Fortunately, however, his mouth was under control of his mind even though his gut shouted accusingly, "Guilty, guilty, guilty." Frowning, he motioned for James to follow him into the office.

"You said to come by today," the suspect began, keeping his voice friendly and upbeat, a far cry from the smarmy arrogance he had presented last evening when he had demanded them to leave his house.

"Yes, Mr. Frazier, I believe you are here to explain your whereabouts after nine o'clock p.m. last Friday night. You were not able to come up with an alibi for Mrs. Vanhuss' murder, let us hope you can do better for Geneva's. So, where were you?"

James, his forehead uncharacteristically creased and lined with perspiration, had shortly lost his usual self-assured swagger. "I'm not a violent man, Roy," he pleaded. "You've known me all your life; have you ever known me to hurt anyone? It's just not in my nature; surely you know that."

Deputy Armstrong, having followed James into the sheriff's office, spoke behind him, "Just answer the question, Mr. Frazier, where were you Friday night?"

Visible pressure was building as James scrunched up his face as though trying to remember his movements. "I just went for a drive and ended up in Columbia. Just messing around, you know? Then I went to a few bars, had some drinks, nothing special. Played the jukebox, drove around again. I got home around two in the morning, I guess. You can check with my wife, she knows when I came in."

"Sounds to me like you've got another no alibi for murder, Frazier," Deputy Armstrong remarked. "I don't imagine you can remember the name of all the bars you visited?"

"Sure I can," he stated, eyeing her with a hint of his former cockiness. "Well, they were mostly in the downtown area, except for the lounge at the Holiday Inn, out on the loop. That's where I started around eight o'clock. Must have been there at least an hour." Appearing to recover some of his composure, he hazarded a smirk. "The bartender, Sandy, she'll remember me."

With a list of six drinking establishments and the approximate times at each, he looked coldly at James. "We'll check it out," Sheriff Gilmore threatened, and then added menacingly, "you can go for now," with the emphasis on "now."

James smiled, nodded his head and headed for the exit.

Outside, he had to admit he was a bit shaky, and as he breathed free air outside the County Office Building, he knew what had to be done, and done soon. The idiot sheriff would never bring him in. He would never be caught and would always be free to assuage his needs. Then, a sudden, inward frenzy began to rack his body and it cried out for denouement. He had no survival skills for the uncommon onslaught of emotional duress except his drug of choice, his addiction, and the fix that could temporarily contain his aching need. He would have to take the chance, now, tonight, to calm the raging storm.

Across the street, a block away in a tan '86 Cavalier, John Westerfield, a laid-back, middle-aged deputy out of uniform, had been waiting impatiently for James. Since the directive to tail Frazier, he had spent the afternoon parked out of sight near the orchard, but downwind of the pond. The sickening stench from the pond had been nearly unbearable, and to lessen it he had had to roll the windows up causing the temperature in the small car to soar. Now, he watched James spring into his red pickup and head toward the interstate. Allowing a good quarter of a mile between vehicles, he began to tail the truck surreptitiously.

* * *

Junior had arrived at Betty's and was attentively keeping her company in the kitchen as she put the finishing touches on their meal. She had never been able to compete with her ex-mother-in-law's cooking, and knowing her limitations, had never tried. She liked good food, but also liked to spend as little time in the kitchen as possible. Tonight, she had decided on something simple, but filling: two broiled Kansas City steaks, and a garden salad, and would top off the meal with a couple of leftover brownies. Contrary to her ex-mother-in-law's belief, she had not found Junior to be particularly finicky about what he ate. He was not simply a "meat and potato" man as Geneva claimed, at least, this had not been her experience. She thought how sad it was that one of Geneva's main reasons for existence had been based on a faulty belief. How sad her life had been in general. Her whole world, after her husband, Ramsey Charles Bryson, Sr., had left her, was built around her son, and for whatever psychological reason, Junior had kept up his part of her false reality. "Another sign of codependency," she thought, and wondered why. "Emotionally healthy young men strive to be autonomous and independent; to break away from mother's apron strings, don't they?" She wondered how deeply he was entrenched in his dysfunctional family's script? And for what parts did he take responsibility? "Maybe Emma was right, maybe I should cut my losses and begin a new life." Realizing suddenly that Junior had asked her a question, she startled back into the present.

"A penny for your thoughts," he offered.

"Oh," she grinned and rolled her eyes, "I'm sorry. What did you say?"

"Nothing important, I just wanted to know if you had a better day than I did."

"It was fine, I guess, nothing special, really. Emma and I got drenched walking to school this morning, but it was kind of fun. Why, what was wrong with your day?"

"For one thing I quit my job. I can't work for Frazier anymore believing he was responsible for Karen's death."

"Oh, Junior." Betty gasped, then walked toward him until only inches separated them and searched his deep blue eyes. "Was he? Do you really think so?"

He paused, quickly researching and cataloging James's past behavior in his mind, as well as today's. "I don't have proof, but I'm pretty sure, dear," he said softly and reached for her hand. She dropped her head and rested it on his shoulder. After a few moments, he lifted her head and kissed her cheek. "Let's not talk about it now and spoil our evening. I've been looking forward to tonight. It's been the one bright spot in a lousy day!"

As they sat down to dinner, Betty asked, "Would you like to say grace?"

"It's been too long," he admitted, then smiled at her, "but I guess it's like riding a bicycle." He prayed briefly, asking the Lord to bless the food and thanking him for His presence in difficult times.

After dinner, Betty left the dirty dishes in the sink, and they took a bowl of ice cream and brownie each into the living room and half turned toward each other on opposite ends of the couch.

Junior scrutinized her face, drumming up the courage to begin a speech he had practiced several times, "Betty, I don't know how to say this," Junior began, staring down at the worn carpet. "But, I know I've been a jerk, not to mention a fool, and I wouldn't blame you if you hated me after the way I treated you. I don't understand why you don't. But I want to know, and you don't have to answer me tonight." He turned and bared his soul, beseeching her with his eyes. "What would it take for you to forgive me and take me back again?"

"Junior, I forgave you a long time ago, but I can't forget. I wonder if it's really in the past. I think it is too soon to talk about the future. I don't know if I'm ready to take that big a step right now. I do still love you." Oceans of meaning passed between them as their eyes bathed in each other's gaze.

Junior moved quickly to her side. "I love you so much, Betty. I would make sure you never regretted taking me back, and I promise never to be so stupid to leave you again."

Leaving their ice cream to melt in forgotten bowls on the coffee table, one became lost in the arms of the other, and time, even eight years of it, was summarily discounted for the moment, and judged inconsequential. For an indeterminate measure of time they remained wrapped together, not sensuously so, knowing that would come some day, but in a state of deep fulfillment. The spell was broken momentarily when the mantle clock chimed eight o'clock.

"Are you ready for some football?" Betty sang, and then teased, "oh, no, I think you missed the kick-off!"

Junior grinned, and then took on a serious look. "I promise you, and I mean it, anytime you want to interrupt a football game, even if it's the Chiefs, do it. I want you to know what my priorities are."

"Now I know you're in love!" she giggled.

"Yeah, the word is smitten, I think. But, if it's okay with you," he smiled, "let's watch the game." He switched on the TV with the remote just as Hank Williams, Jr. was singing boisterously, "Are you ready for some football?"

* * *

In the neighboring town of Hamlet, James pulled his pickup into a hidden parking lot maintained by the porn store, but two blocks from the premises. It was hours before he, and most others, usually frequented such places, preferring the cover of darkness for his visits. But, even in daylight, the many hot-colored neon lights surrounding the clapboard building were glowing and successfully attempted to lure customers with seemingly innocuous words in bright orange, green, pink, and blue: "Theatre," "Novelties," "Arcade," "Videos," "Rentals," "Magazines," and "24 Hours," and "7 Days."

The churches in the county had remained mostly silent regarding the establishment. Yes, there were occasional condemning words spoken from the body of believers, and a couple of letters to the editor had been written in the local paper, but no great outcry was heard or pickets organized. It was acknowledged in religious circles that the Assembly of God pastor had railed against it from the pulpit. However, the "adult" store's business license had been granted with the city's blessing and with little noticeable clamor. "There's nothing we can do about it," was the general sentiment. And the great absurdity of "salt and light" was blended into a tasteless society and well hidden behind stained glass windows.

Reaching the rear entrance, James entered quickly, colliding with a heavily made-up young girl in a black leather second skin with a side slit that didn't stop. He correctly guessed the girl had presented some sort of steamy scene under the heading of "Theatre." Leering at her, he quickly propped his arm across the door, barring her exit.

"Sorry, Dad, I have a date," she said, and quickly ducked under his arm and left, banging the door behind her.

Once inside, patrons were not reminded what time of day or night it was, because every possible link to the outside world was covered with black paint, and the contrasting bright neon and spotlights served to further darken the surrounding space. In the anonymous darkness, various obscene materials were advertised and highlighted from every angle. Timid customers were granted certain anonymity in the darkness and kept their eyes turned from the faces of others as well, seldom acknowledging other habitual frequenters of the business. It was a strange slant on the golden rule: "Do unto others…."

John Westerfield watched the young girl in black leather from his vehicle. She left the back door of the building James had just entered and slid into a red Buick convertible, the only car parked on site. He noted the out-of-state plates as she careened onto the street. Parked between the store's anonymous parking lot, a block away, where James's pickup stood, and the rear door to the store, he radioed Sheriff Armstrong to detail his position, and ask for instructions. "Should I go in, Sheriff? I don't think he'll recognize me since I'm not from Cramer Creek."

After he received instructions, he signed off and entered the adult store. It took several minutes before his eyes focused to the darkness of the large room. As he scoped the room for James, a tall, thin young man with short spiked blond hair approached him. "What'cha lookin for, man?"

Embarrassment rose to the roots of the seasoned patrolman's sand and gray hair. "Uh, I thought I would just look around, if that's okay."

"No problem, help yourself," he said, sizing up the new customer. Then he returned to the area behind the cash register, and picked up a magazine entitled *Hard Core*, and began turning its pages.

The law officer pretended to scrutinize the material on every wall, shelf and aisle, but was actually searching for James, who was nowhere in sight. "Where could he be?" he wondered. Then he noticed several doors lining the back wall or either side of the rear door he had just entered. There had been a narrow hallway no more than five feet long just inside the entrance. Comprehension dawned when he speculated that each of the doorways were entrances into tiny rooms, probably no larger than five by five feet. He figured even if one room was a bathroom, and a large room on one side was a stock room, there was still one large room in the opposite corner and four small rooms in between, three rooms on each side of the rear entrance, which were used for other purposes. "Frazier's in one of those rooms," he calculated. Instead of displaying curiosity about the rooms, he decided to go back to his vehicle and wait for James to return. Wondering if it might be a long wait, he wished he had brought something to eat, especially since his replacement was not due until ten. Then, he looked at the house number near his parked car and had a great idea. He dialed Domino's Pizza and ordered a large sausage and onion, and settled down to wait the twenty-minute delivery time. It would be dark soon, and time for Monday Night Football, he lamented, "Now, if I only had a portable TV!"

Inside the tiny booth, James slipped the illicit tape he had ordered into the VCR and loosened his clothing. The star of the thinly plotted movie was a beautiful Asian child with a dark hooded look interspersed with sudden spurts of laughter. Her co-star was an older man, possibly in his forties, who alternately tickled and gagged her during their activities. The various supporting actors were of various ages and both genders and were seen cavorting in a private playground stocked with a merry-go-round, swings, teeter-totters, and a small wading pool. Disappointed with the tame actions of the XXX rated film he fast-forwarded through most of it.

CHAPTER 15

Waiting for his relief, the middle-aged patrolman tried to keep his eyes open. With his appetite sated and his stomach full of pizza, he was ready for a good night's sleep. "What in the world could keep Frazier busy in there for four hours?" he wondered, looking at his watch. Earlier, only a brief walk around the lascivious. neon atmosphere of the porn store had made his skin crawl and his upper lip curl disgustedly. He was next to certain that more degrading and illicit materials were hidden from sight of the casual and merely curious customers. Something of that nature was probably what had occupied Frazier in one of the small private rooms. "God only knows what a steady diet of pornography does to a man's mind," he thought. Without warning, an unwanted thought flashed through his mind, "Could Frazier have given him the slip and was now somewhere undetected in the community or even back in his own home? Did I let my guard down and doze off? No, I didn't, that couldn't have happened," he affirmed to himself. "I've been within sight of that back door every minute." But just in case, he decided when his replacement arrived, he would locate Frazier with his own eyes.

Actually, it had been twilight, the time of day when muted shadows mingle with gray dusk, when James returned the high-priced rental video to the clerk and followed on the heels of another customer out the back door. Out of the corner of his eye James had noticed the Domino's Pizza sign atop an older model Chevy a street over. Then turning the corner, he had walked east past the gaudy neon building, then south for two blocks, then east again. Then finally, he had turned cautiously onto a tree-lined sidewalk and entered an older established neighborhood and had scanned the street for his prey, a young, dark-haired prepubescent girl, with a ready smile and long tanned legs tapering down into white Nikes. However, she was not in sight just now; not on her red 10-speed bicycle which was lying on its side by the steps, or sitting on her small front porch talking to her friend who lived next door, and not in her bedroom as evidenced by the darkness of her room on the second floor. "She's probably having dinner with the family," he thought.

"Well, maybe after a couple of times around the block...."

* * *

Aunt Lucy was troubled as she knelt beside her bed. Within her righteous mind, a disturbing, but vague vision of emerging clumps of festering slime floated to the surface of a beautiful crystal sea. Slowly, as her vision became clearer, she watched ever-widening circles of small blackened waves of refuge emanate from the core of each slimy abomination, multiplying exponentially as each new clump formed upon the surface. She watched as a myriad of ripples spread over the evil seascape in her mind until the vision plummeted her below the surface of the stagnant water, revealing an even greater horrific scene, one of a lurking iceberg which sported a larger, more dangerous bulk in the hidden depths below. An anvil-heavy burden weighed upon her ancient heart and she prayed earnestly for the Lord's light to shine in the dark and evil world revealed to her.

* * *

At five minutes to ten, Sam Taylor, a thirty-something, good-looking patrolman parked his late model Honda behind Westerfield's Chevy and joined the older man. With a glance, he took in the crumbs fallen upon an ample belly and the empty Domino's Pizza box thrown haphazardly on the back seat. Leaning through the passenger window, he asked, "What's happenin', John?"

"Not a dad-blamed thing. I've been sitting here all night waiting for Frazier to come out of that hell-hole, but he hasn't so much as stuck his head out the door."

"Is that the only entrance?"

"Yeah, well, there is another exit on the front facing the street, but it's an emergency door, a siren sounds if it's opened."

"Okay, have you checked on him?"

"Yeah, I did a few minutes after he went in, but I couldn't find him, he was nowhere in sight. He had to have been in one of those little rooms, watching a video, I guess, or whatever they do in there." He shrugged and shook his head. "That was over four hours ago, I don't know what he could be doing that would take four hours. I figured when you got here, one or both of us should check on him."

139

"Well, since you went in before, let me check it out this time and see what he's up to, okay?"

"Yeah, sure, that's fine with me. That place sours my stomach!"

"I knew you were old," the patrolman joked, "but I didn't think you were that old."

"Yeah, well, there's a big difference between being interested in women and getting involved in pornography."

"Maybe you can explain that to me some day, Pop."

Then, turning from the car window, Sam stroked his blond mustache, comically squared his shoulders, and headed for the rear door of the neon-bright building. Inside, he paused, allowing his eyes to adjust to the shadowy darkness accented by a kaleidoscope of well-placed spotlights. Then, as his fellow officer did earlier, he stalked the aisles and cubbyholes for his quarry, taking a few moments to peruse the magazines and novelties as he passed. Finally, drawing a blank, he sauntered up to the clerk behind the desk.

"Hey, bud," he began casually, "I was supposed to meet James Frazier here a couple of hours ago, but I got held up, is he still around?"

The clerk scrutinized the young plain-clothed officer's face, and decided he was what he appeared, a punk similar to a score of others that frequented the store. "Sorry, buddy, he left a long time ago. Can I help you with anything else?"

Patrolman Taylor grinned conspiratorially. "Nah, not right now, but I'll be back."

'He's been gone for hours," Sam told the older man accusingly when he returned to the stakeout. "You've been sitting out here for nothing. So, what do we do now?"

Shifting his weight uncomfortably, Westerfield contemplated the sheriff's anger when he was informed Frazier was on the loose. "I guess we'd better report it and see what Gilmore wants to do about it." Swiveling his head around he focused on the darkened parking lot a block away, and pointed, "Look, Frazier's truck's still parked in the lot back there."

Officer Taylor looked, and sure enough, the back end of Frazier's red pickup could be seen. "He's on foot! Let's call it in."

Keeping his eye on the truck, John reached the sheriff at home and tried to explain his snafu. The sheriff's instruction, after five minutes of dressing down, was for one of them to keep an eye on the truck, while the other combed the nearby streets and bars in the town of 7,000 people.

The search for Frazier assisted by Hamlet patrol officers was cancelled finally a few minutes after midnight, when he was observed returning on foot from an unknown location to his truck. From there, officer Taylor followed him back to the long driveway of his home in Cramer Creek. When this information was relayed back to Sheriff Gilmore, Taylor was commanded to remain on duty, while the other officers were summarily released from duty and allowed to return home.

Lori observed her husband's frown as he replaced the phone on the bedside table and decided he needed cheering up. To be specific, he needed to cuddle, she thought. She faked an obvious double cough, and when she had his attention, smiled innocently, opened her arms to him, and mimicking the song by Mickey and Sylvia, demanded lustily, "Come here, lover boy!" All was again well with the world as Roy rashly leaped into her arms and began to cover her with kisses, pausing only a moment to ask, "What would I do without you?"

* * *

Early the next morning, Nancy beat the sheriff to the office for a change. She was anxious to study more thoroughly yesterday's fax from the state prosecuting attorney's office. It was only a scanty two-page communication sent in answer to the further information she had requested regarding the "Feeling Wonderful" seminars. She had surmised that the "Feeling Wonderful" group was the main connection between the Vanhuss woman and several prime suspects of her murder. Beyond that, she was personally curious about the content and philosophy of the seminars. She had heard and read various and glowing hype about them on TV and in popular magazines. On the other hand, she remembered Pastor Sharpe's negative appraisal of the group and she was anxious to question him further about his objection to them. Leaning back in the sheriff's comfortable leather swivel chair, she visually scrolled down the pages that described the organization's structure, goals, and formula for happiness in a nutshell. "Feeling Wonderful" was basically a pyramid scheme bordering on illegal, just as Pastor Sharpe had asserted, but was cloaked in a self-help program based on Abraham Maslow's hierarchical stages of self-actualization. Its adherents were people of all ages looking for meaning and direction in life, such as increased psychological well-being, greater success, better relationships and improved health and physical fitness. The program, consisting of seminars, numerous informational CDs, computer software, visual imagery tapes and CDs, and workbooks, is sold to individual members for a steep ten thousand dollars. Then, percentages of that amount trickle down (actually up) to those higher on the pyramid. Nancy, attempting to read between the lines of the report, was unable to ascertain the exact beliefs of the program and its participants, but she found herself interested. On a subconscious level she was looking for something, some kind of meaning, because life to her was mysterious and filled with questions. "What is the purpose of life, anyway?" she posed. "Is it to be attractive to others, to fall in love and have babies? To bring more people in the world to ask the questions?" Basically, in spite of her current train of thought, she was optimistic by nature, and little could hold her down for long, but she had to admit she had a hungering desire for a new direction, although she would adamantly deny she was seeking spiritual answers to the void in her life.

"Self-actualization," she thought, "what could be wrong about that? And even better if money can be made from it." Still, being somewhat cautious, she wouldn't write off Pastor Sharpe's objections just yet. And something else gave her cause to think: of the three couples from Cramer Creek involved in the program, two were dead, one was an alcoholic, one was an adulterer, if not a rapist and murderer, and the two remaining wives were living in nightmare marriages. With these thoughts in mind, Nancy left a note on the sheriff's desk, and drove to Cramer Creek and the Baptist Church.

* * *

In the meantime, Sheriff Gilmore was having a hard time getting out the door at home, and it looked as though both he and Lori might be late for work. Finally, at the very moment when he had forced himself to say the last goodbye after a final kiss, the phone rang. Since Lori was still in her robe and frantically trying to throw herself together, he took the call from Cheryl Patton.

"Oh, hello, Cheryl," he said, rushing his words, "I'm sorry, but Lori's running a little late and I don't think she can come to the phone right now."

"No, Roy, you don't understand. I called to see if I could come by your office during my free hour this morning and talk to you. I'm not sure, and…it's probably nothing, but I think I might know something about that Vanhuss woman's murder. I thought about calling you all day yesterday, but I couldn't decide if I should or not."

Hearing the stress in her voice and curious about what she could possibly know about the murder, he immediately scrapped his previously made plans for the morning. "Sure, come to my office or I can come by the school."

"No, don't do that. I would rather come to your office. It won't take long to tell you what I know, and I don't want our talk to become public knowledge. You know what the grapevine in this town is like, and I am sure Lori has told you about the school lounge, it is a hotbed for gossip. I could be there by nine thirty, if that would be alright."

"Sure, no problem. I'll see you then."

After replacing the phone, he returned to Lori, currently fixing her face at the bathroom mirror, for a final hug.

"Good-bye, sweetheart. I'll see you at Geneva's funeral this afternoon."

"Okay. Bye, honey," she sighed, and slapped more foundation on her face.

He slammed the door and frowned. The appointment with Cheryl would delay his plan to follow up on Frazier's alibi the night Geneva was killed. Now, with her appointment at nine thirty and Geneva's funeral at three this afternoon, he would have to trust his officers to spend the day in Columbia visiting all the bars James claimed to have frequented that night, beginning at the Holiday Inn on the Loop. At least Sarah couldn't attempt to provide an alibi for him this time, as she had the night he was in bed with Rose Findley Vanhuss. His own visit to the Frazier house on Friday night had scuttled her larceny. He had found Sarah alone, relaxing comfortably in her robe, preparing to spend the evening reading a book, and obviously not expecting her husband any time soon. He wondered how many nights Sarah spent in a similar manner.

* * *

Pastor Sharpe welcomed Nancy into his study and indicated one of the mint green chairs she had occupied a few days earlier. This morning, he found himself struck by the deputy's youth and his spirit sensed a vulnerable naiveté about her in spite of her overt aggressive manner. She seemed to him, at this moment, a fragile soul, so much so that he immediately modified his usual objective and helpful persona and became innocuously gentle, determined not to bruise her, "…to do no harm," he thought.

Nancy gratefully accepted the coffee Pastor Sharpe offered, and contemplated how to broach the subject. She began by handing him the fax from the prosecuting attorney's office. "I was wondering," she began, "if you could tell me more about these 'Feeling Wonderful' seminars, Pastor?

When we mentioned the organization before, you were very negative about it. Is that correct?"

"That's right, Nancy," he began, with a fatherly smile. "I'm sure you must be familiar with the term 'New Age'?" he asked.

"Yes-s," she stammered, "but it seems to me it means different things to different people. I've heard that Shirley MacLaine is a spokesperson for the New Age movement, and she believes in spirit guides…channeling, that kind of thing. But, I don't think they all believe in that, do they? I guess I am confused about the whole thing. So, is the Feeling Wonderful organization part of the New Age movement?"

"Well, to answer your last question first, yes, the Feeling Wonderful seminars espouse many of the New Age tenets. I think it will help you if you think of the New Age movement as a wide array of different platforms, as diverse as environmental protection, healthy living, astrology, witchcraft, transcendental meditation, channeling, spiritual evolution, psychological manipulation of reality, and I could go on, but you get the idea. And by the way, some of these platforms are noble and positive, such as loving God's creation and wanting to protect it, and working toward achieving a sound and critical mind, or a fit and healthy body and lifestyle. However, in the more radical outcropping of even these positive platforms, along with more blasphemous others, they are loosely held together by threads of mutual ungodly beliefs."

"That's what I've been trying to figure out, what are these mutual beliefs?" Omitting the adjective "ungodly," was purposeful on Nancy's part because she wasn't sure if something specified as ungodly wasn't at least partially attractive to her.

Jonathan found himself amused as Nancy's transparent thoughts appeared, momentarily, on her face. It was refreshing, even hopeful to see the, as yet, unfiltered conscience active in the young woman. He mused aloud, "I think it's sad when people lose the open countenance and that special inquiring mind of a child so soon. When that happens, they begin to shut their minds to unprejudiced thought and an open search for truth."

Then, noticing she was not interested in his philosophizing, and was waiting for the answer to her question, he refocused and began to expound on the subject. "I suppose the one belief that is common to all New Agers is that god is in everything, and everything is in god. This is not the God of the Bible, mind you, not the Creator of the universe, who knows you intimately, that controls all history, past, present, and future. No, the New Age god is impersonal, not good or evil (in fact, good and evil is denied as a concept), but an infinite consciousness that is a part of all being and awareness. In fact, the bottom line of the 'self-actualization' the Feeling Wonderful group advocates, is simply the recognition that the self is god."

"Yeah, I think I understand what you mean, because we kinda did something like that in school." Nancy squinted her eyes, remembering the incident. "The teacher had all of us lie down on the floor with our eyes closed. Then, she went through this whole dream thing where we imagined we were part of everything and everything was part of us. Like all the molecules of our bodies, the floor, the air, and even the outskirts of the universe were one. We were told there was nothing else, just this oneness. It was really weird. Then, she told us there was a figure coming toward us from a distance away. This being was full of wisdom and knew everything about us, even our thoughts. She said we could trust the being, because it was part of us and would always be our true friend and if we would allow it to, it would guide us to make the right decisions. So, was that New Age stuff?"

"You are very perceptive, Nancy. This type of introduction into New Age beliefs is being insidiously injected, not only through the public school system, but also into corporate retreats, government programs and early childhood education. The experience you had began with a physical fact, a truth. The universe does indeed consist of building blocks that are interconnected. The lie, however, is that the spiritual connection between people and God is based on the same physical phenomena. Quite a jump for anyone to believe, but the reason behind this subjective jump is fairly obvious. You see, New Agers don't want to believe in an objective authority of right and wrong that will hold them accountable. Instead, they are always looking for a mystical, inward, or experiential doorway that will enlighten them, substantiate their own bias, uphold their own authority and autonomy, and disprove the true God. And unfortunately, the downside of these beliefs leads to an ever-deepening and dangerous association with the occult. Because of their disbelief in an objective evil, New Agers easily become pawns to be manipulated by Satan and his demons in the guise of spiritual guides. As a matter of fact, the first lie in the Bible was Satan's lie to Eve in Genesis 3:5. In that passage, he tempted her to sin, saying, 'For God knows that in the day you eat (from the tree) your eyes will be open and you will be like God, knowing good from evil.' So, you see, Nancy, the New Age began in the Garden of Eden. And then, as now, the main problem is pride, wanting to be like God, and denying his righteous authority over us."

"That's horrible!" she cried, then remembering she wasn't at all sure she believed in Satan and demons, added, "I guess. So what else do they believe?"

"Some, but not all, believe in the Hindu belief of reincarnation, or the keep coming back until you get it right' crowd. Positive thinking, or we create our own reality, is another popular one. Here again, since they disbelieve in objective reality, and search mystically within themselves, they are short-circuited in a true quest for truth, which could lead them to Jesus, God's son. And, this brings me to their greatest deception," he continued, "and Jesus, himself, pointed it out by asking the ever-important question in Matthew 16:15, 'And who do you say that I am?' The answer to this question, which was answered in the next verse, is the difference between eternal life and damnation for every person on Earth. Jesus proclaims in many scriptures his Deity, that he is the Christ, the Son of God, the I *am*, God himself, and he says in John 14:6, 'I am the Way, the Truth, and the Life. No one comes to the Father but through me.' This is the tour de force that highlights the New Age lie that Jesus is an ascended master, a teacher, and not God himself. Nancy, you do see the inherent lie, don't you, the discrepancy? If Jesus is not who he said he was, the only way to God, then he is also not an ascended master, but as Ruth Graham pointed out, is either a liar, or a lunatic. They can't have it both ways."

"Yes, I do see that," she said thoughtfully. "But, I can't believe Jesus is the same as God either. I know there is a God. I mean an intelligent being, somebody, or something had to start all this, but I doubt that He would want to know me personally, intimately, as you claim."

At this point, Nancy felt uncomfortable, so she rallied, stood and thanked him for the information and the coffee, and edged toward the study door, falling back on a time-worn prejudice. "To me, pastor, Christianity's just a crutch for needy people who have trouble dealing with the real world."

"Well, Nancy, I want you to know that I appreciate your honesty, as well as your openness in searching for the truth. I hope you'll come back and talk to me again." He smiled, and touched her shoulder.

"I have to get back to the office," she said hurriedly, "thank you for seeing me. Goodbye."

"Goodbye, Nancy. I enjoyed talking with you. Come back anytime," he returned kindly.

* * *

Cheryl Patton arrived promptly at he county courthouse at nine thirty, and because she was on short time, immediately related to Sheriff Gilmore her knowledge of the murdered woman, Rose Vanhuss. "It may not be important," she began, "but I met her at one of the 'Feeling Wonderful' seminars. And I'm sad to say, and, of course I don't want to be a snitch, but it was obvious to everyone there that she and James Frazier were having an affair. A lot of flirting and teasing was going on between them. She was attractive, back then, before the fire, not a knockout, you know, but attractive. Actually, I never saw her after she was disfigured, but I heard that her face was terribly scarred. Anyway, as I said, she was good-looking and was pouring all her charms on James. Poor Sarah didn't seem to notice what was going on between them, and at the time I thought it was probably harmless, that is, until Doug, having had a bit too much to drink, let the cat out of the bag to both of us, Sarah and I, I mean, that they were having an affair. I was shocked, but I can tell you, Sarah was devastated, her face went white as a sheet. Afterward, she ran and kind of stumbled to her room and stayed and we didn't see her the rest of the weekend. James claimed she was sick, had come down with the flu, or something." Cheryl took a long breath and shrugged her shoulders. "This may not mean anything, have no bearing on your case at all, Roy, but I thought I should come in and tell you James knew that woman very well and I just imagine that is why she came to live in Cramer Creek."

"So," the sheriff ruminated aloud, "Sarah was aware of the affair. How about Mr. Vanhuss, did he know about it?"

"I have no idea. I don't think he was around that weekend. Actually, I've never met him, so he might have been. But I wouldn't have recognized him if he had been there. Well, I have to get back to school now, my next class is in fifteen minutes."

* * *

The sedate white stucco funeral home was located in Hamlet. It was a remodeled three-story private home, circa late 1800, graced with an iron-gray slate roof and an enclosed walkway skirted by stucco archways and wrought iron balustrades in between and led to a stain-glass entryway. Gathered there and seated inside a large dark-paneled room were about three hundred citizens from Cramer Creek. They were gathered, not to mourn, if truth were told, but simply to observe the passing of one of their own. During Geneva's lifetime, she had not collected a bevy of friends, but her worthy legacy was the establishment of a lively network of acquaintances, whose only claim to camaraderie were as participants of a juicy grapevine, which kept local telephone lines humming with contempt, innuendo, and maliciousness. She would be sorely missed.

Pastor Sharpe, officiating today, had wrestled for three days over the words he would speak in her behalf. Junior, as Geneva's only relative, as Ram could not be located, stood alone in the receiving line, accepting condolences. Betty, standing near the door off the hallway, looked on with empathic understanding. She longed to help Junior share this burden, but knew she would add more grist to the gossip mill already operating full speed in the flower-filled room. Already, she had observed raised eyebrows and speculative glances aimed her way. Moreover, here and there, calculating heads bowed and hummed together. giving a greater and more realistic homage to the dead than the eloquent eulogy Pastor Sharpe had painstakingly devised for the departed.

* * *

Six deputies filed into Roy's office just before five, as ordered, and just as the receptionist and file clerks were watching the clock, poised to leave for the day. Their report was unanimous: James Frazier's presence in various bars on the night Geneva was killed was substantiated. However, the exact time he had arrived, left and spent at each establishment was unclear, leaving plenty of leeway to return to Cramer Creek at some point in the evening and commit Geneva's murder.

"He's our man!" Sheriff Gilmore announced to the deputies gathered around. "The evidence against him is all circumstantial, so far, but it's piled up high enough to justify a search warrant. First thing in the morning, I will see Judge Raynes, and then, when Sarah and James have left the house, about nine o'clock would be good, I want all of you back here in cruisers, ready to roll. Our caravan to the Fraziers' place is going to be a noisy, visual statement to the town, and will serve notice to Frazier that his days of freedom are nearly over."

CHAPTER 16

For the past week Cramer Creek citizens had been suffering from shock, like battle-weary soldiers overcome by horrific scenes and unutterable atrocities on the battlefield. Their initial adrenaline-producing shock regarding the murders had quickly downgraded into mind-numbing fear. Open, deep cracks had seemingly surfaced upon the town's façade of pastoral, picture postcard tranquility. The easy familiarity and banter between friendly housewives gossiping over backyard fences had disappeared, along with the sight of energetic, free-wheeling children engaged in playing, running or cycling the length and breadth of town. Wary parents, teachers and other caregivers had reined in their charges, as well as curtailed their own activities. Telephones were unnaturally still, and darkening shades were drawn over curious windows, as palpable distrust and fear settled in. Farmers and town dwellers alike had cleaned and loaded their guns, and placed them within easy reach. In only a few days, it seemed the town had closed down and braced itself against any future catastrophe, becoming a mere shadow of its former idealized state.

* * *

With sirens blaring and lights flashing, six official county squad cars dramatically approached and drove through Cramer Creek, intentionally alerting the fearful citizens that local law enforcement was not cooling its heels. Every student in elementary and high school classrooms with windows facing the street rushed to them excitedly to see what the commotion was about, leaving chairs toppled and papers strewn about the floor in their wake. With wide eyes and lessons forgotten, the children and teachers watched the unusual show of local might, and loudly cheered their sheriff and deputies. Aunt Lucy, watching from her high advantage, and listening to the classroom chaos below, shook her head.

Sarah stood pale and silent at the window nearest her desk, allowing her ninth grade Civics class to speculate noisily about the cruiser cavalcade's purpose and destination. As the official cars careened from sight, it became apparent to everyone's listening ears the cruisers had abruptly slowed and turned into the Fraziers' long driveway. Within a minute, the sirens had ceased. Without excusing herself, Sarah blindly left the classroom and in a slow run headed for the only place of solace in the building, the girl's bathroom. She entered a stall, locked the door and sat, head in hands, trying to regain her composure and force her brain to function. She knew only that her husband and their life together was in great danger! Why couldn't James control his appetites? How much did the sheriff know? What were they doing now? Was James being arrested? She had to know, she had to go home.

Armed with the search warrant, Roy, in the lead cruiser, turned onto the long narrow driveway leading to the Frazier home. Then according to plan, the sheriff and another vehicle screeched to a stop in front of the house; the rest surrounded the orchard office and barn.

Dressed in stiff dark blue jeans and a fresh flannel shirt, James stepped out of the wide doorway of the nearest barn in which his office was located. "Mornin'," he smirked to the deputies leaving their cars, then demanded, "what's going on?" Several curious employees in jeans, aprons or overalls stood behind him in the doorway. His familiar swagger in tact, he cocked his dark head and waited for an answer.

"We have a search warrant, sir."

"You have a search warrant, well good for you. Now you can get ready to be sued, Deputy. What's your name?"

"You'll have to take that up with Sheriff Gilmore, sir. He's up at the house," the deputy informed him, and then, followed by the other officers, he edged past James in the doorway and headed toward the office. The deputies followed through with their vague instruction to look for anything suspicious.

Quickly walking the quarter mile and approaching the back door of his house, James was met by the sheriff, who raised the official paper to his eye level. "This is a search warrant, Mr. Frazier," he said forcefully, "and I'll have to ask you to wait outside until we're finished in here," he added, holding his free hand to James's chest.

"And what do you think you're looking for?" he asked slowly, with a superior smile. "Trying to hang a murder on me? I hate to be the one to tell you, my friend, but you're engaging in a exercise of futility."

"Wipe that smug grin off your face, Frazier. You're a murderer and a pervert all right, and I'll have no trouble proving it. If not today, then we'll wait a few weeks when the DNA evidence comes back." Having gone out on a limb, he could not take the impulsive words back, although he wished he could. His excuse for his rashness was he was only human and the man just rankled him. His fists fairly itched to take that smirky, arrogant grin off James's face. Why was Frazier always so cocksure of himself? Then, turning his back to him in frustration, the sheriff reentered the house.

"We found this, Roy," signaled deputy Taylor, holding a black ski mask with red-rimmed eye and mouth holes.

"Bag it," he smiled and nodded, satisfactorily, "And keep looking." Then, walking down the short hallway, he followed his nose to the faint familiar scent of Old Spice. After placing the cologne in another bag, he began absently humming an old familiar hymn, "Will there be any stars, any stars in my crown, when that evening sun goes down?"

Deputy Taylor banged the back door, met Sheriff Gilmore in the kitchen, and promptly plopped down an armload of pornographic magazines.

"Some of the stuff in here is pretty sick, Sheriff. We found them locked in the bottom drawer of a file cabinet. There's more. Some are new, and a few are twenty years old, about to fall apart."

"His favorites, I guess. Put 'em all in a trash bag where they belong, and tag them for evidence."

Walking back to the bedroom, he shouted, "Westerfield."

"Yeah?"

"What was Frazier wearing when you lost him Monday night?"

"Would have been the same thing he was wearing when he left your office," John reminded him. "Just a pair of jeans and a dark shirt. It was a dark color, wasn't it? Maybe gray or dark blue."

"Yeah, I think that's right. See if you can find them in the dirty clothes or in his closet, and bag them. We don't know what he was doing, but I'll bet it was something he doesn't want us to know about."

"Right." John wanted to nail Frazier as much as the sheriff, not only because he might be a rapist and a murderer, but because he was smarmy and arrogant and seemed to be laughing at their effort to bring him down. Then, hearing a car approach, he glanced out the window to see Mrs. Frazier's vehicle coming up the driveway.

The sheriff had also noted her approach, and walked out to meet her. "Sarah," he greeted her.

She echoed the question her husband had asked earlier, but without his presumptuous manner, "What is going on, Roy?"

"Sarah, you shouldn't be here," he sighed. "We have a search warrant to search the house and grounds."

"Listen to me, Roy," she panted desperately, "James has done nothing wrong, you have to believe me. Why are you doing this to us? You humiliated us the way you came through town; everybody knows you came here. How will I ever be able to hold my head up again? You know how people are here, 'Where there's smoke, there's fire!'" she screeched. Sarah was quickly becoming hysterical. "We won't be the pawns in your ineptness, in your failure to find the real murderer. Get out of our house! Leave us alone, James is innocent!"

Feeling somewhat guilty and knowing she was probably right in her assessment of the town's reaction to the show of force instigated against them, the sheriff lowered his eyes. "Sarah, calm down, now." Then he turned back toward the door, where Deputy Westerfield was eavesdropping, "John, would you sit out here with Mrs. Frazier until we're finished?"

"Sure thing," he answered grudgingly, not wanting to stop searching for evidence.

By noon, all six squad cars sedately left the property with their inconsequential booty. Sheriff Gilmore was not overjoyed by their discoveries, suggestive evidence at best, perhaps linking Frazier to the rapes, but absolutely nothing to connect him to the murders, except his own gut feeling, his aversion to the guy, and the more damaging consideration of motive and opportunity. His prayer was forensics would come up with something. The thing he hated most about his impulsive, and perhaps, he had to admit, ill-advised search warrant was the disgrace brought upon Sarah and the panic he had read in her eyes.

James and Sarah, left alone at last, stood several feet apart in the kitchen, and stared at each other for a full minute, neither putting their silent thoughts and accusations into words. Then, abruptly, James turned and banged out the back door, heading for his office. Sarah watched him go, her eyes glassy, and whispered in a childlike voice, "I need you."

* * *

The drama of the morning had not been unnoticed by Cramer Creek's currently leaderless gossip mill, and as glimmers of hope shot flares into the shadows of community fear, its members sought to reconstruct the spokes around their missing hub. After a few hours of fallow repetition, an emerging network, roughly following the Baptist Church's prayer chain, minus a few links of tongue bridlers, was established. A couple of diehards even dialed Geneva's number, but was cut no slack from Junior, who was still hanging about the house since quitting his job at the orchard.

At school, both Betty and Emma were looking forward to their walk home in order to privately confer about and diagnose the meaning of the morning's raid on the Frazier home. Cheryl Patton's suspicion regarding James's possible role as Rose Vanhuss' murderer was confirmed in her mind, but she resolved not to tell Doug of the damning information about James she had given the sheriff yesterday morning. Edie and Brian sighed with relief when the town's critical attention passed from them to the Fraziers. Pastor Sharpe, of course, continued to worry about and pray for all his flock, but now, especially for the Fraziers. More than anyone, however, Aunt Lucy despaired of the mounting darkness and the gathering clumps of evil she surveyed in her mind.

Just back from his four day over-the-road trip, Doug dropped into the Drinking Trough, as was his custom before going home, even though it was early afternoon and he had not shaved and showered for two days. The bartender served Doug's first drink, noting the rough beard, and wrinkled and smelly clothing. In the ten years he had known Doug, he couldn't remember another man who had descended the alcoholic slide so quickly, and, as far as he could tell, without obvious reason. Doug had a beautiful wife who appeared to love him, he made good money considering the depressed Cramer Creek area, and had plenty of friends. However, it was obvious Doug would lose it all if he continued to drink. Overall, the bartender preferred his customers in good spirits (no pun intended) who would drop in to socialize, have a few drinks with friends, and then go home to their families. Doug followed that pattern to a point, until he got sloppy drunk and began to noisily monopolize the attention of everyone in earshot with his version of politics, religion, taxes, fishing, ad infinitum, and allowed no opposite opinion. The drunker he got, and the louder he got, the fewer customers remained in the bar.

When James entered the tavern at seven, having changed into black cords, a smoky blue ribbed sweater and a smooth black leather jacket, his tail parked strategically in the church parking lot. To all observers, James looked and felt self-assured. In fact, the incident with the police was neatly categorized and filed away in his mind as ineptness on their part, bordering on stupidity, and was laughable really. What other people might think about the search of his property didn't bother him like it did Sarah. Rather, he accepted it as a challenge, an opportunity to prove his superiority. He enjoyed looking them in the eye, reading their suspicions, brazening it out, while ridiculing them. The problem with most people was they had no idea how satisfying it was to live on the edge, to be creative, and become a force of your own. Sarah, always concerned about what people thought, disgusted him. In essence, everything was all right with her as long as everything looked okay on the surface. Instantly forgetting Sarah, he smiled, winked, and patted a couple of shoulders as he ambled toward the empty stool next to Doug. Taking in Doug's wrinkled clothes and beard stubble, it was apparent he was nearing the sloppy drunk stage. Nearby patrons had gradually distanced themselves, and were trying unsuccessfully to zone him out of their conversations. James recognized immediately his plan of having a quiet, lucid conversation with Doug was in danger and if it were going to take place at all, he had to get him out of the tavern. When James ordered a Miller Lite, Doug inevitably recognized his voice and turned awkwardly toward him.

"Hey, Buddy!" he bellowed slowly. "Shumbo'e toad me you muhduhd d' G'neva!"

Bending his head back toward the ceiling, James laughed so hard tears appeared in his eyes. Those in the room paused in mid-sentence or with their beers halfway to their mouth. "That's a good one," he roared between laughs, then calmed suddenly, but still smiling, looked around the tavern and said loudly enough to be heard by everyone, "whoever told you a crazy thing like that is going to find himself in court!" Then, James lowered his voice for Doug's ears only. "I got a cold six pack out in the truck, want to join me?" He threw a five-dollar bill on the bar and walked out with Doug struggling a few steps behind.

Half an hour later James had patiently extracted the information he needed from Doug's loose mouth and pickled brain. Although Doug pledged he would take James's secret affair with Rose to the grave, he admitted his gaffe of blurting out the truth to Cheryl and Sarah the weekend of the "Feeling Wonderful" conference. Pleading his case, citing too much to drink as his only crime, he told James he was "sawy." The discovery that Sarah and Cheryl had known of his indiscretion with Rose two years ago caused a chill to run up his spine, not that he was overly concerned. He knew Sarah would die before she would betray him. Of course, Cheryl was another matter. As a favor to her, James dropped Doug off at home with the last of the six pack under his arm. Then, instead of heading for the adult video store in Hamlet as he planned, he decided to go home and begin the process of mending fences with Sarah.

* * *

By morning, James had carried out his maneuver and Sarah had justified, rationalized, and fully excused her husband of any wrong, and was on the offensive. After hanging her coat in the classroom, she walked purposely to the teacher's lounge in the basement. The smokers, as well as most of the non-smokers, were gathered in the too-small room to discuss yesterday's event, and what, if anything, they should tell the students. When Sarah entered the room, surprise was visible on every face, and a palpable silence ensued for a few seconds as the teachers searched for words. Then, Sarah, like a highly motivated courtroom lawyer, broke the silence to begin her husband's defense. Like Marsha Hunt and an avenging angel rolled into one, she confidently proclaimed her husband's complete innocence, a victim of circumstantial evidence, and then, skillfully, Sarah turned the finger of guilt toward the real murderer, Edie Bentley. "Everyone knows," she asserted, "that Edie is unbalanced, living in a make-believe world she constantly reinvents, and she is the only person with an undeniable motive. I feel sorry for her, but not enough to let James pay for her crimes. The fact is, the Vanhuss woman killed Edie's parents in that fire. What better motive to murder her than that? Then, didn't the victim intentionally spill the Vision Cosmetic perfume just before she died, as her final act, to accuse Edie of her murder? And no doubt, poor Geneva was either an eyewitness of Mrs. Vanhuss' murder, or, just as damning, she observed Edie entering and leaving the victim's house at the critical time. As a result, Edie murdered Geneva as well. The sheriff may have been taken in by her youth and her innocent act, but who better to convince him than the greatest little actress to ever live?" Then, Sarah, her tour de force completed, rested her case and sat down, mission accomplished. The official verdict given in the basement enclave was set in stone. Most of the teachers, except Lori, closed rank, and like loyal union members, supported one of their own.

* * *

A dull-eyed depression covered the sheriff's office. Over two weeks had passed since the fiasco of searching the Fraziers' place, and no new evidence had come to light. It was as if a mud hole had dried and caked over the case, and any promising life, however microscopic, had dried with it. The media searched for more creative ways to say nothing about the crime wave in the small town in Missouri, and had begun to decry the incompetence of a bumbling, nearly illiterate, sheriff, serving in an antiquated department in a backward town and county. Again, citizens had become fearful and sequestered themselves in their homes. Nancy and Sheriff Gilmore had gone over the cases, considering every possible suspect and contingency so many times, every scenario was indelibly pictured in their minds. Edie, James, Sarah, Betty, Mr. Vanhuss, Junior, or an unknown and unidentified suspect, were the variables in changing, scrambled equations. They were even considering the coroner's suggestion the county hire a psychological profiler.

The only recent pinpoint of light had been Gencodes' determination that the blood type of the rapist was O positive, the most common blood type, and, secondly, that DNA testing could be done on both the bed sheet from the Vanhuss murder and the eight-year-old sample from Karen's PERK. The results, however, would take at least ten weeks.

"But," the sheriff pounded his desk with his fist, and looked desperately at his deputy, "even if we nail James as the rapist through his seminal fluid, can we prove in court he is also the murderer?"

Looking exasperatedly at her boss, Nancy shook her head, and put into words what they already knew. "Not really, Roy. We know, or we're ninety-nine percent positive, the lab will find James's DNA on the bed sheet because Geneva identified him at the scene, and the victim's own testimony to Pastor Sharpe, and if the DNA from Karen's PERK matches the bed sheet, we know James raped Karen. But, we don't have a witness to place him at the Vanhuss home the next day, sometime around noon, when she was murdered."

"Right. So, if and when we prove James had sex with her, all we have proven is he had sex with her, and if the seminal fluid from Karen's PERK doesn't match, he goes Scot-free."

"Right! But here's the rub, if we do prove that James was Karen's rapist, it follows, he was her murderer too."

"It follows, yeah, but is that enough for a jury? Where's the proof? And how do we connect Karen's eight-year-old murder with Rose's and Geneva's? I'll tell you the truth, Nancy, I don't have a clue. I feel as stupid as the news reporters say I am!"

"Roy," she said compassionately, laying her hand on his arm, "you know better than that. We will figure it out, but maybe we need help. What do you think about getting a profiler, like Dr. Judd suggested?"

"I've already put that in motion, called the FBI earlier and asked them for a referral. Here's hoping they don't drag their feet."

"Don't worry, if they do, I'll become the proverbial squeaky wheel with the grease that gets the job done," she promised.

"Good!" He pounded the desk a second time, turned and walked out the door. When he was out of Nancy's hearing, he contended, "And in the meantime, I think I'll consult our own homegrown psychological profiler."

* * *

Junior, still in his robe watching the early afternoon soaps, continued to be a couch potato, but was bored. Since his mother's death, he no longer felt the need to escape his mother's neurotic smothering, or to experience vicariously the action depicted on the TV screen. He was left in limbo, and felt depressed. This change in his comfort level had promoted a sincere soul-searching, but as yet he had made no astounding discoveries about himself. Initially, his problem was how to replace the useless hours in front of television. Now, a second problem had presented itself, he was eating too much, and mostly junk food. Before she died, he had enjoyed the high fat, high caloric meals his mother had daily set before him, but now he regretted his unrestrained eating and felt it was a symptom of some lack in himself. Betty was a good cook, not great, and he knew a childish part of him wanted her back to feed him and take care of his needs, all of his needs. She used to say she had two children, Karen and him, and obviously, she was right. Betty could take care of his problems, but he recognized something was wrong in that kind of thinking, but he didn't know exactly what. Maybe that was why Betty had been noticeably cool toward him lately, especially since the funeral. Before then, it seemed they were getting close again and she had told him she still loved him. Her friend, Emma, was probably trying to convince her to have nothing to do with him; he could tell she didn't like him. Or, maybe Betty wanted him to know what it felt like to be hurt and rejected. Well, if that was her game, it was working, he was hurting. She was probably laughing it up with Emma about payback time.

* * *

In Hamlet, in a shady, established neighborhood, consisting mostly of older and retired homeowners, Mrs. Jessica Haynesworthy, a thoroughly modern mom, technologically literate and politically correct in her thinking, was sitting at her kitchen table, staring into space. The grocery list before her, listing only eggs, skim milk and whole-grained bread so far, was forgotten. She was pondering anew what had gotten into her daughter. She had considered calling the school counselor this morning to check on Jaime's behavior at school, but was afraid her daughter would throw a fit if she found out. When did it start? she wondered. It must have been a couple of weeks ago she first noticed her puffy eyes and lack of appetite. Then, soon afterward, she became aware that Jaime went right to her room after school, instead of playing with her friends. Moreover, she had not been riding her bike, her favorite thing. When asked questions about these changes: was she sick? Had someone hurt her? Were her grades failing? Jaime, defiantly, asked to be left alone, insisting nothing was wrong. Jessica had taken Jaime's temperature, cooked her favorite foods, asked if she would like to have a slumber party, or take a bunch of friends to a movie, all to no avail. Whatever was bothering her daughter must be emotional. After all, Jaime was a pre-teen, and therefore subject to hormonal mood swings. She remembered her own volatile years of adolescence, uncontrollably jumping from adult-like poise to toddler antics within minutes. But, something told her, whatever was bothering Jaime was more than chemical and she was unable to put her concerns aside. One way or another, she decided, she must penetrate the thick wall of self-protection her daughter had erected around herself.

* * *

"Come in, Roy. This is a pleasant surprise."

"Hello, Aunt Lucy. I think I need to sit in the principal's office, again. The way the news media is pitching me, you should have kept me here more often."

"I don't remember you needing to sit in here all that much."

"Selective memory, you're being too kind, I think!"

"Be careful what you say about my memory, I'm old enough to be touchy on that subject," she chuckled. "But seriously, try to pay no attention what the fifth estate may say about you. I've often noticed that the unknown, or at least the fear of the unknown, usually brings an accompanying need for a scapegoat. All will be forgotten as soon as these crimes are solved. You know, the media does not simply report the news anymore and allow us common people to pass judgment on events; they have to editorialize it, slant it, and spin it, which is another word for lie about it. Most news agencies nowadays consider the average person incapable of deciphering the news, so it is done for them in a politically correct way, of course. Fortunately, since so little is based in reality, it makes the editorializing easier to forget."

"Well, I agree with you, but I didn't come by to protest my treatment by the media, in spite of my pride. Actually, I was hoping you might have some time to give me your 'slant' on the murders."

"Me? Why, I'm flattered, of course, by your faith in my ability."

"The point is, you have known all the people involved in this thing for years, Karen Bryson, Brian and Edie, the Fraziers, Geneva, Junior, and so on, and I trust your insight into people. You've been psyching people out longer than I've been around, and I would like to pick your brain."

"Well, when you put it that way, Roy, I guess that skill is part of the job description. But, aren't there professionals who do this type of thing?"

"Oh, sure, and we've called a professional in to give us a probable psychological profile to help us nail this killer." The sheriff leaned forward, worried creases on his forehead, and appealed to her, "But to tell the truth, I have more faith in what you can tell me about the psychological makeup of the people involved. What do you say, Aunt Lucy?"

Leaning her ancient head back against the back of her chair, and closing her eyes, Aunt Lucy considered what she was being asked to do. In essence it was to come up with the name that had been relentlessly surfacing in her mind, a malevolent entity that had remained hidden beneath a façade of respectability and friendship for years, something she was unprepared to do, yet. On the other hand, if she was right, and she was sure she was, and did not reveal the truth, she would be morally responsible if the killer and rapist struck again.

"All right, Roy," she sighed determinedly, "the best I can do is take you on the path I have taken myself and show you each step of the way."

CHAPTER 17

"What now?" Jessica sighed, as the phone rang. Since her coat and gloves were on, the dry cleaning and car key was in hand, she debated whether to answer it or keep moving. She would have preferred to let it ring, believing if it were an important call, they would call back. But, it was too scary not to answer a phone these days, especially with her husband in D.C., and her daughter at school. "Hello, this is the Haynesworthy residence," she answered.

The woman on the other end identified herself as Jaime's school counselor, and for five minutes Jessica listened with increasing terror as she was informed about her daughter's secret trauma. Aghast, Jessica was in shock and unable to speak immediately, even if she had been given the chance. In addition, she was having difficulty believing the school counselor. As well as her numbed mind could understand, her eleven-year-old daughter had broken down, tearfully, in PE class, and had refused to dress out. She had claimed to be sick when questioned by her teacher, and had, consequently, been sent to the empathetic school nurse, who had offered a listening ear. The counselor described the nurse as kind hearted and non-judgmental, who often found herself in the role of secular priest to the middle school students she served. So, Jaime had succumbed to this accepting atmosphere with tears flowing, and related in devastating detail that a man wearing a ski mask forced her silence by holding a knife to her throat and raped her in her bedroom. When questioned further, Jaime had set the date of the rape two weeks ago on a Monday night. Suddenly, all the pieces of her daughter's unexplained behavior the past two weeks fit together into a certainty, a pattern Jessica berated herself for not recognizing earlier. Was she in denial that such a thing could happen to her own child and cause her to miss it? "Oh, my poor baby," she moaned aloud to the counselor, "I'll come right away and bring her home."

"Well, no," the counselor explained matter of factly, "that isn't possible right at the moment. You see, the school is mandated to report immediately to the authorities when something like this comes up, and, of course, an investigation is currently underway. Jaime is in the custody of the Division of Family Services now, and you will not be able to see her. I suggest you contact them. It's out of the school's hands at this point." Then, as an afterthought, her voice lowered to a softer, more caring timbre, added sympathetically, "I'm very sorry, Mrs. Haynesworthy."

"Excuse me? I don't understand. This is unbelievable," Jessica cried. "Shouldn't you have contacted me, us, her parents, before you called anyone else? She needs her family around her, not strangers. She must be scared to death."

"I'm sorry, ma'am, but it's the law. Actually, we aren't required to tell parents at all. Our main directive from the state is to get the child into protective custody. You have to understand, Mrs. Haynesworthy," she said patronizingly, "parents, or other relatives are often the perpetrators, and to expose the child to that person again would be dangerous."

"That's ridiculous," Jessica retorted, "Jaime has a very loving family, no one in our family would do such a thing, and now she needs us close to her." Realizing her pleas were finding no sympathy, she gave up and rang off abruptly.

Still in coat and gloves, she sat next to the phone quietly, if not calmly, and tried to arrange her thoughts. She felt like the proverbial lioness protecting her cub, and adrenalin was flowing, but where was her child, and who did she have to fight to bring her back home where she belonged? She imagined picking up the car keys off the table where she had thrown them, driving to DFS, and demanding to see Jaime. Her common sense told her she would get nowhere, and the bureaucracy would probably pigeonhole her as a frenzied, half-crazed maniac with something to hide. Okay, so she had to stay in control, seem calm to a dictatorial institution with the power to sweep her daughter away. She quickly made the decision to control her emotions and calmly call the Division of Family Services, but this deed resulted in a dead end. No information was forthcoming from the receptionist, who refused to transfer her to her daughter or the caseworker in charge of the case, and then, suggested Mrs. Haynesworthy wait until someone contacted her.

Abruptly losing her cool, Jessica screamed into the phone, "I can't believe this!" Then, after complaining bitterly to the receptionist, she pleaded, "I know my daughter needs me, I know she is asking for me. Please, help me! Why are you treating us this way? You are making a horrible thing worse. I demand you let me talk to her!"

"I'm sorry, Mrs. Haynesworthy," the receptionist huffed into the phone, "there is nothing I can do. Someone will contact you. Good-bye!"

Confused and angry, Jessica walked the floor as she beeped her husband, who was in Washington D.C. on a business trip. He returned her call immediately, and Jessica, through tears and rage, explained what had happened to their daughter, as well as the further outrage propagated by the intrusive government agency. "Darling, I don't understand why I can't be with her, try to console her. She needs me, and she's alone, somewhere, surrounded by total strangers. John, what can we do?"

"I don't know, Dear, but I'll find out. In the meantime, why don't you call Steve and see what he says. I'll catch the next plane out of here," he promised. "See you soon."

After ringing Police Chief Steven Kopelski, Jessica felt a little better. He was an old friend of the family and he calmed many of her fears, and promised to call her as soon as he had news of Jaime. He had added, "If I might make a suggestion, if I were you, I would file a criminal complaint against a person, unknown, who raped your daughter. This will give us an official entrance into the case. The DFS usually drags its feet before bringing law enforcement into it, and by then the case has often been compromised to the point it is impossible to get a conviction. Off the record, Jessica, they like to do their investigation first, without benefit of a forensic team, and then file a report and make recommendations which many times is biased and based on hearsay and innuendo, nothing that would stand up in court. Being acquainted with their methods I would guess they have already had her examined by a gynecologist."

"Oh, no. That would scare her to death."

"Well, actually, we would do the same thing, although we would allow you to be with her. Unlike DFS, we have to adhere to the constitution and produce evidence before someone is considered guilty. But, for your peace of mind, her caseworker is probably with her."

"Right, a total stranger to her. But, still, thank you so much for talking to me, Steve, I...I...f-feel a little better knowing there is something I can do," Jessica stammered through tears. "I'll come up right away and make out a report, you said against a person, unknown?"

"Yes, that's right. The clerk will give you a form; just fill in what you know, including the information the school counselor gave you."

"All right, and I'll be waiting for your call. Thanks again."

"You're welcome, Jessica." The chief hung up, already suspicious the alleged rape of little Jaime Haynesworthy might be related to the rapes and murders his colleague, Sheriff Gilmore, was investigating. He was aware the prime suspect lived in Cramer Creek, only minutes from Hamlet. Only a couple of weeks ago, his patrol officers had participated in a search for the suspect after he slipped away from the sheriff's stakeout. However, before entertaining that possibility, his first priority was loosening Jaime from the clutches of DFS. To accomplish this, he called Governor Sander, who hailed from the county, to explain the situation and ask a favor. By dinner hour, Jaime was released into her grateful mother's custody and was safe at home. "Mission accomplished," he thought, feeling good. "Now, I'll give the sheriff a call."

The following morning, the county forensic crime team searched Jaime's bedroom, but was thwarted in their attempt to gather evidence. Two weeks had passed since the alleged rape, and Mrs. Haynesworthy, being a conscientious housekeeper, had long since dusted and vacuumed, and washed Jaime's nightgown and bed clothing. Nonetheless, the room was hopefully fingerprinted, and samples of lint from the carpet, blankets and bedspread were collected. It was concluded, the perpetrator had entered the house through the front or back door before the Haynesworthys had locked up for the night. The first and second floor windows, consisting of self-contained storms and screens, were kept locked and remained intact. The approximate timing of the rape on Monday night and the simultaneous disappearance of James a few blocks away were highly suspicious, giving him opportunity. Above all, Jaime's description of the man, the ski mask and the use of a knife in the crime, matched the stories of the other victims.

At the scene, everyone's frustration was apparent. "Here we go, again," Sheriff Gilmore raged to Chief Kopelski, "just circumstantial evidence! Nothing to hang a case on, unless forensics comes through."

"I know," the chief nodded compassionately, "not enough to get him off the street, and maybe save another young girl."

* * *

"So, what do you think? Is Sarah right about her husband? Is the bugger innocent?" Emma put the questions to Betty on their daily trek home after school.

"I don't know for sure. What was that stuff about the victim spilling perfume before she died? I've never heard anything about that, have you?"

"No, maybe she made it up. When Sarah was making her case, I admit, I was swayed, but now, away from her influence, I don't know."

"Well, maybe I'm just too close to the situation, but ever since I've considered James as a suspect in Karen's rape and murder, I can't stand to look at him. My reaction is so strong I want to kill him!"

"Well, you can be bloody certain that Edie didn't rape anyone. I don't know how Sarah could accuse her of murder. Obviously, whoever raped Karen was also her murderer."

"Yes, but Sarah didn't accuse Edie of Karen's murder, you know, just Geneva's and the Vanhuss woman's."

"But, haven't we been operating on the assumption that all of the rapes and murders are connected? It must be the same man responsible for them all, don't you think?"

"I do, but at the same time, there are a lot of inconsistencies."

"Such as?"

"Such as, in the other rapes, the girls were not killed, only Karen. And in the other murders there were no rapes."

"Well, there is one consistent thing," Emma asserted. "This man does not want to be seen. He kills Karen, Rose Vanhuss, and Geneva from the back, and he rapes his victims with his face hidden in a ski mask. It's like he sneaks up on all of them."

"What are you getting at? You mean he's a coward?"

"Yes, he's a bloody coward. He's sneaky, well hidden. The problem with that is, it suggests that James is innocent. He is so arrogant, an in-your-face kind of guy, you could never call him a coward. I think James would want his victims to know who he is."

"I don't think that follows, Emma. It is just self-preservation to protect his identity. Take the rapes, for instance, if he doesn't plan to murder the girls, then he needs to hide his identity not to get caught. That's just common sense. But I think I agree with you about the murders, sneaking up behind to murder someone would not be James's style."

"I know, he is such a sleaze. Can you believe, he made a pass at me in church last Sunday? And do you notice how he tries to make this simmering eye contact with women? Sickening! If I were Sarah, the bugger would have been kicked out on his tail a long time ago, and good riddance."

Betty considered the relationship between Sarah and James. What Emma said seemed so logical. Sarah should have kicked James out years ago. But, if that was true, what good were marriage vows, "for better or worse, 'til death we do part"? However, she remembered the Bible did made an exception, "...except for fornication." One thing she knew for sure, what made sense to observers on the outside, didn't, or was often lost, to those living within. It was the same with her and Junior, during their marriage she couldn't see the sickness of their codependency. If he hadn't left when he did, would she still be making excuses for him, would they still be feeding off each other's insecurities? Breaking the silence and changing the subject, Betty stated the obvious, "You know I still love Junior, and I know you don't want to hear that, but, on the other hand, I would rather stay divorced than end up like Sarah. What do you think, Emma?"

"You know what I think, love. If he truly loves you as much as you love him, He'll want to fix it." Emma stopped, as they prepared to go to their separate homes, and looked Betty in the eyes. "I know I have no life experience, you know, with marriage I mean, and no degree in psychology, but this is my advice: You stand firm until you see what he's willing to do to make a healthy relationship and if you see nothing happening, look elsewhere."

"Emma! I think this is the first time we have agreed on this subject. We have both moved a little, haven't we? You already know I'm going to wait as long as it takes, but you're right, I won't jump into the water again until Junior and I can both swim. It reminds me of the dream I told you about. Remember, Junior and I were climbing a cliff, and as the cliff became more steep and difficult, I had to help Junior more and more, until eventually I was carrying him. Well, I don't know if I'm any smarter, but I know I'm too tired to climb anymore, especially carrying somebody else."

"Good girl! Well, since you seem to be willing to wait forever, let's hope he grows up before your golden years. By then, the only thing you two can do together will be simultaneous rocking in the bloody rocking chairs."

"Thank you so much, Dr. Ruth!"

* * *

"Let's go the next level, Roy," Chief Kopelski was saying. "We'll pick him up on suspicion and put the fear of God in him! I can hold him twenty-four hours for questioning, then you could pick him up and hold him another twenty-four."

The sheriff agreed. "Yes," he said slowly, "that will be forty-eight hours we'll be able to sleep knowing he's off the street."

"Yeah, and give us time to compile evidence. When will the DNA results be in?"

"Six more weeks," he answered mournfully.

"Well, it's up to us to keep him behind bars or on a very short leash until then. I'll have him picked up tonight before he makes other plans, so start looking under every rock!"

"You got it. Okay if my deputy on the case and I observe the questioning at the station?"

"Sure. We'll let him sweat it out over night, and start in the morning about nine. Even if he gets his lawyer involved, with a high profile case like this, he won't walk out of here too fast."

"Right."

* * *

The teachers hoped today's meeting in the teacher's lounge regarding the chili supper would be the last. In three days, on Saturday, the fundraising event would place, and all the plans and preparations were coming together. As chairperson, Sarah was beside herself. She felt she couldn't stand before her peers this afternoon in humiliation and conduct the business at hand. "I can't do it," she grieved piteously. With James taken to the Hamlet jail last night, he could no longer shore her up with his promises and love making, and her world was collapsing around her once again. She had not slept all night wondering what evidence could possibly be stacked against him. She did not understand why the town of Hamlet was involved, but she was very afraid. He had told her as he was being arrested, not to call a lawyer because he was innocent of any wrongdoing and would straighten out whatever it was. But this, on top of the assault on their home, was too much. She just couldn't hold her head up, and she was so tired of trying.

She knocked upon Aunt Lucy's office door and walked in beaten, head down and shoulders slumped, and sat beside the desk.

Aunt Lucy, looking like a wizened owl, viewed Sarah's downcast eyes over her glasses. "What can I help you with, Sarah?" she asked gently.

"I must resign my chair over the chili supper committee, Aunt Lucy," she sniffed into her handkerchief. "With everything happening with James I am too overwhelmed. I can hardly carry on in the classroom. The kids, you know, talk behind my back, are making snide remarks, and laughing at me. They want me to hear what they are saying. I can't take it anymore. I may have to resign my teaching position as well. I know the Bible says we must suffer trials and tribulation such as are common to man, but this is just too much, more than I can face. I cannot hold my head up or look people in the eye. My mother must be turning over in her grave."

"I'm sorry, Sarah, but you mustn't think of James's sins as your own, you know."

"Just what sins are you talking about, Aunt Lucy?" Sarah asked defensively. "James has done nothing wrong!"

"Now, Sarah, remember who you are talking to, I've watched that boy grow up from before he could spell his own name, and I have a good idea what you have had to suffer all these years. You don't have to keep up the pretence with me."

This small bit of sympathetic understanding was all Sarah could bear and her defenses came tumbling down. "Oh, how could you know the pain…the pain…I've had to bear?" she sobbed. "I have loved him so much, but nothing I've ever done for him was appreciated. I was never enough for him, he was always looking for younger and prettier girls, and…and…even little girls. Always showing me that I didn't measure up, that I was a standby when he couldn't find anything else." Anger mixed into self-pity swept over her. "Oh, I've known about his perversions ever since I found the first disgusting magazine with children in it. And now, the worse humiliation has happened, the sheriff and all his people have seen them, and they believe James raped all those little girls. I know he's sick, Aunt Lucy, but you understand, he cannot help himself."

Aunt Lucy stood, her hair bristling at the back of her neck, and spoke with discernment, "Sarah, it is time you quit making excuses for him. How you could have knowledge of what he was doing and do nothing is beyond my comprehension. You're right, and thank God you are, everyone will soon know that James is responsible for taking the innocence of those little girls, and who knows how many others will be saved because of it. And because you have kept his secret, you are an accessory to his crimes, and just as bad as he is!"

Sarah, taken off guard, looked venomously at her righteous attacker through red-rimmed eyes. "You…you…know nothing," she seethed. "It's your word against mine. James has done nothing wrong! I was wrong to trust you!" Arising quickly from her chair, Sarah stood with her head up and shoulders back, and swept out of the office.

Aunt Lucy followed her slowly, making sure she reentered her classroom, and then returned to her desk, wondering how and when this season of evil would end. She kneeled beside her chair and talked to her Lord.

* * *

Pastor Sharpe was preparing for another Wednesday night prayer meeting, raising the thermostat and turning on the lights, when Edie and Brian walked into the sanctuary. He thought to himself how good it was to see Edie smile again.

Brian was also glad Edie was back to normal. She had chirped non-stop about ten different subjects as they walked the two blocks to church. He felt even closer to her since they had shared their heartache again over their parents' deaths, the murder of the woman responsible, and Edie's ordeal of being under suspicion for murder. Although Edie had suffered alone before confiding in him, he didn't think she would keep things from him again.

Emma and Betty strolled in behind Brian and Edie and sat in the second row. Junior followed them just far enough behind it was obvious they had not come together. He slid into the pew beside Betty, whereupon she turned toward him slightly with a cryptic smile acknowledging his presence, then turned back to Emma where the two engaged in a lowered voice, private conversation until the prayer meeting began. Although the crowd was noticeably smaller tonight without Geneva, or James and Sarah in attendance, the prayers were sincere and heartfelt. Pastor Sharpe felt the presence of the Holy Spirit.

CHAPTER 18

Hopefully, Junior waited outside the school for Betty. He had showered and shaved, and shampooed his short dark hair, and even washed his truck. In front of him, his ample belly was covered with a button down shirt instead of overalls. Because Betty had seemed unapproachable last night at church, he had feared asking if she would meet him today after school, and he didn't know when she usually left the building. He was still confused about her changed attitude toward him. Although she had been definitely frosty last night, two weeks before she had been warm and loving, and had reacted positively when he asked her to marry him, but hadn't exactly said yes. Fairly certain it was nothing he had said or done since then, even though he admitted to being obtuse at times, he wanted to get to the bottom of Betty's attitude as soon as possible. He was suspicious Emma had something to do with it. She didn't like him, and he was afraid of her influence over Betty. Not knowing was driving him crazy! Without question, he had been a fool after Karen died, and he knew nothing would ever erase the heartache he had caused. His only defense was insanity begun at his Mother's knee, where the unspoken rules that reigned in his home were blame others for problems and failures, and make excuses for everything else. No personal accountability had been required of him growing up, and concepts like delayed gratification, suffering personal pain, "paying the piper," or "taking your medicine," were non-existent. Several incidents in his childhood had instilled this selfish, no-fault, no-guilt philosophy.

One particular memory came to mind that occurred when he was a young boy, probably preschool age, attending a birthday party accompanied by his mother. During the gift opening, the birthday boy, it might have been Doug, had received a remote control Big Wheel, and all the other little boys were envious. In fact, he had wanted it so badly and put up such a fuss, that he and his mother left the party early in order to buy him one just like it. Another time, when he was a bit older, he and Doug had mischievously written with chalk on the dark brick of the school building, in large letters, AUNT LUCY

IS A WITCH. Doug confessed immediately when questioned, and he never did, but Aunt Lucy punished both of them, obviously knowing the truth. She had prescribed a week of detention, whereupon his mother, protesting his innocence, had caused such an uproar at school that his sentence was recanted. As a matter of fact, he thought, Mother was at school a lot declaring his innocence, accusing teachers of unjustly picking on him, and in general, making sure nothing unpleasant, however much deserved, ever happened to him. Even though he had hated her interference, he was immensely relieved at her successful campaigns. But, now, looking back, he realized his perspective had changed. Time had revealed the pitfalls of his self-centeredness. He had totally screwed up his past by seeking to deny his pain and the dictates of his heart, as well as his responsibilities. By seeking an easy way out of his suffering eight years ago, he had perhaps destroyed his present and future happiness with Betty. The piper had come to collect.

He checked his watch; it was three forty-five. Where was she, had he missed her somehow? But just as he decided to leave and swing by her house, she and Emma walked out the double doors.

"Don't look now, but your boyfriend's back," Emma sang quietly. Junior rolled down the passenger side window, and called out, "Hey," as Betty and Emma walked up to the truck.

"Hey," Betty answered, while Emma stood silently beside her.

"I would like to talk to you," he grunted, and added, looking pointedly at Emma, "alone."

"You know, Junior," Betty said with rancor, "when you are nasty to my friend, I really have nothing to say to you."

Kicking himself silently, he apologized, without making an excuse, "I'm sorry, Emma." And then, turning to Betty, asked simply, "Please talk to me."

She turned to Emma, and asked silently with raised eyebrows.

"No problem, go ahead," she answered, then added with a trace of suspicion, "I'll drop by later for a cuppa, if that's okay."

"Sure, I'll see you later." Then giving her a half smile, she opened the truck door and struggled slightly up the high step. The dubious smile lingering on her lips, she looked at Junior, and said, "What's up?"

"It's a beautiful day and uh, I just wanted to take you for a drive, maybe over to the new lake. I thought maybe we could talk. I know something's wrong between us, Betty, you were so distant last night."

Betty didn't answer his unspoken question, but was wondering how driving down the road with no chance of speaking face-to-face, would facilitate a discussion. She found it difficult to have a serious discussion without eye contact, although she surmised he might find it easier to talk to her with minimum engagement. Although the lake would be a quiet place to park and discuss their problems.

"Why don't we wait until we get to the lake and talk there?" she proposed.

"Okay," Junior agreed, "I haven't been out there for months, I wonder how it's shaping up?"

"I don't know, I've not been there since it was first filling up with muddy water, and the surrounding hills, up to the tree line, were nothing but dirt terraces."

Twenty wordless minutes passed, as both occupants of the truck passed the time thinking about identical goals and wondered how they might be achieved. It was a mystery how the two could be so different, opposites almost, and yet be one mind, focused on the same outcome: their future together. In their turbulent history, and even now, to say opposites attract was an understatement, because the reaction that habitually took place between them was electrical and exhausting at the same time. Their unique magnetic field seemed to confusedly attract and repel at the same time. Sometimes, it seemed what one was missing the other filled the void completely, until they both felt indescribingly whole. On the downside, the same charge that brought such joy also had the capacity to bring pain and despair. What they needed was a safe balance, an even keel. But what mysterious agent was needed to neutralize the destructive tendency of their personalities. Could they find the catalyst, was it even possible, and if they did, would it destroy the special connection, the fire and ice, between them?

As they topped the last hill, they were astonished by the breathtaking beauty of the new lake that lay before them. It was completely filled with the clear, life-giving water of Cramer Creek, the hills surrounding the lake were green with newly sown grass, and the tree line was majestic in fall colors of sienna, yellow, red and purple. Gone was their prejudiced mentality shared with the residents of Cramer Creek, who cursed the Corps of Engineers and their product, and decried the usurping of their beloved flowing creek, and rejected the pitiful pond. Looking down upon the obvious greater good, wherein the bubbling creek had flowed, they rejoiced in the paradisiacal mirror of heaven they beheld. Junior spied a picturesque cul-de-sac ahead surrounded by sun-lit red maples and yellow-leaved birches with a view of the lake interspersed through the branches, and turned into the area, parking beside a sturdy, green-painted picnic table under the trees. They were alone, spying out Eden, and seeking a path to curtail their banishment.

"It's too beautiful for words!" Betty exclaimed. "I never, in my dreams, thought it would be like this."

Junior nodded silently, then boldly reached for her, pulling her into his arms. And, earnestly searching her face, he said, "I don't know what is wrong between us, but whatever it is, we can fix it. I love you. There's never been anyone else for me, and there never will be." He paused, and shared his pain, "All the years without you I've been a walking dead man, empty inside." Tears welled up in his deep blue eyes, and pleaded with hers. "I need you, Betty, can't we put everything back together again?"

Overwhelmed, with her own tears flowing, she wanted to say yes and melt in his embrace, but, this time, reason refused to capitulate to passion. "No, I don't think we can," she said softly, "not yet, anyway. You know I love you and I want to marry you again, but there is something basically wrong in our relationship. Yes, we have great love for each other that sometimes brings me so much joy I think I'm in heaven, but other times, I'm so devastated and in pain, I think I'm in hell. Our marriage couldn't survive like that before, and it wouldn't again."

Junior realized the truth she had spoken, and couldn't deny it, even though he wanted to. "I know you're right," he said with resignation, "but let's not give up."

"We won't, but we need help. We can't do it by ourselves. Are you willing to get counseling?"

Junior, who had never been pliant enough to go to counseling before, but now humble and contrite, and willing, nodded yes. "Where should we go?"

"To Pastor Sharpe."

* * *

Thursday evening, after twenty-four hours in jail at Morley, and another day in the custody of the county jail, James was reluctantly released. The sheriff and Chief Kopelski had pressured the crime lab in Jeff City with numerous calls to streamline their investigation, emphasizing the urgency needed to keep their suspect incarcerated, and without result, had called Gencoles to do the impossible and hurry results of the DNA testing. The rape of Jaime Haynesworthy had brought home the importunity of keeping James caged. One slip in surveillance had brought tragedy to the young girl, and another mistake must not happen. With renewed resolve, Gilmore instructed his officers assigned to stakeout to be highly visible, to advertise their oversight of the suspect and keep him in their direct vision. "Hold his hand in the john, pray with him in church, and follow him up the ladder if he decides to pick an apple," he commanded.

In the meantime, more circumstantial evidence was building. Three tiny blue pieces of lint recovered from James's ski mask exactly matched the blanket on Jaime Haynesworthy's bed. It was enough to convince every officer working on the case, they had the right man in jail, but those experienced in thrown-out court cases knew the defense attorney would have no trouble casting doubt in the minds of twelve jurors.

"But, there is so much circumstantial evidence," deputy Armstrong wailed, "surely the sheer bulk of it would throw out reasonable doubt." She counted the evidence on her fingers. "The matching descriptions, ski mask, no alibis, motive, his addiction to pornography, matching blue lint, Old Spice cologne, his affair with one of the victims, one victim murdered in his orchard. What more do we need?"

"No, Nancy," the sheriff sighed, "we can't take a chance on a trial that could never be retried, we have to nail him for good, even if it means waiting weeks for the DNA results. We just have to do two things: one, be patient; and two, not let him out of our sight!"

* * *

The grapevine, in as good running order as it was when Geneva was alive, lit the phone lines with James's imprisonment, and subsequent release from jail. Then, when Junior abruptly quit working at the orchard, they had put two and two together. As a result, by Friday morning, Junior had been notified by several of the "I thought you should know" crowd that James was now as "free as a bird."

The more he obsessed over Karen's murder and James's release, the angrier Junior became. It was clear the law did not have enough evidence to hold him and Junior wondered how many more rapes and murders James would get away with. His heart ached when he thought about Karen, defenseless and innocent before she was brutalized and murdered. The animal, with his smirky grin, would get away with it. Junior could see him leering in Karen's surprised face before he raped her and apathetically unconcerned about her dead body afterward. "No! He won't get away with it, I'll see him dead before he touches another one." Grabbing his jacket and his Browning Buck

Mark Bull's-eye .22 out of the case, Junior crashed out of the house.

As he turned into the Fraziers' driveway, he noticed the patrol car parked a hundred feet down the road, its occupants openly watching the Frazier property. The presence of the police gave him pause, and he began to rethink his just mission of removing James from the face of the earth. He was not ready to commit murder in front of law officers, and now that he was having second thoughts, he was not ready to be locked up for twenty years throwing away his future with Betty. On the other hand, he wasn't going to leave with his tail between his legs like a whipped puppy. Karen's murderer was going to pay, even if it was only with black eyes and bloody nose. Stopping the truck outside the office, he jumped out minus the gun, and searched the area with his eyes. Spotting James behind the barn giving instruction to the workers, he strode purposely toward him. Without a pause to speak, he flung himself at James, forcefully driving his large body into a punch that knocked James to the ground. Junior then jumped, belly first, on top of him, and pounded him repeatedly until James had ceased moving.

"Junior, stop it, man. You're going to kill him!" Several workers drug him off the still body. "Call 911, quick," someone advised. "Man, his face looks like hamburger."

With his face, hands and bib overalls splattered with James's blood, Junior dug a red bandana handkerchief from his pocket, wiped his face, and then walked nonchalantly back to his truck as he did every day when he finished work and drove home. Halfway down the driveway, he met the police cruiser that had been parked nearby responding to the 911 call. Junior decided to save them the trouble of arresting him, and drove to the sheriff's office.

* * *

Meanwhile, every teacher was busily preparing for the chili supper scheduled to begin tomorrow evening at five o'clock. During lunch hour, the elementary school teachers took turns watching the children and decorating the gym. After school, the elementary teachers would set up the various carnival booths where, for a quarter, participants could fish for prizes, have their face painted, throw darts at balloons for more prizes, or throw baseballs and dunk a teacher, and of course, prepare for everyone's favorite, the cake walk. Some dessert donations were coming in already and covered one long table in the cafeteria. Tomorrow, the high school teachers would cut the pies and slice cakes not slated for the cakewalk. Sarah could be seen going over several lists on her clipboard to make sure nothing was left undone. Betty and Emma were part of the cooking chili and vegetable soup detail, and would begin their job early tomorrow afternoon.

Later, after having straightened their classrooms, they walked together through the double front doors to the same scene awaiting them as yesterday.

"Déjà vu," quipped Emma.

"I know," Betty returned, "but, this time it's planned. We have an appointment with Pastor Sharpe."

"Why didn't you tell me?" Emma asked with hurt feelings.

"I don't know, I thought you would think I was making a mistake."

"Hey, you're a grown lady, and I want you to be happy."

"Okay, well, I'll give you a call later."

Emma waved her on, and walked across the street and entered the market. Betty waved back while she climbed into the truck and greeted Junior with a smile, which faded immediately when she looked at him. Even though he had showered all the blood off and was looking presentable in a long-sleeved yellow pullover and tan Dockers, he couldn't hide the flush on his face, the bruised knuckles, or the sheepish look in his eyes that told her something was amiss.

"Tell me!" she demanded saucily, not thinking he had done anything seriously wrong. "What have you done?"

"I beat up Frazier. I'm not proud of it, but I'm glad I did it. He's in the hospital now."

"Junior, I've never known you to do anything like that," Betty said with wonder. "Why did you?"

"Too much sitting at home thinking, I guess. Seeing how he's probably going to get away with murdering our little girl and my mother. I wanted to see him suffer for once. Actually, I took my gun to kill him, but on the way over there I came to my senses, and left the gun in the car."

"Thank God you did!" Betty exclaimed. "But, you'll probably be arrested."

"Probably. I went to talk to Sheriff Gilmore afterward. He told me to hang around, see if Frazier presses charges. The only thing I can really think about is maybe he'll think twice before hurting anyone else."

"I hope you're right," she agreed. Then changing the subject to the reason they had met after school, she asked, "Are we still going to meet with Pastor Sharpe?"

"Yeah, definitely," he said, and made a u-turn in front of the school, then turned into the church parking lot.

The good pastor was looking forward to the counseling session, even knowing there were problems in Betty and Junior's past, but he believed with the right attitude and motivation they could be overcome. He adopted the realistic therapy of working in the here and now, and not in the sins of the past. If battering was the problem, the answer, according to Pastor Sharpe, was never, under any circumstances, strike a woman, and if it should happen a second time, complete separation was the answer until the abusive party had proven his contrition and attended many hours of therapy. Similarly, if adultery had occurred and the disloyal party repented, and the injured party decided to forgive and continue the marriage, fine. However, should he or she stray a second time, it was Pastor Sharpe's advice to "throw the bum out." He didn't mince words in counseling sessions, and he had no patience with long term, drawn out therapy that dissected childhood, making each counselee a victim and passing out blame to everyone else. His advice to Betty and Junior would be simple: From the first day of marriage, make the decision to never threaten divorce, never go to bed angry, pray together every day, be honest about feelings, talk through each problem as it appears, submit to each other while keeping the husband's headship, and treat each other with love and respect.

CHAPTER 19

James had regained consciousness in the emergency room. As he forced one swollen eye open he looked confusedly around the stark medically equipped room, and wondered where he was. He was chilled under a white sheet that covered his body and he felt tight cords restraining him on a hard narrow table. A nurse seemed to be speaking softly to him, but he had no idea what she was saying. For a moment, everything, including his memory, was a blur; he had no recollection of why he was in the room until the sedative-muted pain coming from his face and upper body spoke conclusively and eloquently. Then he remembered Junior's punching fists and the fiery hatred emanating from his eyes just before he lost consciousness. It was strange perhaps, but he had never been beaten before in his life. His father died when James was only a toddler, and certainly, his mother had never beaten him. She had only sighed, "Oh, James," in a small, pleading, martyred voice when he had callously disobeyed her or gotten into various trouble. He hated her for her sickly voice and her weak-willed mind that held no standard or inclination to govern her son. The ridicule he hurled at her brought her tears, and him, enjoyment. As his vision cleared, he saw Sarah and a doctor approaching.

The emergency room doctor was young, exhausted and gray beyond his years, and he looked out of context with the bright room and shiny metallic instruments. "It would be more appropriate," James thought, "if the doctor was lying on the cold slab table instead of me, or, if he would simply sit quietly in a corner, surely maintenance would soon cart him away with the other used linen and refuse.

In contrast, Sarah was flush and infused with self-righteous energy. She had come directly from school, and her straight gray hair was filled with static electricity. Dressed in the navy blue pinstripe she wore every Friday, she walked stiffly toward James, forgetting the pain in her joints. She was an angry woman. Her husband had been abused, nearly killed by the uncouth Junior Bryson, who was nothing more than white trash, really, just like his father. And his mother, well, the perfect words for Geneva failed to materialize in her overwrought mind. But, to come right to the point, as her mother always observed, "Heredity will out!"

"Oh, James." She sighed exasperatingly.

Sarah was sighing just like his mother, he thought.

"Are you alright? I was so worried when they told me what happened."

"I'm okay," he said shakily, with a hint of residue cockiness.

Then the tired doctor spoke in a monotone, "Mr. Frazier, I'm Dr. Lambert. You don't have any broken bones, surprisingly, although we have stitched several wounds on your face. There were two lacerations on your chin and one on the right cheek. Also, I'm afraid you have a concussion, and now that you're awake I'd like to examine you." Even as he spoke he clicked on the small flashlight already in his hand and began checking the dilation of James's eyes.

Forty-five minutes later, James was wheeled into a private room to spend the night "for observation," and Sarah was sitting in a turquoise padded chair beside him, filling in the menu choices for dinner tonight, and breakfast and lunch tomorrow.

James looked at her sardonically, while holding an ice pack on his cheek. "What do you think you're doing?"

"I'm filling out your menu, why? Do you want to do it?"

"Yes. I believe I do, since I'll be the one eating," he said with a snide simpering tone, which was ludicrous emanating from his swollen bulbous nose and fat lower lip.

"Fine, James. Here, you fill it out," she said, handing him the sheet. "Then," she said, "we can do something about putting Junior Bryson behind bars!"

"Is that what I want to do?" James asked. "He's cooled down by now; I don't think he's going to come after me again. I hope not," he said, touching his chin gingerly.

"It doesn't matter if he would, or wouldn't do it again, once was enough!" Sarah acclaimed shrilly. "He should be in jail for what he did to you. You're lucky you don't have broken bones. Your face looks like a picket fence."

"Sarah, why don't you give it up?" He smiled, shaking his head at her. "You and I both know why Junior attacked me. I'm surprised he didn't do it a long time ago." James sized Sarah up through swollen slit eyes. "You know, sometimes I think I must be crazy to do the things I do. But then, I look at you, and I know, beyond a doubt, you are the crazy one. I'm what I am, and I like it. But you, you won't admit, even to yourself, what I am, what I do,

178

and what I'm made of, because if you did, you would have to admit what you are." His arrogant lips curled up at her. "You are a living lie. Facts are facts, Sarah, and putting on a good face, which I don't have right now," he chuckled venomously, "isn't going to work anymore."

"I don't know what you're talking about, James. What lie? How am I crazy? Up until this last month, I have been so happy. I was living a fulfilling life, the only one I've ever wanted: To be your wife, and to be loved by you. It's still going to be alright, we'll get through this."

"Right! Let me set you straight, my dear, and clarify to your small mind the lie I am referring to. Listen carefully, Sarah, I have never loved you. I married you for two reasons: one, as a cover, because I did not want to draw attention to myself, and of course, two, for convenience, as a poor substitute when I could not have what I really wanted. You, little wife, are a joke. If you think I have ever enjoyed being your husband, listening to your tiresome conversation, or making love to you, then reconsider, because I happen to be a consummate actor, and you are a total fool. I have nothing but contempt for you. So now, since I can no longer hide, shall we say, my predilections, you are no longer of any use to me. So, get out of my sight, and don't dawdle on the way out."

"James," she moaned softly, "you don't mean that. You're in pain and lashing out at me because I'm handy. You'll take it all back tomorrow."

He sneered at her with hatred seething in the slits of his dark eyes, and hissed, "I despise you. You're the one who should be in the grave with your back butchered up instead of Rose, or Geneva, or Karen!"

* * *

The day of the chili supper had finally arrived. Yummy desserts lined the decorated table. There was a tall dark chocolate and blackberry cake with rich chocolate icing, slated for the cakewalk. Betty had made Junior's favorite, peanut butter pie, using the secret method of allowing the pudding, peanut butter and evaporated milk to almost scorch before pouring it into the pie shell. Nearby, was everyone's favorite "dirt cake" made from lots of crunched up Oreo cookies, cream cheese, instant vanilla pudding and Cool Whip, and to make it look authentic the cake had been placed in a clean flower pot with a plastic geranium "growing" in it and a two plastic worms peaking out of the "soil." Two "better than sex" cakes were on hand, as well as the tall and elegant "mandarin orange cake."

Betty and Emma had already begun cutting up vegetables for homemade soup and had started water boiling in two huge kettles used by the school cooks. The chili would come in piecemeal during the afternoon, as large pots of it were being slow-cooked in the high school teachers' homes. Mr. Warmbrough and Mr. Lacey were setting up the many long tables in the center area of the gymnasium floor, while on the periphery, the elementary teachers were constructing various carnival booths. Betty's "Home Living" students who wanted extra credit had agreed to come by later to arrange centerpieces and place settings. Edie had volunteered to create glamorous make-up for the girls and was setting up her booth, while Brian and Elizabeth Lacy were sitting on the stage in front of the curtains enjoying each other's company. Mr. Lacey, spying Emma, deciding to take a break and join her in the kitchen. His attentiveness to the new teacher had been growing over the past few weeks, much to Emma's delight. No one noticed that Sarah, as she should have been busily checking items off on her clipboard, was missing.

Actually, it was almost five when Sarah, looking as dismal and gray as a washed-up piece of driftwood, entered the decorated gymnasium along with an early, steady stream of people from the community. Her face was strained and lacked animation as she coursed slowly through the center of the room incognizant of her surroundings. When she reached the small stage at the opposite end of the room, she stopped, and appeared to be wondering why she was in the room. Several people had watched her dreamlike progress across the room, but only Aunt Lucy approached her.

"Sarah," she said, and touched her arm, "you don't look well. Can I do anything?"

Sarah gazed vaguely at Aunt Lucy until recognition crossed her face. "Aunt Lucy," she spoke as if awakening from a dream, then turned and walked toward the large hall, which held four high school classrooms. Watching her inadvertently, Aunt Lucy saw her enter her Social Studies room and close the door behind her.

Then, Sarah was forgotten as Aunt Lucy turned back to the crowded room, and heard Deputy Nancy Armstrong squeal with delight as she won the cakewalk and watched her choose the mandarin orange cake as her prize. The fishing booth was doing good business with the eight and under crowd, and prizes of glow rings and necklaces, Chinese puzzles, plastic spiders and snakes, and key chain teddy bears were seen everywhere. Mary Thomas was watching mournfully as mischievous Tommy Samp chased Greta Brown with a plastic snake, her screams filling the air.

Betty and Junior had joyfully announced to Emma, Mr. Lacey, Nancy Armstrong, and Roy and Lori Gilmore their upcoming Christmas wedding and the happy news was spreading throughout the festivities. Betty proudly exhibited her old engagement ring, sparkling anew, and Junior, happily puffed up in Lee overalls and white sweatshirt, looked like a rounded Humpty Dumpty with a silly painted smile, and hardly felt his bruised knuckles. It was an evening of fun and celebration, with the fearful events of the past few weeks out of sight and mind.

Later on, the evening was named a success, as the take was counted, and nearing a close when Sarah was sought to accept congratulations for her organization of the event. Aunt Lucy, who had seen Sarah enter her classroom earlier, volunteered to fetch her, and walked down the hall and opened the Social Studies classroom door. Her eye was quickly drawn to a red-stained cluster of rolled-up maps in a chaotic heap on the floor with the unseemly and disjointed body of Sarah piled among them. Aunt Lucy felt every year of her age as she observed her second dead body in only a few weeks. She inched closer to Sarah, taking in her olive green eyes, forever set in a wild, fixated stare and her mouth, crooked in pain. The surplus of blood covering the maps, navy pinstripe suit and finally pooling on the old oak floor boards had flowed from two deeply slashed wrists, now lying peacefully at rest on her blood-stained lap. Aunt Lucy turned shakily on her old legs to summon the sheriff, but first passed Sarah's desk and noticed the bloody razor blade and an envelope addressed to Sheriff Gilmore. She closed the door behind her and, feeling woozy, walked carefully back to the gym.

There, the activities were grinding to a halt as the few diehards drifted toward the front doors. Teachers had begun to dismantle the booths and decorations, and a clean-up crew was hard at work in the kitchen, scrubbing countertops and operating the large commercial dishwasher. Leftovers were being divided among the workers. The sheriff was aimlessly walking about the room waiting for Lori to finish in the kitchen. He looked bored and anxious to leave, and was surprised when Aunt Lucy hurried to his side and pulled on his arm. "Come with me," she said grimly, and led him back to Sarah's forlorn shell.

They stood together inside the classroom like returning POWs discovering their wives had remarried and fire had taken their homes. It was too much to bear. Roy squeezed Aunt Lucy's shoulders solemnly and asked her to lock the door. Then he used the office telephone to call the coroner and crime lab. What was unsure in his crime scene investigation technique a little over a month ago was now rote.

It was midnight when the body was removed, and Dr. Judd and the lab team left. The coroner's verdict was logical, Sarah had committed suicide and left a suicide note/confession addressed to Sheriff Gilmore. After he had photographed and fingerprinted it, Tom Gray handed Roy the letter. Only a small amount of blood had spurt onto the envelope that held the letter, and he sat alone at a lab dusted school desk and spread the three pages out before him. It read in a sloping hand:

> *Dear Roy,*
>
> *I guess my death will come as a shock to you. I don't know anymore why I was born in the first place. Everything I have ever cared about has disappeared into smoke, and now, I look back and see I have set fire to all my bridges and I can't go back and don't wish to go forward. I have been sitting here at my desk where I have spent nearly thirty-five years, and have asked myself, has anyone ever loved me? You might think that is a silly question for a married middle-age woman to ask herself, but when I get down to what I have desired most in my life, it was to be loved. But the answer to my question is, no. I have never been loved and have not even loved myself. So, in the final analysis, here I am, an unwanted, bitter woman with a wasted life.*
>
> *Now, before I die, I wish to set the record straight regarding the rapes and murders in Cramer Creek and elsewhere. I doubt that Karen Bryson was the first young girl that James raped, but she was the first one I knew about. I was late heading for the henhouse to collect eggs the night I saw what he did to her with my own eyes. He was wearing his black ski mask and he threatened her with a sickle we had for cutting weeds around the trees. He had forced her to lie down beneath an apple tree. I was struck dumb by the scene and didn't move a muscle, but I watched horrified as my own husband did disgusting things to her, and I realized for the first time the man I loved, and thought I knew, was a despicable monster. During the rape, Karen was hysterical, and James tried but was unable to keep her quiet, but he didn't seem to worry too much about the noise she was*

making. When he finished with her and was getting to his feet, she suddenly grabbed at the mask he wore and pulled it off his head, and, of course, she recognized him immediately. When she threatened to tell what he had done to her, James only laughed and told her if she ever told anyone, he would rape her again. Then he left her there, crying her eyes out. I knew she could never walk away from there, that she would never keep James's secret, and I knew I had to act in order to save James from himself. I thought to myself, no one must ever know! Then I knew what I had to do, and I crept behind Karen, picked up the sickle as she was pulling on her shirt, and struck her with it several times from behind. She died instantly. Then I finished dressing her, and because I was afraid the dog or another animal might get to her, I wedged her between two boughs in the tree. And that was where Betty and Junior found her later that evening. James was so surprised when the sheriff told us she had been murdered in our orchard. Of course, we were questioned but James and I provided an alibi for each other, and I don't think we were ever seriously suspected in Karen's death anyway. But, after the sheriff left, I'll always remember how James smiled at me and treated me so sweetly. I think he knew the truth then, but he has never said a word.

After that, I thought James had stopped his perverted activity, until I heard through the grapevine about Mary Jane Oglesby's rape a couple of years ago. Although I suspected James, I didn't know for sure, and soon forgot about it. But a bit later on, when I was looking through James's file cabinets in his office, I came across the nasty magazines he had hidden, and I began to wonder. The magazines were full of children of all ages in disgusting poses and having all manner of evil being done by them and to them.

It was while we were at the "Feeling Wonderful" seminars in Kansas City that I found out James was having an affair with Mrs. Vanhuss. I didn't know the Vanhusses but had seen them at some of the meetings. I had noticed the wife and James were flirting openly, but that was nothing new for him. He had never let the fact that I was around curtail his flirting with other women. I have had to put up with that all our married life. But, I'm fairly certain the affair ended after the hotel fire that killed five people that weekend, including the Bentleys. I had read in the newspaper reports that Mrs. Vanhuss was responsible for the fire, and had been horribly disfigured by it, and after that, I never saw her at another seminar. Then, soon, James also seemed to lose interest in the meetings and we dropped out of the group, even though we had sunk a hard-earned ten thousand dollars into it.

It was only by chance I visited Mrs. Vanhuss while procuring dessert donations for the chili supper. She lived in the neighborhood that had originally been assigned to Betty, but I had taken it so Betty wouldn't have to visit her ex-mother-in-law.

Mrs. Vanhuss was calling herself Rose Findley, and although I recognized her immediately, I pretended I didn't. I welcomed her to the neighborhood and even invited her to our house for dinner. I could tell she recognized me as well, but she also kept it to herself. That was the very evening James was out almost all night and I was certain they were together. He denied it, of course, but I knew.

It had been eight years since I had been called to murder Karen, and I hadn't enjoyed it, naturally. I had considered it a duty, really, a clean-up duty after a naughty little boy. And now, I knew I had been elected for the job again. This time, however, I felt a bit different about it. Maybe enjoyment is too euphemistic, but I must say I set about my plans with a lightness of heart. You see, I have always been well organized and have liked things with no loose ends. I suppose that is why I like to read murder mysteries. Because when the murderer is finally discovered and caught at the end of the book, the killer's motivation, why the victim was chosen, how the alibi was manufactured, and so on, is explained completely, a very satisfactory way for a book to end, I think.

Now, as I have intimated, I set about the task at hand with some relish, but also with determination to construct as near a perfect plan as I could. It seemed the obvious time to carry out the murder would be during the day when I could get away from school and when Mrs. Vanhuss' next door neighbor, the pit viper, Geneva, would be occupied with cooking Junior's dinner. As I studied other possible witnesses to the crime, I discovered the only houses with an uninterrupted view of my victim's house were unoccupied during the day. Mr. Lacey and Elizabeth would be at school; you, Roy, and your wife would be working, as would the other close neighbors. So, from my analysis of the situation, the exact timing of the murder, and my most critical exposure time, had to be when Geneva would be hell-bent on getting Junior's dinner on the table at noon. This would stretch my third hour free period at school, but because my lunch hour follows I would have a few minutes lee time, and if I didn't return until nearly noon, no one would notice. I also had my entire third hour to construct my perfect alibi, seemingly, leaving me no extra time to commit murder. To make certain I wasn't seen getting back to school late, I reentered through the janitor's room knowing he would be busy in the noisy cafeteria, and then slipped along to my classroom where I had left a sack lunch. By ten minutes after twelve when the first bell rang I had eaten a quick lunch and was ready for my fourth hour students, with no one the wiser.

The actual murder was simple. I brought a newly sharpened butcher knife from home, and wore tight fitting gloves. I removed the knife from my purse after asking Mrs. Vanhuss for a glass of water, and struck her from behind as she started for the kitchen. She crumbled to the floor immediately, and then I stabbed her a few more times making sure I had perforated her heart and lungs. After I watched her for a few moments, I was satisfied she was dead or dying. Next, I noticed the small sample of Vision Cosmetic's perfume that I was sure Edie had given her, and I saw an unplanned opportunity to implicate Edie in the murder, especially since Mrs. Vanhuss had caused the fire that killed Edie's parents. So, I opened the bottle and spilled the contents in front of

Mrs. Vanhuss' head, and then squeezed her fingers around the bottle and let it drop to the rug.

It was uncanny how contained and complacent I was the rest of the afternoon as I taught my classes, and even later on, fixing dinner and talking to James at home. This time, I don't think he had a clue that I was the avenging angel. That's just how I felt, Roy, like an avenging angel righting wrongs, making things the way they should have been. I'm sure you must feel that way sometimes, when you are able to eradicate at least some of the filth that runs rampant, even in our almost perfect little town. And that is exactly the reason why I also had to kill Geneva.

I was really frightened for myself when Lori told us all in the teacher's lounge that Geneva knew the identity of the murderer, but I guessed that was just so much hot air on Geneva's part, wanting to be the center of attention because the murder had the audacity to occur next door to her and she hadn't even been aware of it. As the captain of Whoremongers Anonymous, she was found lacking. In fact, her only reasons for existence seemed to be to spoil her son, spread rumors and perpetuate filth. After you told me Geneva knew about James's late night visit to the Vanhuss house, I knew she would never keep silent about their affair and it would soon be general knowledge. Also, I thought she might try to implicate him in the murder and James would not be able to hold his head up in town. I had to protect his good name, didn't I?

Anyway, Geneva's death was very straightforward, and it's a good thing it was, because I didn't have time to plan it. When you left my home that night, informing me that Geneva witnessed James's late night visit to the Vanhuss house (and you had, by the way, provided me with a perfect alibi), I dressed quickly, and wearing gloves again, grabbed a sickle from the shed and followed the path along the old creek bank until I came to Geneva's house. Imagine how surprised I was, when she came out her front door and walked to Betty's house. I watched their little "set to" with enormous enjoyment and waited behind a tree for Geneva to walk back *to her house. I saw her grinning to herself, probably planning how she would fabricate, to Junior and the infamous grapevine, the details of their fight, making Betty look as bad as possible. At that moment, I struck with the sickle several times. And then I hurried back home, tossing the sickle near the Samp's back yard on my way; it always looks like the city dump anyway. I must admit, I was petrified when Aunt Lucy's car lights picked me up on the trail, but I prayed that her eyesight was bad enough she would not recognize me, and I guess that turned out to be the case, as nothing ever came of it. Again, James, I am sure, had no idea of my extracurricular activity, just as he thought I had no idea of his.*

Reading back through my letter, I think I have stated nothing but the truth, which should wrap up the murder investigations. As for the rapes, I don't know how many girls James violated, probably more than you will ever discover. But, what I hope for, more than anything, is that you will see that everything I did, I did thinking of others, without consideration for myself. Each time, by taking a life, I was able to prolong another one. Well, I see the hour is getting late, and it is time to say goodbye.

Yours truly,
Sarah A. Frazier

The sheriff refolded the letter and reinserted it in the envelope, and sat silently for some time looking around Sarah's classroom. He remembered twenty years ago when he had sat in this very room studying history and government, and was taught by an enthusiastic and knowledgeable teacher. As he tried to piece his memories together with what he had seen tonight, he faltered. Then, a slight knock at the door got his attention, and Aunt Lucy tucked her head in the room.

"Roy, I don't want to disturb you, but it's after one, and I guess I should get on home. I thought I would just leave the key to the front door with you and you can lock up when you leave." She held the large key out to him.

"Oh, I'm sorry. I didn't realize anyone was still here." He gave her a half smile. "I'm sure it's way past your bedtime."

"Yes, that's true, probably yours, too. Carman will be wondering where I am. Although, when I get home I'm not sure I'll be able to sleep."

"Well, if you feel like staying a bit longer, I'd like to get your reaction to Sarah's suicide letter and confession. It appears she has set the record straight, and it seems your suspicions were correct all along."

Taking the three-page letter from his hands, Aunt Lucy read it slowly, alternately shaking and nodding her white head. When she finished, she handed it back and lamented aloud, "Isn't it amazing? All I can think of is the wasted lives, all the pain, and done for crazy, skewed definitions of the word, 'love.' Poor Sarah. Tell me, Roy, why do we lump sex, lust, and codependent needs under the same name: love?"

"Yeah, I know what you mean. And I suppose my question is, where does love draw the line? Like, when does love for a spouse or a child deteriorate, or escalate, from caring and wanting the best for that other person, into overprotecting, controlling, and manipulation?"

"Well, I would guess when it is consciously, or unconsciously, done for selfish reasons, Roy, and that usually involves pride. Overt pride in self, but sometimes it's the opposite: the individual ego is so deflated that the only life one is able to live is through pride in another person. In Sarah's case, she made excuses for James's behavior, covered up his crimes, and even killed in order to maintain and protect her vision of him and their standing in the community. To her, as long as the façade was unblemished, it didn't matter what evil lurked beneath the surface."

"But it seems James's crimes stem from different reasons."

"Yes, I believe we can safely say he is a true sociopath. He simply feels no remorse. Which means it is psychologically impossible, although he may have desired it, to put himself in his victim's place or to feel their fear and pain. To know heartache and pain, or true love and joy is antithetical to him. He has no more idea, than Sarah, of the sacrificial nature of true love, our Christian example being Christ's death on the cross for us. In fact, their complementary hidden psychoses fed on each other."

"Aunt Lucy, I think you should take one of those high paying jobs with the FBI. You would be their best profiler."

"You're teasing me. But, I must say I feel sorry for anyone in that line of work, to be a human dredging machine. At least in my job, I don't run across too many bottom-dweller types, plus, I get the cream of the crop as well. Seeing lots of variety in the human condition makes for an interesting life."

"Well," he stood, and stretched his tall, handsome frame, "I guess I'd better get out of here and let Lori know what's going on. Tomorrow, if James can leave the hospital, he will rot in jail where he belongs. I don't think he'll be surprised about Sarah's death or her confession. With her letter added to all the circumstantial evidence we've collected so far, we have a good case against him. Then, when the DNA results come in, that will seal it. I don't think he'll be hurting any more little girls. Do you need an escort home tonight, Aunt Lucy?"

"Oh, no thank you, Roy. Right now, I feel like Cramer Creek is a safe place to live again."

CHAPTER 20

"It's a perfectly wonderful day for a wedding, don't you think?" Betty asked Emma, her maid of honor. She stared out the window of the church classroom, designated as the bride's dressing room, at rounded white swirls of snow covering the beginner hills of the churchyard. "What a wonderful, wonderful day! Should I break out in song?"

Emma smiled widely at her friend and thought she had never seen her look so beautiful with her clear, and usually calm, gray eyes, now full of twinkles. Betty still was not fashionably svelte even after losing twenty pounds over the past three months, but her white satin wedding gown with thousands of seed pearls over the bodice fit perfectly over her full figure and she looked absolutely majestic with the three-foot train flowing behind her.

Betty's parents had flown in from their retirement home in Brownsville, and were finally okay with the wedding. They wanted their daughter to be happy, and this marriage was what she wanted, but they had not completely forgiven Junior for his past abandonment of her. Waiting outside the dressing room, her father looked elegant in his white tails and dark red rose. Her mother, dressed in a two-piece silk suit, the color of wine apples, had already been escorted to her position in the front pew.

Junior, succulently handsome in white tails and dark red rose, nervously waited at the front of the church with Doug and Pastor Sharpe. Like Betty, he had tried to lose a few pounds for today, but had failed and actually gained another five. Presently, he was holding his stomach in tightly, hoping the white vest buttons were not too obviously stretched over his girth. At this moment, more than anything, he wanted the wedding to be over without a major blunder on his part. Last week, at the small rehearsal dinner, he had actually bungled up some words, and skipped over others, causing Betty to blush. Yes, he did have the ring, no, he didn't, he had already given it to Doug, his best man. And, today, instead of the traditional best man helping the bridegroom, he and Cheryl had watched Doug, making certain he had not a drop of liquor before the ceremony. Not an easy task, since it was Doug's practice to celebrate Christmas day with a few drinks. Suddenly, the door opened from the vestibule and Emma, dressed in a shimmering dark red, almost black gown, began her slow descent to the front of the glowing candle lit church. All along the center aisle, attached to the pews, and in each stained glass window were dark red roses tied in bunches with dark, hunter-green velvet, flowing ribbons. Then, as Emma reached the front, and at a sign from Betty's father, the organ began the processional, and the guests stood. Junior's gut wrenched, but when his eyes rested on Betty's glowing face, he knew he was the luckiest man alive. Thirty minutes, forty-five tops, this would all be over, he thought, and she would be his wife, again. He promised himself to work at their marriage like he had never worked at anything before.

Pastor Sharpe smiled at the bride and groom as they stood before him and believed it was going to work this time.

* * *

The wedding reception, held in the fellowship hall, was a joyous celebration for everyone. Festive Christmas music was piped in from the sanctuary sound system, and toasts to the couple were made with plastic cups holding dark strawberry punch. Doug, who seemed to be getting louder, wished Junior and Betty "lotsh of luck." Pastor Sharpe blessed them with the scripture from Numbers 6:24-26, "The LORD bless you, and keep you; the LORD make His face shine on you, And be gracious to you; the LORD lift up His countenance on you, and give you peace." And Aunt Lucy toasted them with her old world wisdom, "May you never go to bed angry."

At a long damasked covered table, the Gilmore's, Nancy Armstrong, Emma, and John Lacey were discussing Frazier's upcoming court trial.

"The jury will have a lot of evidence to mull over," Nancy affirmed. "The DNA results are in, proving James raped Karen, the lint fiber found on his ski mask matches the lint on the little Haynesworthy girl's blue blanket, Sarah's incriminating letter, of course, and a bunch of circumstantial evidence."

The sheriff agreed. "Yes, we have a good case. I believe the judge and jury will put him away for a long time."

"I hope you're right," John reasoned. "Then, maybe, this town can get back to normal."

"That's assuming it ever was!" Roy noted.

"Well, I will never think of it as normal again," mused Lori. "My eyes have been opened now, and I've learned what you see on the surface around here is just a cover. People I thought I knew and called my friends and colleagues, turned out to be hidden perverts, and murderers. I'm a lot more skeptical than I used to be."

"Yes," agreed Emma, "I know what you mean. But when I look at Christmas that we are celebrating today, as well as a beautiful wedding, I just can't believe Cramer Creek is all bad."

Aunt Lucy, hearing the discussion as she passed, stopped to listen, and added her piece of cautious optimism. "I think Cramer Creek is pretty much like all the world, Emma, good and bad. In Galatians, Paul pointed out the deeds of the flesh were immorality, sensuality, impurity, idolatry, sorcery, jealousy, outbursts of anger, dissensions, and I can't think of all of them, but the point is they exist everywhere. There is a spiritual battle going on. If Cramer Creek is different, it is because more people try to hide their sins, so, on the surface our little town usually looks wholesome and innocent. Of course, God sees all the hidden muck. The amazing thing is, and it's called grace, is that He loves us."

Printed in the United States
808900003BA